The shining splendor of our Zebra Lovegram logo on the cover of this book reflects the glittering excellence of the story inside. Look for the Zebra Lovegram whenever you buy a historical romance. It's a trademark that guarantees the very best in quality and reading entertainment.

SWEET SURRENDER

He lifted a finger to her lips. The bottom one was swollen, and a tiny drop of blood was welling from a cut. "Does this hurt?"

"Yes," she said softly, her breath touching his hand. "Am I under arrest, Rance?"

He tugged at her lower lip with his finger, moving the little cut out of the way so he wouldn't hurt her. "I can't let you go, Carrie."

Her eyes were so wide, he could see all the way to her heart, which was beating as fast as his own.

"But my uncle—"

"Now now," he said with his lips so close to hers, he could almost taste them. "I don't want to hear any more stories about Dutch uncles or shouting preachers, Carrie. I don't want to hear anything at all."

Her mouth was cool and soft and he covered it gently with his kiss.

I'm doing this for my country, Carrie told herself, but it wasn't Abraham Lincoln or the Union she was thinking of when Rance's tongue touched hers and her knees gave way beneath her.

KATHY JONES

REBEL'S MISTRESS

ZEBRA BOOKS
KENSINGTON PUBLISHING CORP.

ZEBRA BOOKS

are published by

Kensington Publishing Corp.
475 Park Avenue South
New York, NY 10016

First printing: November, 1991

Printed in the United States of America

This book is dedicated to the memory of my grandparents, Grandma and Grandpa Pauley, my grandmother, Rubby Jones, and grandfather, Daddy Jones. They are all gone now, and I miss them.

I want to thank my editor, agent, husband, and my parents and family, especially my aunts Eula Litton, Betty Pauley, and Bobby Simmons, who, along with my parents, provided invaluable assistance with my research for this book. I also want to thank Stan Cohen and Terry Lowry for their excellent books on West Virginia Civil War history, and the staff of West Virginia's state archives library for the aid they provided not only with my research, but also my constant explorations for a place to plug in my computer.

Note to Readers:

I would like to offer some assistance in the pronunciation of a frequently used place name in this book, Kanawha, one of the most beautiful words in American geography. Webster's recommendation for the correct pronunciation is so confusing I can't even type it, much less say it. Being a native of Kanawha County, I'll try to coach you on the way I say it:

The K is firm, as in Kennedy.

The first two A's are soft, as in "ahhh, that feels good."

The W and H are thought about but not said.

The last A is also soft, but a bit shorter as in "ah, yes."

To indicate the syllable breaks, Ka-naw-ha, let your breath softly hesitate, then flow forward.

Isn't it lovely?

West Virginia & Virginia

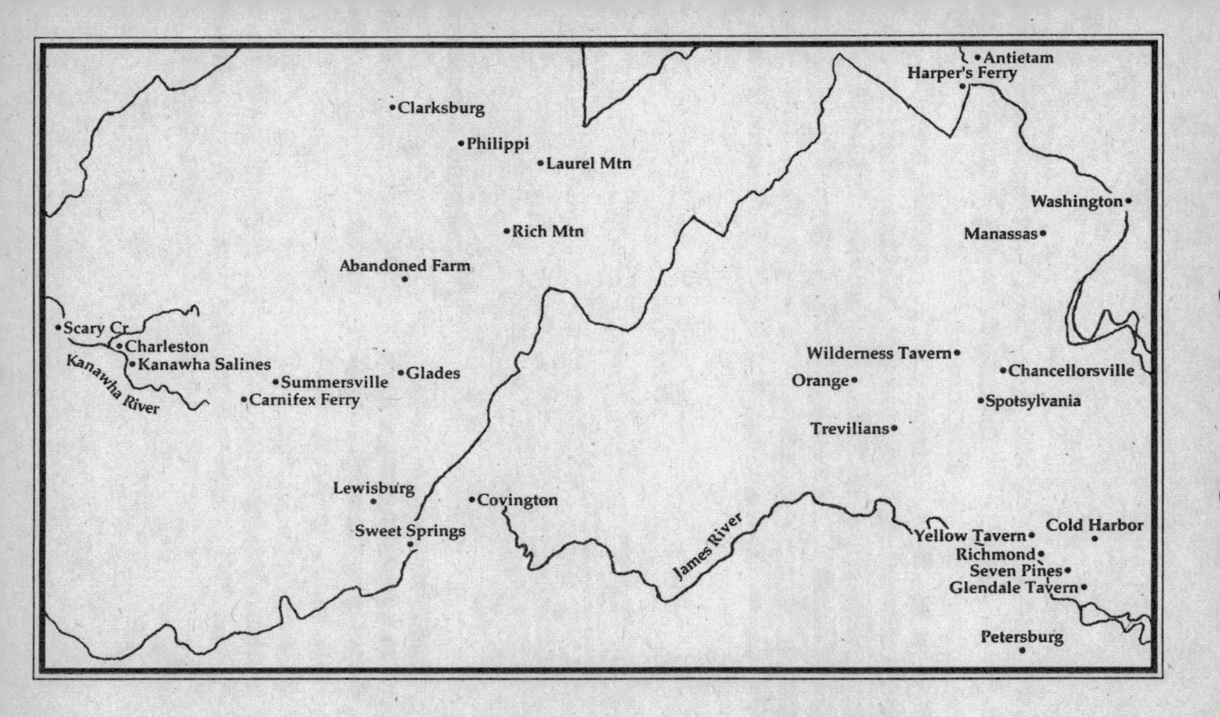

Chapter One

The night air smelled of the distant river. Carrie Blackwell leaned into the breeze, letting its cool caress wash away the cloying stink of secession that clung to her like cheap perfume. The ballroom of the Stanard House, on whose balcony she stood, shone like a bright diamond in the velvet darkness. Similar diamonds sparkled all across the hills of Richmond tonight. The streets of the city were also lit with parades and parties, illuminations and speeches, as Virginia celebrated its separation from the Union.

The sound of bands playing and people shouting their joy at finally being free of the overbearing demands of the Union hovered over the city like an ocean fog. That secession also meant war didn't affect the excitement. Everyone was ready, even eager, to fight to defend that freedom.

Everyone except Carrie.

For her it wasn't a war to defend freedom. It was a war to suppress it.

One moment she was alone on the balcony grieving over what she'd been pretending all evening to rejoice. The next she was being crushed against the decorative iron of the balcony's railing as other partygoers crowded around her, each eager to catch a glimpse of history.

Decca Blackwell slipped an arm through her daughter's. "Isn't this exciting, darling? I'm so happy that I am here to share this moment with you. Do you remember how depressed I was when we missed Charleston's celebration over South Carolina's secession?" She didn't give Carrie a chance to answer. "How silly of me. Of course you don't remember. You were with—" Decca stopped suddenly, leaving the unfinished sentence dangling between them.

It was the closest Carrie had ever heard her mother come to acknowledging the existence of her estranged husband, Carrie's father.

"You know I wouldn't tell Pops if you accidently said his name, Mother."

Decca dropped her arm from Carrie's. "This night air is too cold for you, darling. We should go inside before you take ill." Decca gathered her crimson skirts and made her elegant way into the ballroom.

It was a large room, long and wide and filled with so many candles that it really did sparkle like a diamond, the flickering light playing across the painted walls and cupola-carved plaster of the high ceiling like sunlight off clear water. Yet as large as the Stanard ballroom was, tonight it was filled to overflowing with billowing hoopskirts and untried uniforms.

Carrie and Decca paused to watch dance partners being saluted and exchanged in response to the orders of the husky-voiced caller of a Virginia reel. The chandelier under which they stood sent a spill of shimmering candlelight onto them, its glowing brightness such a perfect complement to Decca's classic beauty that Carrie knew they were not standing there by chance.

"He has breakfast in your bedroom every morning, Mother," she said. She'd been saving that tidbit of news for years, waiting for just the right moment to drop it into conversation. "He talks to the empty pillows as though you were sitting there."

"I can't hear a word you're saying, darling. The band is too loud."

When a heartbeat later the music crescendoed to an end, Decca drew Carrie into the promenade of guests circling the room. Though promenading was customarily performed at a slow walk to allow participants to see, be seen, and to socialize, Decca set such a quick pace that Carrie had no chance to repeat her revelation about Harris Blackwell's breakfast habits.

Instead, she concentrated on ignoring the glares of disapproval cast her way. While every other woman at the ball, including Decca, was dressed in red and white to honor the Confederacy, Carrie was wearing a brilliant pink creation that had been flounced, ruffled, puffed, and beribboned within an inch of its life.

"Stop blushing, darling. You look beautiful in that dress."

"I look like an out-of-season valentine. Why didn't you bring my red gown?"

"For the same reason I have been repeating to you all evening, Carolina Grey. Your wire didn't say you needed the red, only that you wanted it, and I knew this dress would look much lovelier on you. If you had not waited until the last moment to prepare for this ball, you would have had time to obtain proper attire."

Decca's use of Carrie's full name instead of the usual "darling" indicated that the subject was to be dropped. There wasn't much she could say anyway, especially since she hadn't even sent the wire. Hannah, her personal maid, had sent it after the invitation to the Stanards' celebration ball arrived at Carrie's hotel room a few hours after Virginia's vote for secession two days ago.

Carrie hadn't known about either the secession or the invitation until her clandestine arrival in Richmond minutes before the ball was to begin. She'd barely had time to dress, much less obtain another gown. If the affair had been hosted by anyone other than Eleanor Stanard, she would have refused to attend. The caliber of guests a Stanard invitation would draw had made the social sacrifice seem worthwhile. So far her humiliation had resulted in learning nothing that couldn't have been obtained by reading tomorrow's *Richmond Times*.

"Look, darling, it's Franklyn Bredon!" Decca floated to a graceful stop beneath another chandelier to await the object of her delight.

Carrie's pink gown, which her mother had designed, had a waist two inches smaller than she was accustomed to wearing. As a result, her corset was pulled so tightly, she was certain that at any moment the upper half of her body would break away from the bottom half.

She took advantage of the cessation of movement to hide behind the privacy of her painted silk fan, where she allowed herself the pleasure of an unladylike gasping intake of air. The cinched laces of her corset refused to yield to her desperate need, though, and she was horrified to hear herself making a noise like a landed fish. She flicked the fan faster, hoping the sound of its fluttering would drown the sound of her floundering.

Franklyn Bredon was a South Carolina rice planter and politician, both professions having brought him great renown and even greater respect. He was also one of Decca Blackwell's most favored admirers.

He took both her hands in his. After looking her over with an appreciative eye, he gifted her with a pleased smile. "My dear Decca, now I know why the Yankees are so eager to reclaim the South."

Decca's face, so prettily framed by point lace and diamonds, flushed. "Franklyn, you should have been a poet instead of a politician."

"So there you are, Carolina, I've been looking everywhere," a deep masculine voice said, its richly timbered tones drawing the attention of every female within overhearing distance. The perfect voice materialized in the form of James Bredon, who stepped out of the masses to stand for a posed moment at his famous father's side.

After every tittering gossip in the vicinity was given the chance to witness the moment, James relinquished his place in the spotlight to move closer to Carrie. She should have been thrilled. He was handsome and charming and the only son of a rich father, everything that every Southern girl wanted.

Everyone except Carrie.

She stopped the frantic waving of her fan, refusing to allow him the assumption that she was too warm because he was so near. "What is the news from Montgomery, Governor?" she asked his father.

Franklyn Bredon had held almost every political office South Carolina offered, except governor, a post he'd never sought and had repeatedly refused. And yet the title was still his. "I don't know why. He's just always been called the Governor," James had said years ago in answer to Carrie's questionings.

Franklyn Bredon's gray eyebrows lifted to heights as familiar as his friendship. He released Decca's hands to grasp the lapels of his jacket and raised himself onto his toes in the manner of a campaigning politician. "In less than sixty days," he proclaimed, "the Stars and Bars will be waving over the White House in Washington City!"

It was the same boast being shouted from every street corner south of the threatened city. Not only did Carrie not believe it, it wasn't the answer she'd come here to obtain.

"Do you really believe there will be a war?" Decca asked in a trembling voice.

"There already is a war, Mother," Carrie said.

Franklyn shook his head. "That little show Beauregard put on in Charleston harbor was merely a declaration of intent, Carolina. The real war is yet to begin."

"But there will be one?" Decca persisted. She had paled from what Carrie knew to be pretend fear. Her mother had been eagerly anticipating the promised clash with the Union army ever since South Carolina seceded four months ago. Decca had even boasted of being among the civilian observers on the artillery line when Confederate gunners opened fire on Fort Sumter.

"Yes, there will be a war," James said. "And I shall be on the front line giving those Yankees hell!"

"I thought you were paying a man to fight for you," Carrie said. It was one of the few sins he'd been unable to hide from his father. She wasn't about to let an opportunity go by to point it out.

He wasn't listening to her, though. His attention was on Decca, who was reeling in a faint. Franklyn cupped a hand of support around her right elbow.

James mirrored his father's concern. "Please accept my apology for using such strong language, Mrs. Blackwell." He turned an assessing eye on Carrie, who had been left alone to brave the horror his use of the word *hell* should have caused her to suffer. "I hope you aren't too upset to dance with me," he said, referring to the next scheduled selection by the orchestra, which was one of three he'd claimed on her dance card.

Carrie gave a few exaggerated waves of her fan. "I shall try to recover before then," she said, delighted by the excuse he'd accidently handed her to beg off what she'd unwillingly granted.

When she'd first learned of the reason for tonight's ball, Carrie had sworn an oath to dance with no man wearing a Confederate uniform. But in the two days since Virginia declared her rebellious intent, her favorite sons had turned up in such uniformed force that Richmond had taken on the appearance of an armed camp. And because the Stanards had invited every one of these aristocratic seekers of bloody glory to tonight's ball, Carrie's private protest had resulted in James Bredon's unprecedented claiming of three dances.

More determined than ever not to let tonight's miseries go unrewarded, she turned her attention, and the conversation, back to his father. "What I wanted to know, Governor, is whether there has been any official talk of the Confederate capital leaving Montgomery?"

Franklyn bestowed a paternal smile on her. "A girl as pretty as you should be thinking about making eyes at my son instead of wanting to talk politics."

"Dear sir," she said in her best imitation of Decca's molassas-thick drawl. "Y'all know that Southern girls have no need to practice making eyes at handsome young men: we were born knowing how to do that." She dropped the exaggeration, returning to her normal voice, which was flavored with just enough sultry Southernness to make most men act like fools. "Did Jefferson Davis tell you, or did he not, that he planned to move his capital to Richmond now that Virginia has seceded?"

The question rang out like cannon fire in the suddenly silent ballroom. Carrie was caught between horror and curiosity. The end of the orchestra's foot-stomping rendition of "Old Dan Tucker" was part of the reason for the silence, but this intense graveyard quiet wasn't normal.

Franklyn Bredon, along with Decca and James, was staring over Carrie at the room beyond. She turned, but all she could see were the backs of a hundred heads. "What is it?" she asked.

Her only answer was what sounded like a pack of hounds being denied entrance to the ballroom. Unhappy whinings were punctuated by howls of despair. A sharply spoken command ended the pleadings and loosed in the room a hum of whispered conversations.

Carrie laid a hand on Franklyn's arm, using him as an anchor while she teetered on tiptoe in an attempt to see what was happening. Her efforts were in vain, and she was forced to ask again, "What is it?"

"Ransom Fletcher." Franklyn covered Carrie's hand with his. "I couldn't be more surprised if Lincoln himself were to walk in."

"Ever since Fletcher inherited that tobacco plantation from his father, he never leaves it except on business, and then reluctantly," James said. "He didn't even attend his brother's graduation from West Point last year."

Carrie realized that Franklyn had transferred her hand to James' arm. She pulled free of his unwelcome embrace of her fingers and wiped off the memory of his touch on the flounces of her dress.

"That must have been a terrible disappointment to his mother," Decca said while trying to maneuver Carrie's hand back onto James' arm.

Carrie resisted the not-very-gentle pressure of Decca's urging. "I'm certain he had good reason, Mother."

"Fletcher's in uniform," Franklyn said. "Apparently he has chosen to recognize our cause as his business."

"My," Decca breathed in an undertone. She was staring over Carrie's head again. "What a splendid specimen of the male animal!"

Carrie strained to see what her ever-flirtatious and enviably taller mother was appreciating. But her only contact with the source of everyone's excitement was the sound of boots clomping across the marble floor in the direction of the resting orchestra, which Carrie also couldn't see.

"Mama heard," said a feminine voice from among the masses blocking her view, "that his gallant offer to raise a cavalry regiment was turned down."

"And *I* heard," another girl said, that embarrassingly blunt refusal was occasioned by President Davis wanting bad-boy Rance just awfully for a tremendously *special* appointment."

Carrie pushed toward the familiar voices. "What as?" she asked.

Lisset Lewis slipped her arm through Carrie's and pulled her close. "You poor thing," Lisset sympathized. "I suppose you don't know even a single thing about gorgeous Rance with all the time you spend in those dreadfully wild hills of yours. Well, let me tell you that he is *simply* the *most* excitingly aloof man you can *imagine!*"

Alice Barton put on a conspiratorial expression and leaned closer. "Mama says he has a winning way of earning everybody's detestation."

Lisset clicked her tongue in disagreement. "Not everybody. My sister Melina was frightfully in love with Rance before he was expelled from West Point for dueling. And that wasn't the *first* time he'd paced the deadly distance, either."

"Nor the last," Alice added. "Mama says he takes offense as easily as he gives it."

Carrie subdued her eagerness to know more about the presidential appointment while she eased her way back into her friends' gossiping confidence. "Why did your sister let herself fall in love with a man like that, Lisset?"

Rebecca Pringle gave Carrie's dress a condescending smirk before asking, "And why shouldn't she fall for him? He is very sound on the goose."

Lisset gave Rebecca a chilling stare. "Our little Carrie prefers the pursuit of *business* accounts, not *men* with *bank* accounts. What Becky means—"

"Is that he has a plantation and no end of Negroes," Carrie said, finishing the distasteful slang expression with the last of her patience. "What kind of appointment did Jefferson Davis want this Fletcher for, Lisset?"

The Virginia belle pointedly glanced at Rebecca Pringle, who had become immersed in whatever secrets Susan Dinwiddie was whispering, leaving Alice, Carrie, and Lisset free to whisper their own.

"Melina says that temperamental Rance is frightfully clever at mathematics, and President Davis wants him to use his intimidatingly wonderful brains to find deceitful *spies* and break their traitorously clever *codes!*"

"Espionage," Alice sighed in a breathy whisper while her eyes rolled up in a spasm of ecstasy. "Isn't it just too romantic?"

"Yes, too romantic," Carrie said, her voice as flat as her heartbeat.

"Melina says," Lisset continued, "that poor Rance was given a whole *list* of people to investigate whose loyalty to our government is suspect, and he is every bit as mad as a swatted bee over the whole *exciting* affair!"

Carrie felt suddenly smothered by the overheated room. "How does your sister know this, Lisset?"

"By a stroke of the *most* incredible luck, Melina just happens to be best friends with Sallie Brockenbrough, who is engaged to that noble-looking Tom Reynolds, who is second cousin, thrice removed, from a very uninteresting girl who actually lives in that humid old Montgomery. Can you *believe* it? Anyway, it was she who found out about adorable but dangerous Rance from a house servant whose mother is actually owned by the delightful Mrs. Davis *herself!*"

"From God's mouth," Carrie said and Lisset hugged her.

"Exactly! Oh, Alice, you are so deliciously right, it is just *too* romantic that wicked Rance is actually *here!*"

"I wonder why?" Carrie asked, but her heart wasn't in the question. She already knew, with numbing certainty, why Ransom Fletcher had broken his self-imposed hermitage to attend this particular ball.

Her father was as famous for his opposition to secession as he was for putting Carrie in charge of his successful salt business. Harris' Union sympathies had already caused his daughter no end of trouble.

Now, with the ink barely dry on the contract she'd signed with the Confederacy to sell them her salt, and with Ransom Fletcher making his booted and spurred way across the floor in her direction, Carrie realized that her troubles were just beginning.

Chapter Two

Rance knew her the moment he saw her. Recognition came not from reports he'd received on her physical description. It came from the laughter that sparked like lightning in her eyes when she turned from the whispering of the youngest Lewis girl and met his damning stare.

He had already been angry that his offer to command a regiment had been ignored in favor of this ridiculous assignment. Now, to discover that his disgrace had already become a subject for schoolgirl gossip, his anger turned to rage.

"You must handle this matter with delicacy," President Davis had instructed Rance. "The Confederacy needs Miss Blackwell's salt, but not at the cost of treason."

The need was a vital one. Horses and cattle required salt for proper health. Salt was used to cure fish, pork, beef, and mutton. Hides were preserved in salt until they could be turned into leather. Salt was used in the dying of homespun cloth. Butter was salted to prevent deterioration. Eggs were packed in salt to exclude air.

Now that war was imminent, the Confederacy could no longer rely on the uninterrupted importation of salt from its current supplier, England. They needed an abundant and reliable source closer to home. The biggest supplier of salt in America was Kanawha Salines, a small river community in western Virginia. And one of Kanawha Salines's biggest producers was Blackwell Salts.

Just looking at the heiress to the Blackwell dynasty was enough to irritate Rance almost beyond control. There were men who would tell any secret to a woman like this. Perfect innocence was a Southern gentleman's Holy Grail. Everything about Carolina Blackwell, from the soft twinings of satin ribbons in her yellow hair to the corsage of pale pink rosebuds pinned to the waist of her overdecorated gown, promised a very perfect innocence. Everything, that is, except her eyes. They were filled with too much dark charm to be anything except dangerous.

"Do I know you, Captain?"

Her voice was beautiful, too, sugared and soothing and accented with deceptive gentleness.

She underlined the laughter in her eyes with a smile that reeked of smugness. "It is *just* Captain, isn't it?"

To hell with delicacy. He gripped the handle of his saber in a deadly embrace and advanced on her.

Carrie held her ground as Ransom Fletcher stalked toward her. Boots clung thigh high, rich wool stretched across mountainlike shoulders, wide and unbendable. Hair, almost black, almost tamed by a piece of leather that held it tied at the back of his head beneath a hat pinned with gold and crowned with plumes as dark as his hair. Face, rugged and strong, carved by distrust and set in lines of anger.

And his eyes, blue eyes, wonderful eyes, eyes that seemed to be speaking directly to her heart, telling it secrets, telling it lies.

Threatening my life, Carrie told herself firmly and refused to listen to anything else her heart or his eyes had to say.

"I ask you again, Captain, have we been introduced?"

"No, Miss Blackwell." Rance glanced at Lisset Lewis, then back to his enemy. "I am certain you know *of* me, however."

Amusement deepened her smile. "Is that why you were staring at me? Because you thought my friends and I were talking about you?"

He released his saber and grasped her wrist, the rough leather of his riding gauntlet crushing the ruffled lace of her glove.

"Dance with me," he ordered. Without waiting for a response, he dragged her onto the dance floor, where they were confronted by a man as tall as Rance and almost as angry.

"Unhand her, Fletcher."

James Bredon was the mongrel's name, at least the first name was his. The last was a gift from his father. Rance doubted that James would ever live up to it.

"The next dance is a quadrille. I'm on Carrie's dance card for all the quadrilles."

Carrie had often daydreamed what it would be like to have two men fight over her. "Unhand her, Fletcher, the next dance is a quadrille," didn't quite live up to her imaginary challenges, though. But then, James Bredon was nothing like her fairy-tale prince. Once upon a time, maybe, but not any more.

"It will be a waltz," Rance said.

She couldn't bring herself to say James was right even though it meant proving that this overbearing spy catcher was wrong. "A quadrille is scheduled next," she said in a compromise. "They never alter the program."

Rance increased the pressure of his grip on her wrist until her eyes flashed with fire. Only then did he lessen his hold and give a nod of acquiescence as though she had asked for relief.

His little game of dominance irritated Carrie into a frown. Her reaction must have pleased him, for his eyes turned suddenly dark. A chill of anticipation shivered through her heart.

"A true daughter of the South, Miss Blackwell, would never refuse an honorable request from a man wearing a Confederate uniform."

It was the most elegant insult she'd ever heard. That it was directed at James Bredon made it even more enjoyable. However, it was the perfection of Ransom Fletcher's challenge to her loyalty that charmed her the most.

"I will dance with you, Captain Fletcher," she said without even the slightest regret at having to break her oath.

James was not in the least charmed. His face twisted into a mask of anger so horrible that it made him appear possessed by madness. Carrie would have been frightened if she hadn't seen him this way before. It had only been once, but that one terrible time had changed her life.

"I forbid this, Carolina."

"How fortunate that I am neither your wife nor your slave, James, for I have no interest in what you do, and do not forbid."

She turned from him and into Ransom Fletcher's waiting arms. The first note of "The Evergreen Waltz" swept into the room, and they began to dance.

It was like dancing with the devil. From the first touch of his hand on her waist, her soul was his, and her only regret at its loss was that this dance would not last forever. The light in his eyes was as cold as mountain ice, numbing her senses. And his touch set those same senses on fire. She didn't care that he hadn't bothered to take off his hat, she didn't care that everyone in the room was staring at them. She didn't care about anything except the exquisite sensation of being held by this powerful and overwhelming man.

Lilacs, Rance thought. *She smells of rain-washed lilacs.*

Carrie floated through the first steps of the dance, exquisitely aware of her hand resting on his shoulder and the spinning beauty of the music that surrounded them.

And her hair. Rance couldn't decide what to compare it to. Freshly minted gold? Moonlight on daffodils?

It was the pain that snapped Carrie out of her fairy-tale enchantment. Not just one pain, pain that exploded anew with every heavy-booted step he took, all of them on her slippered feet.

The first hay of summer, Rance decided. *Sweet, sun-warmed hay.*

"Which was it, Captain?" Carrie asked. "Bribery or threats?"

He moved his gaze from the soft shine of her hair to the soft curve of her lips. "Neither, Miss Blackwell. I merely asked the conductor, who wants my permission to marry one of my sisters, if he would play a waltz."

"How ingratiating of him to comply."

Rance wanted to laugh. Instead, he whirled her faster. It was almost impossible to dance in riding boots at all. Doing it at this speed was suicide. But at least the effort of trying to maintain his balance gave him something to think about other than how perfectly this little Yankee fit into his arms.

The unprecedented change in the music program had caused a social revolt among the ball's guests. Men ignored both dance cards and women's protests to follow Ransom Fletcher's lead by claiming their desired partners with a laying on of hands. The dance floor was soon filled to overflowing with triumphant men and blushing women.

At the end of their first circuit of the room, the combination of his skidding boots and the crowded floor overwhelmed Rance's efforts to stay upright. To avoid falling, he turned her off the floor and into the orchestra.

"Why are you selling salt to the Confederacy for fifty cents a bushel when everyone else is demanding a dollar?" he asked as they danced past his hopeful brother-in-law-to-be, who had been knocked off his conductor's perch by a fleeing violinist.

"I am flattered by your interest in my business, Captain Fletcher."

"My interest is in the answer to my question, Miss Blackwell."

"I fear you shall be terribly disappointed then, for the reason is no more interesting than I wanted to make my mother happy."

It was true that Decca had asked Carrie to be fair in her dealings with the Confederacy. Undercutting the price of her competitors had less to do with pleasing her mother; though, than with Carrie's desire to win the contract, since with it came a pass allowing her unrestricted travel in the Confederacy.

"See, you are disappointed, Captain. I can tell from all those ugly creases in your forehead. And I did so want to amuse you in the hope that someday you might again honor me with a dance," she said as they waltzed through the cornophone section.

He was a menace to society, a hazard to women everywhere. To make horrible matters worse, when he dragged her out of the orchestra and back onto the dance floor, his spurs tangled with the puffed crape on the hem of her gown, and she heard the unmistakable sound of shredding satin.

As they sped down the long length of the ballroom at what had become a breathless pace, Carrie realized he was turning the dance into a Langaus, the object of which was for a man to waltz his partner from one end of the hall to the other at least six times at the greatest possible speed, each couple on the floor trying to outdo the others.

The last time she had been in one of these hoop-skirted horse races, she'd fainted dead away at the end of the dance in what her mother had described as "an apoplexy of the lungs, darling." Carrie had sworn an oath that night to never again participate in a Langaus, or in any situation that might even remotely result in a similar humiliation.

If I live through this without fainting. I promise that I'll never swear another oath as long as I live, she pledged.

"This is delightful," she said to Rance.

He scowled at the dimple which her obvious lie had caused to appear in the center of her chin. It was tiny, perfectly centered, and in the most ridiculous place he'd ever seen for a dimple. She was most likely inordinately proud of it and purposely told lies just so the silly thing would appear.

Why is he staring at my chin? she wondered.

"How are you planning to smuggle those Negroes out of Richmond, Miss Blackwell?"

She almost bit her tongue off. "I don't know what you're talking about, Captain."

He smiled as her dimple deepened. "I'm talking about the three runaways you brought up the James River in the hold of a fishing boat this afternoon. I assume you are planning to smuggle them out of Richmond on the train, taking them first into the western Virginia wilderness, then into Canada to join the other slaves you've stolen during the last two years."

Carrie was very close to fainting. The edges of her vision were blurring into blackness and her heart was hammering so hard she couldn't hear the music. "Western Virginia is not a wilderness, Captain."

"Any place without a telegraph is a wilderness."

"Does your plantation have a telegraph?" she

asked. Her taunt was rewarded by another tear in the hem of her gown.

"Are you aware, Miss Blackwell, that every train, carriage, and wagon leaving Richmond for any destination other than directly south is being searched for runaways?"

"As well they should be," she said. The only other way out of the city was the Kanawha and James River Canal. She would have to leave before they began checking the canal boats. "I'm certain one of those searches will reveal the true identity of your Negro-smuggler, Captain. When that happens, I shall enjoy hearing you beg my forgiveness for your false accusation. I shall not grant it, of course, but please don't let that stop you from trying."

He was smiling at her now, a nasty, threatening smile. "I'm going to break you, Miss Blackwell."

"You would have to hold me much tighter to break me, Captain Fletcher."

He pulled her so close to him that it felt like she'd been impaled on the handle of his sabre.

"I didn't know captains were high enough in rank to command a regiment," she said, parrying his thrust with the only weapon she had at hand. "That is the position you asked President Davis for, isn't it, Captain Fletcher? A regimental command? Rather daring of you considering your expulsion from West Point. But then, the Confederacy's empty treasury would cause the president to look with favor on anyone's offer to privately equip a company, so it isn't really so surprising that your request for a command was accepted."

His ferocious scowl almost made up for having to pretend she enjoyed being galloped around the room in a shredded skirt and a too-tight corset while being held so close against the front of an enemy uniform that the impression of its buttons would be on her breasts the rest of the night.

"Your request *was* accepted, wasn't it?" she asked, determined to drive the stake all the way through his pride.

Rance stopped dancing so abruptly that every couple on the floor was staggered. He didn't release her, but stood motionless with her crushed against him, the hurricane eye in a storm of frenzied dancers.

"I'm going to enjoy putting a hangman's rope around your neck," he said.

She looked up at him through dark lashes. "I prefer pearls," she said softly.

The music ended and a shout proclaimed victory in the Langaus.

"You didn't win, Captain Fletcher."

Rance released her and took a step backward. "Our dance isn't over yet, Miss Blackwell," he said, and walked away.

Chapter Three

Carrie waited until the dark plumes of his hat reached the front entrance. Then she began to laugh, forcing the sound to ripple and curl with deceptive gaiety, determined that it would be the last thing Ransom Fletcher heard as he left the hall, even if it killed her.

Decca and Lisset rushed to her side. Exhausted and completely out of breath, Carrie welcomed their supporting embraces, letting them lead her off the floor and into a private alcove. The window in the alcove was open. She collapsed gratefully onto the seat beneath it. In deference to her stays, she inhaled the cool, fresh air in small, ladylike gasps until her dizziness passed.

"That man should be horsewhipped," Decca said. "He should be drawn and quartered and fed to his dogs. I'm going to send Franklyn after him and have him shot!" She rushed off, her face glowing with indignation.

Lisset gathered Carrie's hands into a clinging embrace. "Wasn't I right? Isn't Rance just an *absolute* dream?"

"More like a nightmare." Carrie looked down at her boot-trodden slippers. "My poor feet." She tried to wiggle her toes. They were too bruised to respond.

"Your *dress!*" Lisset leaned over to examine the shredded crape. "It's ruined!"

Carrie pulled aside the drapery that sheltered the alcove. Her mother was nowhere to be seen.

"Lisset, I have to leave. Will you tell Mother that I was overcome by what happened and went back to the hotel to recover? And don't let her go rushing after me. I need a hot bath, not hysterical mothering."

"I shall not let the worried Decca out of my sight," Lisset said. "I am ever so surprised that beastly Rance treated you like this, Carrie. He was always such a perfect gentleman to Melina. Too perfect, if you know what I mean. I must confess, I had a tiny little doubt about that handsome devil's manhood until I saw him look at you tonight. If a man ever looked at me like that, I would swoon *dead* away! Didn't you just want to *die?*"

"That wasn't exactly what I was thinking," Carrie said. "Would you do me another favor, Lisset? I'm leaving tomorrow morning for home. Would you—" She hesitated, but ever since the first Confederate shot was fired at Fort Sumter, it had been too late for hesitation. "It's about Rance, Lisset. If you hear anything else about him, from Melina or from anyone, would you write me?"

Lisset's eyes opened wide. "Why, you *secretly* romantic *thing,* you! I never would have guessed that *anyone* could sweep levelheaded Carrie Blackwell off her feet!"

"Please, Lisset, don't tell anyone, especially not

Alice. You know she tells her mother everything, and Mrs. Barton tells everyone everything."

"You are a silly duckling, but I promise anyway. You have to promise me something, though. I want to know simply *everything* that happens between you and the boringly boorish but terribly dashing Rance."

Already more had happened than Carrie herself wanted to know. "I promise," she said anyway. Just before she slipped out of the alcove, she turned back to Lisset with the glimmerings of an idea. "Tell Alice to write me, too," she said, and let the damask drapery fall back into place.

Rance knew it was Carolina laughing, for in the laughter that followed him from the ballroom he heard the same false bravado that had kept her smiling even though he'd spent more time dancing on her feet than the floor.

When he stepped outside the Stanard house, his dogs clustered at his heels, their sensitive noses picking up the scents of the ballroom from his boots. He slung his caped coat about his shoulders. Another parade of celebrators was clogging the street. Fireworks sparkled overhead like bursts of cannon fire, and the city was infected with the discordant noise of dozens of bands unsimultaneously playing "Dixie."

Rance put a hand on the neck of his stallion to calm the nervous beast. Cain had been in a state of constant agitation ever since Rance left his plantation. The stamina and speed of the ebony stallion would be assets in the days to come, but if Cain didn't settle down soon, Rance would be forced to send him home.

From the shadows at the side of the Stanard house came the sound of a match being struck. The lit match was lifted and lowered, then lifted again.

Rance retied Cain's reins to the post and ordered the dogs to stay. He glanced around. When satisfied no one was watching, he stepped into the dark garden. The smell of a freshly lit cigar greeted him.

"I never thought you a foolish man until tonight, Fletcher."

"Carolina Blackwell is the one being foolish."

Moonlight shimmered on the smoker's brows as he lifted them in an expression of surprise. "You have proof already?"

"She has three slaves hidden in her father's warehouse beside the canal right this minute. I telegraphed President Davis. He refuses to issue an order for her arrest."

"And you don't agree with his decision."

"I don't agree with ignoring facts to chase rumors."

"If that girl has been stockpiling salt, and if that stockpile is even half as large as our informer suspects, it is worth a lot more than three Negroes." He knocked cigar ash into a bed of dormant roses. "Find that salt, Fletcher, and I will see to it that you are given the command you want."

There it was. The promise Rance had demanded from Jefferson Davis and been refused. The word of this man, however, was more valuable. He had no constituents to please.

"I'll have the foolish Miss Blackwell's salt in Confederate warehouses before the first drop of Yankee blood stains Virginia soil."

"Don't underestimate her, son. Carolina is not your typical Southern belle."

Rance gave a derisive laugh. "There are two things in this world of which I'm most certain. First, the Confederacy will win this war. Second, it is impossible to underestimate a woman."

The glowing end of the cigar revealed its smoker's smile. "Interesting theory, Captain. See that it isn't your downfall."

Rance waited until the old man's footsteps faded into silence at the back of the garden before he returned to the street. Cain had settled with the passing of the parade. Rance's relief was undermined by the behavior of his hounds. The pup rushed to his side, where the stupid creature trembled in whining agitation. Ruth was in a point directed at the closed front door of the Stanard house.

Rance gave a hand signal to the other dog to stand quiet before he stepped back into the shadows beside the garden gate. The front door opened, and a froth of pink satin burst into view.

"Carolina," Rance said, breathing the word into the river-scented wind.

Her flight down the steps stopped. She stood poised with one slippered foot extended and her hands filled with the cascading flounces of her skirts while she searched the night for the source of her name.

Rance remembered how the trailing ribbons of her gown had tangled with the gold braid on his uniform sleeve when they were dancing. It had been a small thing, an insignificant thing, but thinking of it now caused his hands to tighten into fists as he fought to dispel the feelings that entwined intimacy caused within him.

Apparently satisfied that she'd imagined hearing her name, Carolina ceased her search of the silent shadows to continue down the stairs. The wait had been too much for Rance's pup, though. He ran toward her, flinging his gangling paws up onto her dress and almost knocking her over with his boisterous attack. Though her dress had already been ruined by Rance's spurs, he still expected her to be angered by the pup's mauling. Instead she knelt to draw the big-boned beast closer.

"What a great oaf you are," she said and tickled his ears. The black and brown coonhound lapped at her face with a tongue as pink as her dress. "I haven't time for kisses, so you'll have to find someone else to drown in slobber, baby."

She held the pup at bay while she finished her flight toward a waiting carriage. Just before she entered it, she glanced back at the pup. The hood of her cloak fell back. Light from the street's gas lanterns fell softly on her hair, making it glow like candle-warmed brandy while she laughed at the pup's mournful expression.

"We'll have to hurry," she said to the coachman, then slipped inside the carriage and was gone.

When the patched pair of dappled horses harnessed to the rig had drawn it out of sight, Rance whistled the pup back and knelt to rub Ruth's head. "Good girl. As for you," he lightly cuffed the cavorting pup, "I think I'll keep Cain and send you back to Tory instead."

A gangly boy in a private's uniform was riding

down the street, not that what he was doing could really be called riding. "Cap'n Fletcher?" he asked, his voice almost as uncertain as his seat in the saddle.

Rance nodded.

"Orders from headquarters." He handed Rance a sealed envelope.

"What's your name, Private?"

"Kitchen, Allison Winslow Kitchen."

"Where are you from, Private Kitchen?"

"Alabama, but my ma's from Virginia. That's why I come here to join up."

"Didn't they teach you to ride in Alabama, Private Kitchen?"

"No, sir. They taught me to plow."

"Why did you join the cavalry if you couldn't ride, soldier?"

"I didn't join, I mean I did join, I just didn't mean to." His face went scarlet. "There was this girl on the train. She had paint on her face, sir. I never seen no girl that painted her face before. She said cavalry men was the most handsome men in the whole world and she just knew I must be comin' up here to join the cavalry." The boy looked miserable. "So I did."

"What happened to this 'girl,' Private?"

The boy turned even redder. "She took up with a navy officer, sir."

"Never listen to anything a woman tells you, Private Kitchen. You'll live longer."

"Or at least in less pain," the boy said and rubbed at his saddle-offended rear.

Rance frowned as he read the order Kitchen had brought. North of Richmond, a slave had been caught carrying coded messages inside a dead chicken. Both messages required Rance's deciphering efforts.

"Tell the colonel that I'll report to him within the hour. And Private Kitchen, you are to report to the stables tomorrow morning, where my man Task will teach you to ride. Meanwhile, try to remember you're not a plowboy anymore, you're a Confederate soldier astride a Virginia horse whose ancestors can be traced back further than yours. Dismissed."

Allison Winslow Kitchen rode away, his back a little straighter but his seat just as unsteady.

Rance snapped his fingers. "Follow him," he said, and the two dogs bounded off after Kitchen. When they were out of sight, Rance mounted Cain and spurred the stallion in the direction of the river, the same direction Carolina Blackwell's carriage had gone.

Chapter Four

A cold wind was whipping up the canal's dark water, sending plumes of even colder water splashing against the sides of the freight barge. Every few minutes, Carrie was christened by one of the spewing plumes.

"Last one," Jack Douglas said. He followed the announcement by rolling a man-sized barrel onto the deck of the *Adda May.* After the barrel was fitted into place beside five identical barrels, he pulled off his knit cap and wiped the sweat from the top of his hairless head. He was built like a barrel, big-chested, stout arms and legs, no neck, and a keglike head. He was also gruff-voiced, gruff-tempered, and gruff-minded toward everyone and everything, except Carrie.

The first time they'd met was when he was working at Kanawha Salines loading salt onto river barges. She'd been five years old at the time and had looked Jack Douglas up and down, then announced, "I like you, but I sure don't know why." Their friendship had been instantly cemented.

"Did you give my letter to your wife?" she asked him now.

"I've been loading barrels."

"So that's what you were doing. I thought you were showing off to impress me."

"Upstart female."

"Bad-tempered grump." Carrie patted the nearest barrel. "Now that they're loaded, you can take my letter to Mrs. Douglas. She needs to take it to Mother's hotel as early as possible, not that it will help much."

Jack checked his shirt pocket to make certain he had the letter, then huffed his way off the boat and west along the berm, the strip of land fronting the canal.

Decca would be furious at Carrie's abrupt departure from first the dance and then Richmond, but it couldn't be helped. There was no time to spare for placating her mother. She wouldn't even waste time sending a letter if they didn't have to wait for Hannah. In addition to being Carrie's maid, Hannah was also an excellent forger. She'd learned the art when still a slave and had used her skill to aggravate her merchant master first into fits, then bankruptcy.

Jack Douglas had been gone less than a minute when Carrie began to pace the deck with worry. "Hurry, hurry, hurry," she chanted in rhythm to her pacing. "We have to get away before—"

She fell silent as a chill chased up the back of her neck that had nothing to do with the wind. She turned and searched the shadows fronting her father's warehouse.

"Captain Fletcher," she said, knowing somehow he was there even though she couldn't see him.

He moved out of the shadows and into the spill of light from the bow lantern on the *Adda May*. "Miss

Blackwell." He stepped onto the boat. "Before what?" he asked. "Before you are stopped and searched for contraband cargo? Before you are arrested for stealing slaves?"

She rubbed her sweating palms on the skirt of her blue velvet traveling dress. "Is that an official accusation, Captain, or are you trying to flirt with me?"

He moved so close to her that she instinctively took a step backwards, and almost into the canal. The barge's low railing both stopped her and tripped her. To avoid falling, she grasped the front of his caped coat, which he hadn't bothered to fasten, a discovery she made when she continued to fall.

Rance caught her with one arm and his coat with the other.

Carrie threw the handfuls of coat at him. "Didn't your mammy teach you how to button your clothes?"

"Only my pants."

She wanted to laugh. She also wanted to look to see if he was right. It took a lot of self-control to do neither.

He began rummaging in the low-ceilinged wheelhouse. "I want to see the shipping order for these barrels."

She pushed in beside him and pointed at a packet propped behind an empty coffee mug.

Rance untied the red string and opened the packet. Inside was a six-month-old copy of an order from a winery in Kanawha County, Virginia for six oversized white oak barrels. Also included in the sheaf of papers was a shipping order, dated today, contracting with the *Adda May* to take the barrels to the head of the canal at Covington.

"What's in them?" he asked.

She leaned over his elbow and read, "Six *empty* barrels. Didn't your mammy teach how to read, either?"

She looked up at him for a reaction, only to realize that there really wasn't very much room in the wheelhouse. They seemed to be even closer now than when they were dancing earlier, and that had been too close for comfort. And the way he was looking at her made the space seem even smaller.

"You remember your mammy, don't you?" she asked. "Big black woman who changed your diapers and wiped your nose and told you not to look at young ladies as if they were a chocolate eclair of which you were about to take a bite?"

"Is that how I'm looking at you, Miss Blackwell?"

"That's exactly how you're looking at me, Captain Fletcher."

He leaned down until they were eye to eye. "I think there's something you should know."

Carrie swallowed so loudly it sounded like she was drowning. "What? What should I know?"

"I don't like chocolate eclairs." He turned his back on her and walked over to the closest barrel. "I want your empty barrels opened, Miss Blackwell."

"My buyer won't take them if they've been opened," she said. "You'll just have to trust me."

"Your buyer is your concern, Miss Blackwell. My concern is those runaway slaves."

"And you think I have them hidden in these barrels?" Her laughter sent a flush of anger across his face. "You've been reading too many romantic novels, Captain. We slave smugglers rarely conceal our cargo in barrels. Hay wagons are our preferred mode of transport, although onions will put a dog off the scent much better. Speaking of dogs, that wouldn't have been one of yours that molested me back at the Stanards', would it? Cute creature, a bit too demonstrative for a hunter, though."

"Open those barrels," Rance said, "or I will."

"What will I tell my buyer?"

"Tell him to order his barrels from a local cooper the next time so he doesn't have to wait six months for them."

Carrie wished that she had fallen into the canal. Then he would have been too busy saving her to bother with the barrels. Maybe it wasn't too late. She edged toward the port side of the boat. Just as she was about to tip herself over the rail, she noticed him watching her with a smile in his eyes.

"There's something else you should know about me, Miss Blackwell. I don't rescue maidens in distress."

"How unheroic of you," she said.

Before she could think of a way to move away from the railing that wouldn't look like a confession of her previous intent, he took down the axe hanging from the side of the wheelhouse and prepared to break open one of the barrels.

"No!" She threw herself between the barrel and axe, which wasn't a very safe place to be. The glittering blade had stopped its downward swing mere inches from her face. "If anyone's going to ruin them, it's going to be me." She slipped out from under the blade and went into the wheelhouse, emerging a moment later with two pistols.

She took aim at the barrel Rance had been about to split open. With her eyes squinted almost closed and her extended hand wavering like a flag in a rainstorm, she pulled back on the hammer.

Rance stepped between her and the barrel. "What are you doing?"

"You wanted them opened, Captain. Get out of the way so I can open them."

"With a bullet?"

"I'll tell Mr. Friend that they're bungholes," she said, referring to the hole put in wine barrels so they could be filled with grape juice for fermenting. "You can stick your shiny sabre in the hole, Captain, and thrust about until you relieve your suspicions. Now move or I'll bung you, too."

He pushed the gun down with one hand. With the other, he touched the side of her face. Her skin was soft and cool, and as he caressed it she didn't flinch away. She kept her gaze locked with his, those dark eyes like mirrors, reflecting everything around her, revealing nothing inside her.

"I know you're stealing Negroes, Miss Blackwell, and I know this isn't the first time. It will, however, be your last. You've pulled the wool over everyone else's eyes, but you can't outwit me." He stroked her cheek again.

Carrie jerked away from him and took another bead on the barrel.

Rance grabbed her arm. "Don't do this, Carolina. I don't care about the slaves."

"That's the difference between us, Captain. I do care. I care very much."

The pistol exploded in a discharge of bullet and gunpowder. Once, twice, again and again. First one pistol, then, left handed, the other, the firing continuing until all six barrels had been shot, two of them twice. It was the worst job of bunging Rance had ever seen. The holes, which should have been made with a bunging tool, should also have been placed in the exact center of the main stave. Carolina's pistol holes looked like they'd been drilled by a drunk. The barrels were not only ruined, they were also most likely empty.

It was possible, however, that she placed those holes just where she wanted them. His youngest sister could plug a fly on the wing at a dozen paces. There was no reason to believe Carrie couldn't miss a stationary slave at less than three.

She put the pistols back in the wheelhouse. "Now, Captain, I'd appreciate your help in pushing these barrels overboard." She pressed her shoulder against a bullet-riddled barrel and before Rance could react, the barrel was floating down river.

"This isn't necessary," he said.

"Not only are they empty, Captain, they're also ruined. Are you going to help me or not?"

He did, and soon two more barrels were floating downstream.

When she moved to shove the fourth one overboard, Rance stopped her. "All right. I was wrong. The barrels are empty, you've proved it beyond even the most reasonable of doubts."

Her smile was so smug that he laughed. It might take more effort than he'd anticipated, but it was also going to be a great deal of fun knocking Carolina Blackwell's pride out from under her.

"It's good that you take defeat so well," she said. "You're going to have a lot of it to deal with before this war is over."

He could smell the intermingling of gunpowder with the sweet lilac scent of her. It was a strangely intoxicating combination. "You're very sure of yourself, aren't you, Miss Blackwell?" The soft curves of her lips beckoned him. He wondered what would it be like to kiss a girl with eyes that sparkled like a mischievous cat's.

"I thought you didn't like chocolate eclairs, Captain Fletcher."

She looked so pleased with herself, he almost expected her to start purring.

"It must be all that celebration champagne I didn't drink which made me forget." He stepped off the *Adda May* and, from the superior height of the berm, looked down on her. "Before I leave, Miss Blackwell, I want to compliment you on your trick with the barrels. Perhaps someday you'll explain to me how it works."

Her eyes widened. "You can't still believe—"

"We pushed three empty barrels overboard, which leaves exactly three. And since I don't believe in coincidence, I have no choice but to believe what you believe I couldn't possibly believe." He winked at her. "Good night, Yankee."

Her eyes crinkled prettily at the corners, and she laughed up at him. "Turn around, doubting Thomas, and behold the error of your ways."

He followed her glance. From out of the warehouse came not three, but four Negroes. One was a woman, which his agent had not reported. The men were looking at him as though he were about to bullwhip them. The woman never even glanced at him, but went straight to the boat and climbed aboard.

"The papers?" Carrie asked. Hannah handed them to her. She handed them in turn to Rance. "I believe you'll find them all in order, Captain."

He looked through them. Bills of sale for three male Negroes with Carolina Blackwell listed as buyer.

"Forged, of course," he said.

"This time, yes," Carrie answered. "Next time, maybe not."

"Is this the one you was tellin' me about?" Hannah asked in a whisper that could be heard all the way to Washington.

Rance's eyes flashed with laughter, and Carrie decided she liked him a lot less than any person she'd ever met in her entire life.

"You told your maid about me?" he asked with a disarming grin. "How untypically feminine of you, Miss Blackwell."

"I told her that I was mauled by a beast at the dance. Yes, Hannah, this is he."

Jack Douglas was running down the wharf toward the *Adda May,* his knit hat askew and his eyes wide. "What's happened, girl? What were you shooting at? An alligator? A crocodile?"

"Suspicions," Carrie said. "But I didn't kill them. Speaking of killing something, Captain Fletcher, I hope you didn't punish your dog for jumping on me."

Rance shook his head. He knew what was coming next but couldn't think of a way out of it, so he stayed silent and waited.

"Perhaps you could tell me his name so if he attacks me again, I can call him off before he knocks me down and tries to lick my face off."

"Peanut," Rance said, spitting out the word like the foul thing that it was. "My youngest brother named him."

She gave him a smile of pity. "Try not to sound so defensive, Captain, it's most unattractive. Could you untie our bow line before you leave? Jack Douglas still looks a bit harried by my shooting, and I wouldn't want him to fall in the canal."

Rance untied the line and tossed it to the burly barge pilot, who looked more threatening than harried. As the boat drifted away, pulled by mules on the first leg of the long journey to Covington, Rance pulled his coat close about him and began to wonder just how long it would take to wipe that smirking smile off Carolina Blackwell's pretty face.

Chapter Five

Carrie knew the little town of Charleston in western Virginia as a peaceful place of quiet streets and gentle people. The town was situated on the northern bank of the Great Kanawha River, where it was joined by a smaller river known as the Elk. The narrow valley where they merged was embraced by mountains so richly covered with forests that in most places the slopes were impenetrable, as was most of the Appalachian mountain range.

Charleston owed its existence and most of its commerce to its famous salt business, most of which was located in nearby Kanawha Salines. The town's social set was dominated by salt manufacturers who were themselves dominated by a desire to follow the manners and customs of eastern Virginia aristocrats.

The most elite of Charleston society built mansions and owned slaves and affected plantation manners, but no matter how hard they tried or how determinedly they pretended, they were still the small-town residents of a backwoods hamlet. And no matter how many times Carrie denied the accusation, this was still a wilderness. It had no railroad, no telegraph, not even a post office that could be used to deny the unwanted moniker.

Mail was addressed to Kanawha Court House, and from there distributed to the few residents who had contact with the outside world. Freight arrived from the west on steamboats whose range was restricted to only a small portion of the Kanawha's mighty length, or from the east on wagons braving the long and lonely miles of the James River and Kanawha Turnpike.

News often arrived slower than mail, freight, and travelers. In the April 23rd issue of the *Kanawha Valley Star,* Fort Sumter's bombardment on April 12th and its surrender on the 13th were both in the headlines, along with the results of the April 17th vote in Richmond calling for Virginia to secede from the Union.

When Carrie arrived in Charleston a week later aboard a bateaux named *Potbelly Prue,* she realized her hometown had changed. People were everywhere, not singly or in pairs, but in groups and mobs. The valley vibrated from the noise of so many people. To Carrie, the sound was like the menacing and unwelcome drone of swarming bees.

Even the river had changed. The broad expanse of the Kanawha where it flowed past Charleston was not a stranger to river traffic, but now it was untypically crowded with steamboats, barges, and ferries. Despite the crush, the *Potbelly Prue* bullied her way up to the landing and discharged her passengers, then skimmed back out into the center of the river, where she caught the current and continued her journey west toward the Ohio.

On shore, more changes awaited Carrie's discovery. The cargo stacked on the landing was not typical. Normally there would be manufactured goods arriving, things like sewing machines, farm plows, and medicine to stock the shelves of the drugstore and the black leather bags of local doctors. Waiting to be shipped out would be kegs of salt, barrels of wine, and thousands of board feet of lumber smelling of the forest and stained by the sweat of the axman's brow.

There were still a goodly number of salt kegs awaiting shipment, most of which, Carrie was pleased to note, were from Blackwell Salts. Wine and lumber were in such short supply, however, both were almost nonexistent. And arriving at the landing were casks of gunpowder and lead shot, crates of rifles and sabres. A shipment of gray uniforms was being unloaded from a barge, the bulky wool tied into a gigantic bale so heavy that the dock workers groaned at the lifting of it.

Confederate insignias brightened the dull color of the uniforms. Carrie moved closer to see the place of origin for the rebel clothing. Philadelphia, the label read, a town loyal to the Union. War might be a terrible thing, but profit was profit.

Web Sinnet, the freeborn Negro foreman of Blackwell Salts, drove the company wagon onto the landing with a clattering of steel-clad wheels and iron-shod horses. He stepped down beside Carrie, who was making a mental inventory of the incoming freight. She looked up from counting sabre crates to welcome him with a smile.

"I see you got my letter," she said.

He nodded, then took off his felt hat and waved it at the incoming freight. "Things changed 'round here while you was gone."

An ear-splitting explosion filled the valley, the terrible sound ricocheting off the surrounding mountains and echoing back down onto the cringing town.

Carrie waited until the noise had died down before saying, "Apparently not for the better."

Web grinned. "That's Doc Hale's doin'. He turned his salt furnace into a foundry and made himself a cannon. So far the only thing it's good for is makin' noise, but he swears it'll be workin' in plenty of time to kill any Yankees that come callin'. Your daddy's threatenin' to make his own cannon so he can blow up Doc's."

Carrie started to laugh until she remembered that her father always made good on his threats. She grabbed Web's arm. "Pops not really making a cannon, is he?"

"I told him I wasn't havin' no part in it 'cause it was a crazy idea."

Carrie groaned. The easiest way to get Harris Blackwell to do anything was to tell him it was crazy.

"It was that Lucy Bream that stopped him."

Now Carrie did laugh. Her father hated Lucy Bream. In the twenty-odd years since Decca Blackwell first brought Lucy into the house, Harris had fired the bossy housekeeper at least a thousand times. But because she didn't believe in listening to anyone except herself, Lucy was still there, running both the house and Harris' life.

"How ever did she manage it, Web?"

"She moved his wheelchair ramps away from the doors so he can't get out of the house."

He left Carrie laughing and went to get her baggage, over which Hannah had been standing guard. While he loaded their luggage, Hannah supervised the three runaways' boarding of the wagon.

"Keep them eyes down and shoulders slumped," she told them in a threatening whisper. "You ain't free yet."

On the other side of the landing, a young man wearing a long coat of dark green cloth and a dashing black hat decorated with ostrich feathers was comparing the contents of a list he held with a pile of death-dealing supplies. Apparently everything was to his satisfaction, because he turned away with a smile on his face.

His gaze fell on Carrie. His eyes narrowed in pleased recognition before taking in the Negroes in the back of the wagon. "Surely you haven't brought in more workers, Carolina. Your father must already have two men for every job in his furnace."

It took her a moment to recognize her interrogator as George Patton, who owned a very pretty house in Charleston. The last time she'd seen him, though, was in Richmond last year at a Christmas ball. Since then he'd grown a dark curly beard that made him look quite handsome.

She let her gaze slide down to the green uniform, which was a striking complement to his fine figure. The short cape attached to the uniform coat had been flung back over his shoulders, giving him an even more rakish look. A black stripe ran down the sides of the slender trouser legs, and his boots were so highly polished they reflected light like the oily surface of the river.

"When did you join the Kanawha Riflemen, George?" she asked, referring to the volunteer company formed by the male members of Charleston's upper crust society earlier that year.

"I did more than join them. I'm in charge of them. These," he waved a hand at the surveyed supplies, "are our new weapons."

She pretended not to be able to see so far away. He offered his arm, and together they crossed the landing to take a closer look. Once she'd maneuvered him so that the wagon was no longer in his line of sight, she turned her attention to the supplies. George was watching her too closely, though, so she said, "I've never seen so many shotguns before," to give him something to talk about while she took mental inventory of the items George was claiming.

"Rifles," George corrected her. "I ordered them from Harper's Ferry. I was afraid Lincoln's men would confiscate them, but we were lucky." He patted the top of the nearest crate like it was a favored dog.

Carrie finished her inventory and turned her attention back to George. She ran an inquisitive finger along the twin rows of braid on his sleeve, then looked up at the three gold stars on his collar. "Does this mean you're a general?"

"Merely a captain, I'm afraid."

She put on a lip-softening pout. "I wanted to impress you. Instead, I've made a terrible fool of myself. Whatever must you think of me?"

He covered her hand with his and gave it a gentle

squeeze while smiling indulgently down at her. "Dearest Carolina, you are the furthest thing from a fool that I shall ever have the good fortune to meet. As for your charming mistake, I would be honored to personally instruct you in everything you need to know so you can avoid making future errors."

She turned her pout into a grateful smile. "You are a darling, George."

"May I call for you tomorrow morning for our first lesson? I shall have my men put on a special drill for your benefit, then we can tour the camps of the other companies in town."

"I shall not sleep a wink all night in anticipation."

He escorted her back to the wagon and helped her onto the seat beside Hannah, who was rolling her eyes in silent comment.

"Until tomorrow, Carolina," George said, his gaze never once straying from her face to the wagon's human cargo.

Web shouted the draft horses into motion, and the wagon rolled onto Front Street. When George Patton was no longer in sight, Carrie pinched Hannah's arm.

"You know that always makes me laugh. I almost bit my tongue in two trying to keep silent. Web, please get us out of town before anyone else has a chance to wonder why we're bringing in new workers. I don't want to have to flirt my way out of trouble twice in one day."

Chapter Six

Riverway Cabin was built by Harris Blackwell the same week he sunk his first well into Kanawha Valley mud and struck salt water. The one-room log cabin was intended as a home for a bachelor, but the following year while on a business trip to South Carolina, Harris met Decca Grey. He fell in love instantly, courted her unmercifully, and married her a month later. When he brought her to his home in the western Virginia hills, his bride pronounced the cabin primitive and promptly moved into the Kanawha House, Charleston's biggest, and at the time, only hotel.

To please his estranged bride, Harris had commissioned a local carpenter to add room after room until the cabin became a beehive of rooms: bedrooms, dressing rooms, dining rooms, sitting rooms, drawing rooms, and music rooms, until Riverway was unequaled in size by even the grandest plantation in all of Decca's beloved South Carolina.

Despite the drastic change, Riverway had still

retained its title of cabin. That was because even though Harris had given into his wife's demand that the cabin be turned into a house, he'd built every room, from the largest drawing room to the smallest privy closet, the way he wanted them built, and that was the same way he'd built the original cabin, entirely of logs, hand-hewn and caulked with mud, bark unpeeled, sometimes even with limbs untrimmed.

Delicate crystal chandeliers were suspended from ceilings of roughbarked cedar logs. Fine woolen carpets covered floors of split walnut logs. Imported French furniture looked even more fragile when set against walls made of massive chestnut logs.

It was a strange combination and Carrie loved it. She missed Riverway even if gone from it only a few hours. Long trips left her aching to return. Now, as the road wound closer and closer to home, she leaned so far forward in the seat to catch that first precious glimpse of the cabin, she almost fell out of the wagon.

A curl of chimney smoke was the first thing she saw. It drifted against a backdrop of mountains where maple and dogwood trees still slept in winter barrenness. The laughter of water coursing along the stony path of a tiny creek welcomed her next. The wagon followed the deep ruts of the road around a boulder so huge it was like a building, and there, just ahead, was Riverway rising grandly from the center of a patch of cleared ground.

It was just as beautiful as she remembered it, but then she'd only been gone two months, not enough time to forget even the smallest detail. Still, those two months had felt like forever, and she drank in the sight and the smells and the sounds with desperate excitement.

Web brought the wagon around to the front door. Carrie bounded out and ran past the naked branches of lilac bushes that chattered in the wind. With her skirts lifted to her ankles, she took the steps two at a time. At the top, she threw open the door and shouted, "Pops, I'm home!" The cry was answered by the crowing of a rooster from behind the house just as Lucy Bream came out of the kitchen.

"You haven't murdered Samson yet," Carrie said as the rooster crowed again.

"Tomorrow," Lucy said, but it was an empty threat.

Lucy Bream didn't like animals. The only way to get her to tolerate them, which meant not kill them, was by giving them Biblical names. As a result, the breeding sows were named Jezebel and Delilah. Goliath was their surly mate. The plow mules were Matthew and Mark, the carriage horses, Luke and John. The milk cow, for some unremembered reason, was Peter. And while Samson ruled the chicken coop, it was Eve, Mary Magdelene, Esther, Naomi, Dorcas, and Eunice who did all the work by laying eggs and raising broods to fill Lucy Bream's skillets and soup pots.

"Thanks for taking Pops' ramp away," Carrie said. "Where is he?"

"Pouting," Lucy said and waved away the word like a bothersome gnat. "Crazy man."

Carrie took off her hat and and coat and tossed both items onto a chestnut limb before beginning her search. She'd wound her way into and out of half of the rooms on the ground floor before she found him.

He was in the smallest of the three music rooms, all of which had been converted to other uses, since no one in the family had even the slightest musical ability. His wheelchair was pulled close to a battered oak desk covered with stacks and mounds and heaps of papers and books and ashtrays. He was making notes along the side of a gigantic piece of paper, most of which was covered with what looked like a blueprint. The window behind the desk was open, but not even the forest sweet breeze pushing through the curtains was able to subdue the rank smell of smoke that filled the room.

Carrie crossed to the desk, picked up a mouldering cigar, and stubbed it out. She then began to rearrange the clutter on the desk, shuffling and reshuffling until finally her father dropped his pen and sat back in his chair to look at his daughter, who stopped straightening the desk to look at him.

Harris Blackwell was a big man. The wheelchair he'd been confined to for the last six years had taken nothing away from his size, nor from his ability to dominate a room simply by entering it. It was a trait that came as naturally to him as it did to Carrie.

She also had her father's eyes, pirate-eyes Lucy Bream called them, dark and full of fire, another Blackwell trait that could be traced to ancestors who not very long ago had indeed been thieves of the sea. The rest of Carrie's features were inherited from her mother. The combination of Decca's beauty and Harris' personality had created what Hannah Matthew described as "trouble looking for a place to happen."

"Mother's well," Carrie said.

Harris turned back to his drawing. "I've wasted enough time gabbing," he said and dipped his pen in the ink well before scratching a new string of words across the paper.

"She came up to Richmond to attend the Stanard ball celebrating Virginia's secession."

More scratching.

"She was the most beautiful woman in the room. Men were having duels to see which one would dance with her first."

Furious scratching.

"Franklyn Bredon was there, too."

The scratching stopped so suddenly that a dark blob drained from the pen onto the paper. Harris impatiently dumped sand on the spreading blot. With a weighty sigh that implied he'd never known a moment's peace in his entire life, he rolled his chair back from the desk and glared up at Carrie.

"Did you get the contract?"

"Did you think I wouldn't?"

"Were they suspicious?"

"I wore a secession badge on my dress collar and a rosette of palmetto on my bonnet, and I swore an oath that I was as every bit as Southern as cotton. The lot of them were still bug-eyed with suspicion, though, so I repaid their lack of trust by stealing three slaves out from under their traitorous noses."

Harris nodded approval.

"They've put a bloodhound on my trail, Pops. A tobacco farmer named Ransom Fletcher."

"I knew his father. Decent man. A bit too decent for my taste. What's his son like?"

"Not decent at all." She turned her attention to the paper on the desk, brushing away the sand to reveal a drawing of a cannon. "You're not really thinking about making one of these, are you, Pops? You know we can't spare a furnace for you to use as a foundry. As it is, I'm thinking about leasing the old Daniel Boone furnace. We have enough workers to man the kettles, and we could use the extra salt to bribe the rebels into trusting me."

"Are you scared of this Fletcher, girl?"

"You know I'm not afraid of anything except snakes, Pops."

"Why did you pick up that rattler last year?"

"I didn't know it was a rattler, and I picked it up because you bullied me into it."

"What if Fletcher tries bullying you?"

It wasn't the possibility of Rance Fletcher bullying her that frightened Carrie. It was the smile in his eyes and the touch of his hand on her face and the way he'd haunted her dreams, both waking and asleep, every minute and every mile since she left Richmond.

She covered her mouth and faked a yawn. "I'm tired out from traveling. I think I'll take a nap before supper."

She was surprised by how fast her father moved to block the doorway. She didn't have time to take even a single step before the only exit in the room was rendered impassable by his wheelchair's bulk.

"Answer me, Carrie. What are you planning to do if Fletcher tries to bully you?"

She leaned over, grasped hold of the wheelchair, and pushed it, along with its occupant, out of her way. Then, still leaning over so she would be eye to eye with her father, she met his sparking stare. "I'll bully him back, Pops, just like you taught me."

For the first time since she'd entered the room, Harris Blackwell smiled. "Good to have you home, girl."

"Good to be home. Don't relight that cigar when I leave the room."

As she started up the stairs to her bedroom, her grandfather, Peach Blackwell, appeared on the landing and began descending toward her. Peach wasn't really his name, at least he didn't think it was. People had been calling him Peach for so long, he couldn't remember his real name.

"Where have you been?" he demanded when they met on the steps.

"Richmond," she said.

"Damn rebels," he said and started down the steps again.

"Where are you going, Peach?"

"Coon hunting. Want to come?"

"Maybe next time."

"I'll hold you to that." He hefted his shotgun in one hand and a jug of home brew in the other. After casting a glance over his shoulder, which Carrie knew was to be certain Lucy Bream, who also didn't like whiskey, hadn't seen the jug, he threw Carrie a wink. "You keep quiet about this, Mosquito. That colored woman is almost more than I can tolerate without having her riled up about my whiskey."

"Good luck with the raccoons, Gramps."

As he started to leave, she stopped him by calling out, "Peach!"

He turned back to her.

"I looked in the Blackwell family Bible that Mother has down in South Carolina. There was someone named Almarene Blackwell listed on the birth record page. Do you think that could be you?"

He looked horrified. "Almarene? Lordy, I hope not!" His eyes rolled back in his head, and he gave a howling groan of laughter before heading out the door.

In the resulting silence, Carrie heard the popping sound of a match being struck in the little music room.

"I told you not to relight that cigar!" she shouted at her father.

"Mind your own business!" he shouted back.

She smiled. It *was* nice to be home.

Chapter Seven

It didn't take Rance long to discover that the Great Kanawha River Valley was as Southern in its sympathies as Richmond. Charleston was the center of the area's poor attempt at civilization, and it was on fire with secessionist fever. Empty town lots bloomed with the camps of would-be Confederate soldiers. Fields, some so swampy they were like giant mud puddles, were the scenes of drills and gunnery practice. If it wasn't for Harris Blackwell's reputation as a Union loyalist, it would be easy to believe that Carolina's proclaimed Confederate sympathies were real, based purely on the enthusiasm of her hometown for the cause.

James Henry Jones met Rance at the edge of town. He worked for the Blackwells as teamster for their salt shipments. Unknown to them, he also worked for the Confederate government.

"This is their only warehouse," Jones said. He limped heavily on his wooden left leg as he led Rance into the two-story warehouse on Kanawha Street. "They doubled the output from their furnace last year, and production was up the year before that, too. Only I hauled less."

"How much less?" Rance asked.

"Half as much last year as in '58. Maybe a third less in '59."

There was more than enough salt here for Carolina's first scheduled shipment to Richmond, but not nearly enough to make up for that much of a drop in shipping. Rance pried the lid off one of the barrels. The salt inside was the rusty red for which Kanawha Salines was famous. This mineral-rich salt was considered superior for curing meat.

A roar of excitement was heard outside the warehouse. Rance went to the window. In the field that adjoined the warehouse, a band of backwoods recruits were putting on a shooting exhibition, to the obvious delight of a crowd of onlookers.

"That's the Logan County Wildcats," Jones said. "They've been showing off all week. Can't nobody beat them."

"Let's have a look," Rance said. "There's nothing else we can do until it gets dark."

The leader of the Wildcats was a wild-haired, wild-eyed, lanky-framed mountaineer who, with an antique flintlock squirrel rifle, was out shooting every man in town. He was also taking them for everything they were gullible enough to bet.

Rance watched the captain of the Kanawha

Riflemen take aim at the top branch of a wind-hassled pine tree at the opposite end of the clearing two hundred yards away. He missed.

Anderson Hatfield put the hammer on his flintlock at half-cock, poured powder into the barrel, and tapped it to settle the charge. He put a patch of cloth over the muzzle, dropped a lead ball onto it, and rammed it home with his ramrod. Instead of using a percussion cap, he primed the flash pan with gunpowder. He lifted the squirrel rifle to his shoulder, sighted along the barrel at the tossing tree limb, cocked his hammer back all the way, and pulled the trigger.

The flint mounted on the hammer struck the hinged cover of the pan, spraying sparks onto the priming powder, which ignited with a flash the powder in the breech. The gun discharged its lead ball with a belch of noise and smoke. A moment later, the end of the limb was missing its needles. The branch itself was untouched.

Someone in the crowd let go a screech that sounded like a tribe of wild Indians being massacred. Laughter followed the yell, and as it was dying away, Rance heard her.

"Stop pouting, George, and pay Mr. Hatfield. It's much too lovely a day to be shot as a welsher."

Rance raked his gaze through the crowd, and there she was, a cocky pheasant feather dancing in her hat and a smile sparkling on her upturned face. The defeated captain was the object of her teasing attention. He handed Hatfield a handsome pocketknife.

"Nice doin' business with you, Cap'n," Hatfield said and began to look for his next victim.

Carolina's eyes flashed like midnight moonlight as she linked her arm with the captain's, then turned away from him to speak to a pretty girl beside her, who hid a fit of giggles behind a gloved hand.

The expression on Carolina's face suddenly changed. Rance saw again the cautiousness she had displayed when his whispering of her name had caused her to pause on the Stanards' front steps. He moved to the back of the crowd while her gaze flicked across the meadow. Where he had been standing, her glance hesitated, then passed on, her suspicions fading only when her escort insisted on leaving the scene of his defeat.

Rance approached Hatfield. "Think you can shoot the feather off that girl's hat?" he asked and pointed at the retreating Carolina. The tip of the brightly colored feather bobbed inches from her ear as she carried on a laughing conversation with the captain and the girl who accompanied them.

"Sure," Hatfield said.

"Without her knowing it?" Rance asked and the mountaineer's black eyes sparkled with confidence.

"What are you bettin'?"

"A fitting replacement for that peashooter you're wielding."

"Deal," Hatfield said and loaded the flintlock

with amazing speed. He used a smaller load of powder and a lead ball so small it looked like a gnat.

The gun barrel gleamed like dark danger in the Kanawha Valley sun as he lifted the rifle to his shoulder. A flash of fire, a spitting of smoke from the end of the barrel, and Carolina Blackwell continued her flirting stroll, completely unaware that she was no longer adorned with a feather.

Rance threw back his head and laughed. She'd be angry as a hornet when she found the feather missing. The only thing that would make the joke better was if he could sign his name to it.

"Great shot," Rance said and slapped Hatfield on the back. "I have the perfect rifle for your skill at the livery."

Cain was trying to kick his way out of the stall at the stable. "Easy there," Rance said and pushed the stallion out of the way so he could get to his gear. "This is the best weapon on the market today, Hatfield." He handed the mountaineer a Sharps rifle. "Breech-loading, .52 caliber, accurate to six hundred yards, and can fire up to ten rounds a minute without jamming."

Hatfield ran a hand along the deadly length of the Sharps barrel. "It's a beauty," he said. "I can shoot a lot of Yankees with this."

"If you're looking for infantry work, try the 8th Virginia," Rance said. "Good men in that outfit. You'd be a welcome addition."

Hatfield's face grimaced into a grin. "Since

when did horse soldiers talk proud about fighting men?"

"It doesn't take a genius to see it's going to take more than a few brandishes of cavalry sabres to win this war," Rance said. "If I get into a situation where brandishing mine won't get me out, I'd like to know you and that Sharps are covering my back."

Hatfield nodded. "We'll be there, friend."

Chapter Eight

Candlelight and the smell of hair tonic. Roasted duck, fried mushrooms, sweet potatoes browned in a butter and sugar sauce. Claret soup and lettuce salad, baked onions, almond cake, and apple brandy. And served with everything, a generous helping of discussion, argument, and compromise, along with plans, plots, and promises.

It was a small gathering. That was the only kind Riverway Cabin could host. The dining room was the cabin's biggest room, but it also held the biggest table Carrie had ever seen. Made of cherrywood, the table was so large the room had been built around it. Neither chairs nor guests had been taken into consideration during the construction. As a result, diners had to squeeze around the table's ponderous girth to reach their chairs, which they then had to squeeze into. Because there was no room for Lucy to serve, guests had to hand the food from one to the next like a bucket in a fire brigade.

Carrie wore a green velvet dress so rich in color it resembled spring-fed moss. Her father said she looked like something growing on the log behind her. "I don't know whether to feed you or scrape you off before you spread."

"Does that mean you don't like my dress?" She liked it, or had before his comment. Now it felt moist and spongy.

"I don't have anything against moss, but maybe you should sit on the south side of the room just in case that Lucy Bream has something against it."

While the evening's debate progressed, Carrie took plates from her father at the head of the table and passed them to Dr. Spicer Patrick on her right. Next in line at the table was George Summers, who with Spicer had attended the Richmond Convention as Kanawha County delegates. They had both voted against the Ordinance of Secession. And across the table sat Maj. E. J. Allen and Francis H. Pierpont.

Everyone except Major Allen, who was a visitor not only to Harris Blackwell's table but also to Virginia, entered the heated discussions. The topic—the refusal of the western counties of Virginia to be subjugated by the state's secessionist government.

Of the forty-seven representatives from the west, thirty had voted against withdrawing from the Union. Now, not only here but everywhere in the loyal counties, meetings were being held to defy their mother state and setup a loyal government of their own. Maybe even a new state. It wasn't a new idea. It was an old and much discussed idea whose time had finally come.

When the meal had ended and brandy was being

enjoyed at the table, for everyone had eaten too much to attempt an exit from the room, the talking continued.

"Setting up a restored Virginia government is just a stepping stone to claiming our independence from the Old Dominion," Harris said. "It won't be long before we'll be lifting our glasses to toast the new state of Kanawha."

Carrie was sipping cherry cider, a poor substitute for brandy but the strongest drink Harris allowed her. ("I don't care if you're a *hundred* and twenty, you're not drinking brandy!" he'd told her before their guests arrived. She had accepted her defeat gracefully. It wasn't the first time she'd lost an argument with him, and she'd bet her best petticoat it wouldn't be the last. Besides, she didn't like apple brandy any better than she liked apples, which wasn't at all. The only reason she started the argument was because she thought they were going to have imported brandy.)

"One thing at a time, Pops," she said in response to his enthusiastic support of a new state.

Spicer agreed with her. "We have to get back in the good graces of the Union before we start writing a constitution for a new state."

"Whatever we do," Harris said, "we'll have to do it in Wheeling. That's far enough out of the reach of the Confederacy to avoid any trouble from Governor Letcher."

"Richmond is already buzzing with talk of holding the Kanawha Valley," George Summers said.

"And President Lincoln can't help us until we prove we want it," Pierpont added.

Major Allen had finished his brandy. Now he wipcd his beard and squeezed out of his chair. "Gentlemen, and Miss Blackwell, I am grateful for the opportunity to have shared a meal and the thoughts of so many loyal Virginians. This evening has been a pleasure and an education. I wish you luck with your ambitious plans. Good evening."

The other men left, too, each one thanking Harris and Carrie, the brave among them also offering praise to Lucy Bream, who hovered just inside the front door of the cabin like a disagreeable watchdog. Harris finally shooed her away, and Carrie stood at his side as they bid Spicer, the last to go, good night.

"It will be a hard fight, Harris."

Her father scrolled his thumb along the arm of his chair. "All fights are hard. This one won't be any worse than the rest of them."

Spicer took Carrie's hand in his. "I know you support us in wanting a new state, my dear, but I wish you were on our side in the bigger fight that's coming."

She'd known him all her life. He'd set the arm she'd broken when she was seven. He'd treated the pneumonia that almost killed her at eleven. He had pulled ticks from her hair, laughed at her childish jokes, and had been disappointed when she didn't marry his son, Spicer Jr. He'd seen her through mumps and measles, had gone fishing with her and spent many nights sitting on the cold ground with her and Peach, listening to their dogs trail raccoons across hill and valley.

She respected Spicer Patrick and she loved him. And now, as he stood holding her hand, she would have given anything in the world to be able to tell him the truth. But not even he could be trusted with that secret.

"I'm afraid I'm too much my mother's daughter, Doc."

He turned her hand over and traced the heart line on her palm with his index finger. "I've never known this line to lie, Carrie, and it runs true to north."

She closed her fingers over the telltale line. "I never would have taken you for a witch doctor, either, so I guess we've both been mislead."

Spicer laughed. "I don't care what you want me to believe, Carrie. In my book, you're all Blackwell, and that makes you as Union loyal as your old man. Good night, my dear." He kissed her cheek. "As for you, Harris, stop smoking those rot-gut cigars. If you have to disobey my orders, at least get something that smells better than those things you buy."

He left, and Carrie closed the door behind him, then turned to her father. "I told you he'd know you hadn't stopped smoking."

"Stop your fussing and get to bed, girl."

"Not yet. One of our guests is coming back. Let's wait in the music room."

"I don't trust this Allen character, Carrie. He doesn't know enough about the military to know which way to point a firing squad. I don't want you risking your life to get information for him."

Carrie's assessment of Major Allen was not too far different from her father's. Allen was really the famous detective Alan Pinkerton, and even though he'd saved Abraham Lincoln's life by exposing an assassination plot prior to Lincoln's inauguration, Pinkerton had no military skills. He had, however, offered Carrie a chance to serve the Union, and through it, the abolition of slavery.

Harris had been studying her face. "Maybe that Fletcher boy will change your mind about this craziness."

"I can outsmart Rance Fletcher every day of the week and twice on Sundays with half my brain tied behind my back."

"It's not your brain he's gonna be trying to outsmart, Mosquito." It was Peach. He was sitting in the little music room, feet propped up on the desk and a dog stretched out on the floor beside him.

"Catch anything?" Carrie asked. It was the first time she'd seen him since he left to go hunting yesterday.

"A doozy of a hangover and a no-account rebel captain. I came into town this afternoon and saw him watching you. I've been returning the favor."

So, she hadn't been imagining things. Rance had been there today. She held her breath; forcing her heart to slow its fevered rush of beats. "He was at the exhibition of the Logan Wildcats," she said.

Peach nodded. "He paid Hatfield to shoot your feather off."

She thought George Patton took it as a token.

"Where is he now?" Harris asked.

"Philip Snell's office, only Snell doesn't know it."

Snell was the salt inspector at Kanawha Salines. It was his responsibility to judge as merchantable all salt being shipped for sale to towns of more than two-thousand inhabitants. He weighed the salt, determined product quality, and collected fees.

"And guess who's been giving this Fletcher the town tour? Peg-leg Jones."

"James Henry Jones?" Carrie couldn't believe it. James Henry had been working for her father for more than fifteen years. He might be as stubborn as the mules he drove, but he was also just as loyal.

A teamster who hauled salt and a salt inspector's office. What was going on?

"What could Fletcher possibly want in Snell's office?" She paced the short distance across the room. "I thought my contract with the Confederacy was just the excuse he used to approach me at the dance."

Harris started to light a cigar. Carrie caught his eye and lifted a threatening eyebrow. He scowled at her, but blew out the match and tossed the cigar on the desk beside his father's feet.

"We won't learn anything from James Henry," Harris said. "He's more tight-lipped than a lock-jawed donkey. We'll have to keep an eye on him and see if we can figure out his connection with this Fletcher."

"Maybe it's those boys you stole," Peach said to Carrie. "Peg-leg would be the first one in line to join the rebels if he had all his parts."

She shook her head. "Rance had a chance to stop me in Richmond and didn't take it. It has to be something else, something to do with our salt. But what?"

A knock on the front door drew Harris out of the room.

Peach gave Carrie a hard stare. "You be careful of this Fletcher, girl, and remember what I said about what he's going to be after. You and I both know you'd slit your own throat just to prove you're not afraid to do it, and what he's going to be challenging you with is a long sight more tempting than a knife in the neck. I wouldn't feel right about killing a man that you opened the barn door for, Carrie. I'd do it, I just wouldn't feel right about it."

"Don't worry, Gramps. Rance doesn't like chocolate eclairs." She winked at him and turned to greet their late-night guest. "Major Allen, this is my grandfather, Peach Blackwell."

"I know you," Peach said. "You're that Pinkerton who saved Lincoln in Baltimore."

Pinkerton assumed a noble expression and overlaid it with a humble smile. "I must insist that you call me Major Allen. That shall be my only name until this war is over."

Carrie unearthed chairs for him and herself. "I

have a clever idea for the code you wanted me to use in my communications, Major." She leaned forward and launched into an enthusiastic explanation.

"Excellent!" Major Allen exclaimed. "If there is no courier available, you can send it through the post like a regular letter without worrying about detection. Even if it should be opened, it will offer no reason for suspicion."

Harris hadn't been so easily convinced. "You sure this will work, Allen? My girl is already under suspicion. I don't want her putting her head any deeper into the noose than it already is.

"Tell me, Mr. Blackwell, would you look for military secrets in a letter filled with gossip and fashion news?"

"If I was fighting a war, I'd suspect a horse's ass if it showed up where it didn't belong. Anyone who knows my daughter will wonder what she's doing shoveling manure."

"Don't worry so much, Pops. Not even their best bloodhound will see anything except what I want him to see. I'll address the letters to Mary Allen, Major, and send them to the address you gave me in Washington."

"You are a lovely and valuable asset to my corp of agents, Miss Blackwell. Your connections with the Confederate government, as well as your acceptance in Southern society, will open many doors." Major Allen stood. "Now I must bid you farewell. My boat leaves early tomorrow, and I mustn't miss it."

After he and Harris left the room, Peach chuckled under his breath. "Pretty good, Mosquito. Where'd you come up with that idea?"

She leaned back in her chair and grinned. "From a chocolate-eclair hater, Gramps."

"What are you talking about with this eclair business? I don't even know what an eclair is."

"It's a flaky pastry filled with rich cream and smothered in chocolate. They're quite the rage in Richmond. And that's the way Fletcher looks at me, like I'm a chocolate eclair he'd like to take a bite out of, only he doesn't like eclairs."

"You remind him if he ever gets close enough to take that bite."

She jumped up and kissed Peach's scratchy cheek. "You've got my word on it, Gramps. Good night." She skipped out of the room and bumped into her father's chair. "Sorry, Pops. See you tomorrow," she said and ran up the stairs.

"Stop running in the house!"

"Grouch!"

"Gossip!"

Carrie laughed as she entered her room and shut the door behind her. The hat she'd worn that day was on her bed. The stubby end of her feather stuck out like a frozen frog's tongue. It was a good thing Anderson Hatfield was a better shot than George Patton. Otherwise she'd be too dead to wonder why Ransom Fletcher was poking around the salt inspector's office.

* * *

The office was stuffy. Smells of dust and ink, coal-oil lanterns and some other undefinable stink caused Rance to want to rush through this tiresome task. He denied the urge and settled down to work.

One hour, two, almost three passed before he finished auditing the last four years of salt inspection records for Blackwell Salts. Rance tabulated the last column of figures, wrote the total, and sighed as he sat back in the chair. There was no doubt now. Carrie was definitely up to something.

In 1857 and 1858, Harris Blackwell sold one-hundred twenty-five thousand pounds of inspected salt. In 1859, and again in 1860, the figures dropped to ninety-thousand and fifty-thousand respectively. But according to James Henry Jones, the furnaces had not only maintained production levels during those years, the volume of salt produced had been increased. Not even by adding the salt reported by Blackwell Salts as being sold without inspection did the figures for the last two years approach previous sales records.

Carolina had taken over management of her father's company just prior to the first quarterly drop in inspected salt sales. Even though that was two years ago, most of the country had long been convinced of the inevitability of civil war. The logical reason for stockpiling was speculation. Salt was one of the most important products on the market. If the war lasted even a year, the price would skyrocket. The piece of the puzzle that didn't fit was why a potential speculator would contract to sell her product at half the market price for the duration of the war.

Rance frowned at the figures spread before him. He was going at this from the wrong direction. Trying to figure out why a woman did something was a waste of time. Why Carolina was stockpiling salt didn't matter anyway. Only where.

He put the ledgers away, closed the ink, and turned down the lantern wick. The flame faded and died, releasing a streamer of white smoke. Outside, the only sounds were the quiet lappings of the Kanawha River against its banks, and somewhere in the night, a bullfrog croaking his contentment.

James Henry was leaning against the office wall. He flicked the ash from his smoke. "Well?"

"You were right." Rance buttoned his coat against the chill wind blowing down from the mountains. "Now comes the hard part—finding that missing salt."

Chapter Nine

The trip to Wheeling was interesting, and it had also been productive. Harris Blackwell took part in forming the Reorganized State of Virginia. Francis H. Pierpont was named governor of the provisional government, and newly elected senators were on their way to Washington to seek admittance to Congress. The men who had participated in the political mutiny had dreamed of this day for so long, the reality of it was hard to grasp.

Carrie had spent a few days watching the reformation politics, then left for Cincinnati to work with Major Allen on polishing the code she would use to relay whatever Confederate secrets she was able to uncover. When all was said and done, her part was going to be easier than Major Allen's, who had to ferret the secrets out of her letters.

Now the Blackwells were on their way home, after a short visit with the Union's newest hero, General George B. McClellan. His victory at Philippi in the northern part of Virginia was the war's first military engagement west of the Alleghenies. The press had christened him "Little Napoleon," elevating him to the heights he believed he deserved.

"Stop strutting and start fighting," had been Harris' advice to the general. Because Major Allen worshipped McClellan almost as much as McClellan himself, Carrie had kept her opinion of the game-cock general to herself.

Now, as the *Julia Maffitt* steamed within sight of Charleston, Carrie wished that she had told McClellan that a little less planning and a lot more action would be preferable. The reason for her change of attitude was waving in the warm June breeze above the Kanawha Court House. Until this moment, she'd never realized that each time she approached Charleston, it wasn't the town itself that drew her eye, but the flag that had forever waved over it. During this absence from home, those beloved Stars and Stripes had been replaced with Stars and Bars.

A terrible ache tore at her. She'd thought her loyalty to the Union was founded only on her determination to see slavery abolished. Now she knew that wasn't the only reason she was willing to risk her life as an agent for the Union.

The *Julia Maffitt* pushed confidently through the Kanawha River's greasy water, the steamship's bow slapping at the current in her eagerness to make dock. The landing was too crowded with barges, though, and as Captain Nat Turner held the *Julia Maffitt* in midstream, he spat curses at the fresh coat of oil adhering to his ship's hull.

Carrie frowned at the greasy stains, too, The oil was an unwanted by-produce of pumping brine out of the valley depths and was allowed to overflow the settling vats at the salt furnaces. The smelly substance then spilled into the Kanawha, giving rise to the river's nickname of Old Greasy.

The oil was a fact of life in the valley that she never thought about except when on the *Julia Maffitt,* for it was on this ship's decks where Carrie had first "seen the comet." The term had been coined when a comet so bright it could be seen even during the day had appeared in the sky over America.

While the superstitious, including Lucy Bream, saw marching armies in the comet tail that were claimed to be a prediction of the end of the world, young people all over the country had spotted in the comet's tail an opportunity not to be missed. Whenever a couple wished to steal a private moment away from ever-watchful elders, they pleaded a desire to "see the comet."

It was during a trip to Cincinnati aboard the *Julia Maffitt* that a dark-eyed gambler with a smile that would melt solid steel had shown Carrie just how exciting comet watching could be. It had not been her first kiss, but it had been the first time she realized a kiss could be much more than just a pleasant diversion on a moonlit stroll. That devil-hearted gambler had inflamed her with the first feelings of passion she'd ever experienced. She'd come so close to swooning in his arms that just thinking about it now made her feel faint. The very thought of being backed against an unyielding wall by a man, the way that gambler had backed her against the wall beneath the deck stairs, and Carrie's knees threatened to collapse. Recently, instead of the wild-eyed gambler, her dream kisser had become Ransom Fletcher.

"What's wrong with you, girl?" her father asked. "Your face just turned beet red."

She snapped back to reality so quickly she had to grasp the railing to keep from falling. "I'm seasick," she said.

"Bull. You're mooning over some man. Stop acting like a lovesick heifer and grab hold of this chair. We've been docked for almost five minutes."

She pushed her father to the ramp, where Captain Turner took over the task of maneuvering the wheelchair off the boat and onto the landing, where Web Sinnet waited to assume command.

While Web lifted her father into the carriage, Carrie glanced back at the *Julia Maffitt,* her gaze catching and lingering on the shadowed alcove below the stairs to the second deck. Her face flushed hot, and she whipped around, irritated by the disturbingly persistent image of Rance Fletcher, and found herself face-to-face with him.

"Why is your face so red?" he asked.

"She's seasick," Harris announced from his perch in the carriage. "At least that's the lie she told me. Who are you and what business is it of yours why my daughter's face is red?"

Mortified by her father's bluntness, Carrie didn't even bother to wonder what Rance was doing there.

"Captain Ransom Fletcher," she said, "this is my father, Harris Blackwell. He's loyal to the Union, so watch your back. You'd best watch your front, too. Pops likes to look his enemy in the eye while he's stabbing them in the back. If you're ready, Pops, I'm eager to get home. Good day, Captain Fletcher."

"I'm not ready to leave yet," Harris said, "so calm yourself, girl. I want to know what this Fletcher is doing in Charleston." He looked Rance over. "I knew your father. I don't think he'd approve of you waiting on this landing to ambush my daughter, and I don't hold with it, either. State your business, and let's clear the air."

"Pops, whatever his business is here, it's none of our business. Let's go home."

Rance grinned. Harris Blackwell was a bigger-than-life version of Carolina. Right this minute, they had identical scowls plastered on their faces. The only difference was hers sent Rance's pulse racing while Harris put him on his guard.

"Too bad you're a Lincoln lover, Mr. Blackwell. Jefferson Davis could use a man like you on his cabinet. We need more bluntness and less politics."

"I don't know if you're insulting me or complimenting me. I do know you're avoiding my question."

Carrie's insides were twisting into knots. Every

time she looked at Rance, which was at least once for every breath she took, she felt again the caress of his hand on the side of her face. Memories like that weren't good for her health. She tried staring at her hands, the rear of the horses, even the accursed Confederate flag wagging in the wind over the court house. Her gaze refused to stay away from him, though, and her mind refused to think about anything other than what it would feel like to be kissed by Ransom Fletcher.

"He's probably here looking for recruits, Pops, not me."

"Your father's right, Miss Blackwell, I was looking for you. Your last two shipments to Richmond have been short by a few hundred pounds."

Carrie crushed her reticule in angry hands. "How dare you accuse me of undershipping my salt!"

"That's enough," Harris said.

"He just called me a thief, Pops!"

She looked so indignant that Rance almost laughed. The way she was clutching her bag, though, made him wonder if it held something more deadly than hair ribbons and lace handkerchiefs, so he stifled his amusement in favor of looking offended.

"My orders are to escort your next shipment to guard against highwaymen, Miss Blackwell, not accuse you of speculation."

"Speculation!" she cried. "I sell my salt to the Confederacy at a loss and you accuse me of speculating? If I had a gun, I'd bung you so full of holes you'd be leaking like a ferry with termites!"

"That contract might have been a ploy to gain Confederate trust," Rance said. "You put part of each shipment aside, blame it on theft, then later sell it an inflated price. For all I know, you might already have thousands of pounds of salt hidden away waiting to do just that."

From the clipped way he spoke, Carrie could almost believe he already thought her guilty of just such a plot. She met his glaring stare with a sudden smile. "That's an excellent idea, Captain. I wish I'd thought of it. Not only would it make me rich, it would make my father very happy, wouldn't it, Pops? I'm certain you'd much rather have a dirty, low-down speculator for a daughter than a rebel." She kept her smile trained on Rance. "Now that you've amused us with that delightful little flight of fancy, Captain, why don't you tell us what you're really doing here so my father's curiosity will be satisfied and we can go home?"

"I was waiting to find out when your next shipment is leaving Charleston."

"Are you staying at the Kanawha House?" she asked. He nodded. "You should ask them for the weekly rate then, Captain, because the next shipment isn't until Tuesday." She gave him a smirking smile. "I do hope you find someway to amuse yourself until then. Good day, Captain. Web, we're leaving now."

"Wait," Harris ordered. "What did I teach you about suspicious people, Carrie?"

Now she was certain she didn't like her father's bluntness. She glared at him, then turned to Rance.

"When I was ten, I was caught trying to steal an apple from the grocer. Pops took the strap to me, not because I'd tried to steal something, but because I did it on the sly. He said if I was going to do something illegal, do it in the open. People won't expect it, so they won't notice it. In other words, instead of sneaking that apple out of the store in my pocket, I should've eaten it right in front of the grocer. His natural inclination would have been to think that I brought it into the store with me."

"To stop her from stealing apples," Harris said, "I made her eat them until she got sick." He nodded. "Stopped her from stealing."

"It also stopped me from eating apples. To allay your suspicions about my sending those shipments out short, Captain, I'll give you a guided tour of our operation to prove we have nothing to hide."

"Is tomorrow too soon?"

Carrie already had an appointment tomorrow, one which Rance's presence in Charleston made even more vital. "Perfect," she said, deciding as she spoke that Rance Fletcher was a lot more aggravating than her faceflushing daydreams had allowed her to remember. "The blueberry pancakes at the Kanawha House are the best in

Virginia. I'll meet you there for breakfast."

Rance had been watching the dimple in her chin. Obviously, tomorrow was far from being her preferred day for the tour. His presence in Charleston must be putting a serious crimp in her schemes.

No sense in pushing her too far, he decided. She still had a pretty good grip on her bag. "How about ten o'clock?" he asked. That would also give him time to do a little exploring on his own.

Harris snorted out a derisive laugh. "I thought farmers got up with the sun."

"Not the ones who have slaves to do all the work," Carrie said.

Her eyes were cold as they dared Rance to respond to the taunt. He held his silence.

"Ten is fine," Carrie finally said.

"Until tomorrow," he said and touched the brim of his hat to her. "Good day."

Carrie concentrated on remembering how much she didn't like him as she watched him stride away.

"Now I know why your face keeps turning red," her father said.

"You're wrong, Pops," she said, but even to her own ears, the denial lacked conviction.

Chapter Ten

Carrie didn't know what to do. Pryce Lewis couldn't have just fallen off the face of the earth, and yet that was how it appeared. Last night he'd dined with George Patton at Camp Thompkins. He'd left there early this morning for Charleston, a mere twelve miles distant, where tomorrow he and Carrie were scheduled to have a "chance" encounter.

After that chance meeting, she would have introduced him into Charleston society as a friend sympathetic to the Confederate cause who could be trusted with even the most intimate Southern secrets. If she couldn't find Lewis before tomorrow and cancel their meeting, Rance's doubts about her loyalty to the South would make Pryce Lewis suspect, too.

She paced the three steps across the little music room, turned, and paced back. "I don't understand, Pops. I've checked every hotel, every inn and saloon, every nook and cranny from Coal Mouth to here, but no one has seen either him or

Sam Bridgeman." They were both agents sent by Major Allen to scout the valley. Lewis was posing as a titled Englishman, Bridgeman as his servant.

"Sit down," Harris ordered, "you're making me dizzy. We'll post Web Sinnet on the west side of town. When Lewis shows up, Web will tell him not to acknowledge he knows you, that way Fletcher won't have someone else to be suspicious of." Harris smacked his hand on the arm of his wheelchair. "Problem solved."

"There's more to it than that, Pops. I have to find another way to get them into the good graces of General Wise so Lewis can take over my assignment of prying information out of him." Henry Wise was the ex-governor of Virginia. Because of his respected reputation in the Kanawha Valley, he had been put in charge of the Confederate forces there. His arrival was scheduled for tomorrow, which didn't leave Carrie much time to think of a plan.

She started to pace again. "Who do people trust completely without knowing a single thing about them, Pops?"

"Heroes," Harris said.

Carrie stopped pacing. "Exactly!" She hugged her father. "I'll tell Web our plan tomorrow morning. Good night, Pops."

"Wait a minute. What plan?"

"To find Pryce Lewis and make him a hero."

"How are you going to do that?"

"I haven't the slightest idea. But I'm certain I'll

think of something. Don't let the bed bugs bite, Pops."

A half-hour later as Carrie curled into bed, her hair brushed and braided, her nightgown tied snugly around her wrists and neck, and her feet warm inside woolen socks, she still hadn't thought of a plan. She had, however, thought a great deal about Rance Fletcher. Seeing him today had brought back with disturbing clarity the memory of those first few moments of their dance when she'd been willing to sell her soul to spend the rest of her life in his arms.

What would she do if he made an advance toward her tomorrow? There were so many secluded, dark corners at the saltworks. He was just the kind of man to take advantage of an opportunity like that. The first corner they encountered, he'd probably press her back against a convenient wall and have his way with her right there in her own father's saltworks!

"How disgusting," she said aloud and hugged herself to stop the fevered rush of chills that had claimed her.

Chapter Eleven

Rance had never seen anyone so pleased with herself. Carrie virtually glowed with self-satisfaction. She was sitting across the table from him at the restaurant in the lobby of the Kanawha House eating pancakes and flirting with every man in the room, including the waiter, who was eighty if he was a day, and excluding Rance.

He wanted to strangle her.

"What's going on, Carolina?"

She opened her cat-bright eyes wide. "What do you mean, Captain? Oh look, it's Pamela!"

She rushed to meet her friend. Pamela Weese's dark hair and pale green eyes had been the undoing of every boy in town and quite a few of the men. Carrie brought her to their table and introduced her to Rance. Pamela dropped her gaze beneath his daring stare.

"Delighted," he said, standing up to tower over the blushing beauty. He even went as far as to press a kiss to the back of her hand.

Carrie wanted to strangle him.

Just because this was what she wanted, which was for Pamela to distract him so she could concentrate on what to do regarding Pryce Lewis, there was no reason Rance had to enjoy it so much.

"Pamela is joining us today, along with her brother, who will be our chaperone."

"Barton is waiting for us outside," Pamela said in her breathy whisper of a voice that caused Rance to stand a little taller.

Perfect, Carrie thought. *He's forgotten that I exist. Now if I can just stop clenching my jaw so tightly, I'll have plentv of time to figure out what to do next.*

Kanawha Salines was six miles east of Charleston. Tall chimneys marked the location of the furnaces that lined both sides of the Kanawha River. Only eleven of the seventy-two furnaces were in operation. Coal-oil production had become the newest industry of choice in the valley. Many of the salt barons had turned their attention to that growing business. Still, last year alone, those eleven furnaces had produced a million and a half bushels of salt.

"Pamela and I have to change before we go in," Carrie said. "Barton, maybe you can acquaint Captain Fletcher with the owners of the chimneys he can see from here."

"Carrie," Pamela said. "I think I'll stay here

while you take the men through. You know how I dislike those terrible leather things you wear, and I really just came along for the ride."

"I'll stay with my sister," Barton said.

Now for the true test of Pamela's power. Carrie turned to Rance. "What about you?"

"As delightful as the alternative is," he said while practically devouring Pamela with his eyes, "I would like to see the saltworks."

"I'll be right back," Carrie snapped.

Once inside her father's office, she stripped off her riding skirt and put on a stiff leather skirt. When it was secured, she took two deep breaths to calm her skidding heartbeats and went to join her nemesis.

Rance took in her costume change with a questioning glance. "Why the strange garb?"

Not only did she not answer, she didn't even slow down as she passed him. "This way," she said and kept walking at a rapid clip into the rear yard where the wells were located. "The deepest is eighteen hundred feet. There's also a pocket of gas at that depth. It brings our brine to the surface without need for a pump."

Rance couldn't stop staring at her bulky leather skirt. What ever had possessed her to put on such a thing?

"Who drilled the first saltwater well in the valley?" he asked.

Carrie tapped her foot impatiently at his delaying question. She had intended to discard the rest of her tourist speech about the wells in favor of moving onto the next step, the collecting cisterns, which just happened to provide a view of the area where Pamela and Barton were waiting.

"Two men named Ruffner in 1808," Carrie said. "It was the first rock-drilled well west of the Alleghenies, if not in America. It took months to drill and they sold their first product for four cents a pound. Anything else, or can we move along?"

Without waiting for an answer, she rushed toward the cisterns, where she explained how the brine brought up from the wells was put into the cisterns where the accompanying oil was allowed to run off into the river.

Barton must have said something funny, because Pamela was filling the air with her seductive laughter. Rance was more interested in the oil running down the side of the cisterns. Carrie didn't understand why her plan wasn't working. Pamela attracted men like skunk cabbage attracted flies.

"How many barrels of oil do you bring up in a day?" Rance asked.

She stopped glaring at her friend and turned to answer him. He was standing so close, she could see the sunlight reflecting in his eyes. She'd spent the whole night worrying about keeping him away from dark corners, yet here they were in broad daylight and in full view of two people and he was standing so close to her that if Peach saw him, there would be one less captain in Jefferson Davis' cavalry.

"Twenty-five to fifty," she said, exhaling the answer in a rush. "The wells that use steam pressure to raise the brine bring up the most oil. In our gas pressure well, it's just the weather that affects the flow. Winter turns it thick as jelly. In the summer it's a lot thinner and easier to raise."

She looked scared out of her wits, which Rance found charmingly attractive, and he bent to kiss her.

"We also pumped up a dead fish once," she said in desperation. She was fighting for her life now because she knew if he came even a fraction of an inch closer, she would die on the spot. "It was solid white and blind. Pops said it was a cavefish and couldn't figure out how it got in our well."

Rance couldn't decide whether to laugh or kiss her into silence.

"I think Web put that fish in the well as—a—as a—" His lips were so close Carrie could almost taste them.

"Joke?" Rance asked.

Her mouth was watering. "Yes, as a joke."

"Carrie?"

"Yes?"

"Why are you wearing that ugly leather skirt?"

She instinctively glanced down. Her forehead collided with his jaw.

"I didn't think the question was cause for an attack," he said, and she covered her mouth to keep from laughing.

"I'm sorry, Rance. I forgot how close you were."

"First you break my urge to kiss you with a story about a dead fish, then you break my jaw with your forehead. Now you're breaking my heart by saying you forgot I was here."

Now she did laugh. It caused her tension to disappear, putting her comfortably back in control. "Come on," she said and taking him by the arm, lead him into the main building.

There were four sections of the furnace. Each section consisted of ten cast-iron pans, each measuring eight by three feet, which had been bolted together. The sections were filled with brine, which was boiled over gas-fed fires.

"This is why I wear this!" Carrie said, shouting to be heard over the roar of the fires and boiling brine. "Six years ago, I was in here with my father and my skirt caught fire!"

She went into the next room, which was quieter. It was filled with settling vats, each ten feet wide and a hundred feet long. The boiled brine was sent through copper pipes from the furnaces into these vats, where the excess water was encouraged to evaporate by steam heat while the salt was allowed to settle.

"Pops stripped the burning cloth off me before I could get hurt," she said, going on with her story in a quieter voice. "He was so worried about me, he didn't notice how close he was to the boiling brine. He tripped, fell into one of the pans, and his legs were badly scalded."

Rance's stomach clenched and his palms broke into a sweat. "Is that why he was in that wheelchair yesterday?"

"The scar tissue is so tight that it's terribly painful when he tries to straighten his legs. We have eight women working here, including me. Ever since Pops' accident, we always wear an 'ugly leather skirt' when we go into the furnace room."

Rance put his hands on her waist. "Now that I know the story behind it, I think it's beautiful."

Carrie was painfully aware of his touch, and of the workers watching them. She stepped away from him to point at a row of shallow vats.

"Once a day, the settled salt is dipped out of these vats with long-handled shovels. That's what those men are getting ready to do. They'll put it on this salt board," which was suspended above the vats, "where the final draining is done. From there, the salt is trundled off in wheelbarrows to the adjoining salt house, where it's packed in barrels for inspection and shipment."

She led the way out of the main building to

the salt house. It was really just a small warehouse. Empty barrels on one side, filled ones on the other. Right now, there were more of the latter than the former.

"This is what you'll be accompanying to Richmond." She patted one of the sealed barrels.

"There's more than enough here for the next shipment," Rance said. "Why are you waiting until next week to send it out?"

"Because these haven't been inspected. See? No brand." She waved a hand at the unmarked barrels. "Someone broke into the inspector's office." She looked at Rance as though trying to nail him to the wall. "The burglar didn't take anything, just went through the account books. Mr. Snell had to do a complete audit to see if anything was changed and hasn't had time to inspect our salt. He promised he'd be caught up by Monday, so we scheduled our shipment for Tuesday. Shall we go, Captain?"

"I liked it better when you called me Rance earlier, Carrie."

She was hoping he hadn't noticed. "I liked it better when you called me Miss Blackwell."

"Too bad," he said and gave her a devastating smile.

She smiled back at him. "My sentiments exactly, Captain."

When they reached Charleston, Carrie suggested that since it was such a beautiful day, why didn't they visit George Patton's camp? She offered Rance the opportunity to beg off, "I just know you'll be bored silly," but he insisted on going, too, "It's not like I have anything else to do until Tuesday." Short of borrowing Barton's pistol and shooting Rance, there didn't seem to be anyway to get rid of him.

Web was still standing watch beside the turnpike on the western edge of town. Carrie reined in Malachi, her roan mare, so she could talk to Web while the rest of her party rode ahead. The mare protested being left behind. She sidestepped and pranced, trying to break Carrie's grip on the reins.

"Easy, Mally, it's just for a minute. Have you seen him yet, Web?"

"No, but I heard talk about some English lord stayin' last night at somebody's house just east of Camp Thompkins."

"That explains why I couldn't find him last night. He has to be on the road by now, even English lords don't sleep past noon. I'm riding that way, but maybe you should stay here in case I miss him." She set Malachi into a gallop.

Her party had stopped because Barton wanted to turn back. "The roads are too muddy, Sis. Father would never allow you to ride under these conditions."

Carrie noticed a well-appointed carriage approaching from the west. The gray horses pulling it were the same exquisite pair that had been stabled beside Major Allen's horse in Cincinnati. It was time to put her plan into action to warn Pryce Lewis not to recognize her and to make him a hero. The problem was, she still didn't have a plan.

"Please, Barton, just a little farther. Carrie is right, it is such a beautiful day and the valley is so pretty along this part of the road."

"And you know Pamela is an excellent rider," Carrie said, and suddenly realized the solution to her problem.

She had brought her friend along as a distraction, which is exactly what she needed right now. She created one by kicking Pamela's gelding in the rear. The startled beast broke into a gallop, and Pamela proved Carrie's claim about her horsemanship by managing to keep her seat while the beast bolted straight toward the approaching carriage.

Carrie had already put Malachi into a run after Pamela. Behind her she heard the men shouting. The driver of the carriage, who Carrie could now see was indeed Sam Bridgeman, had apparently assessed the situation of the runaway horse.

He turned his team across the road, blocking the gelding's path. Pryce Lewis jumped out of the carriage and ran to meet Pamela's horse. The gelding slackened his pace at Lewis's approach, and Carrie pushed her mare to top speed. In a blur of motion, she saw Lewis spring for the gelding's head. He pulled the animal to a stop, and Carrie saw Pamela fall from the saddle.

Carrie's heart stopped. She pulled Malachi to a rearing stop, threw herself from the saddle, and ran the few long feet to where her friend had fallen. She almost fainted herself when she saw that Sam Bridgeman was holding the unconscious Pamela in his arms.

"Thank you, God," Carrie whispered, her relief so intense she felt ill. "I swear I'll never involve anyone in my schemes again."

While Pryce Lewis tied Pamela's horse to a tree, Carrie spread her cloak on the grass beside the road. Sam laid Pamela on it while Pryce ran to join them.

"Only a minute," Carrie said, her words coming out in breathless gasps caused by the sight of Rance's swift approach. "Cavalry captain—is trouble—I can't get to Wise—you have to—you don't know me—"

It was all she had time for, because Barton and Rance were already off their horses and running to join them.

"Pamela!" Barton cried and dropped to his knees beside her.

"She just fainted," Sam said.

Pamela's eyes fluttered, then opened. She looked around in bewilderment. Then her gaze fell on Pryce Lewis and her face softened as though she were about to cry. "You saved me."

Pryce looked properly humble. "My man Sam had a hand in it, too. Most strange how your horse bolted like that."

"Yes," Rance said. "Most strange. Wouldn't you say, Carrie?"

She ignored him. "How do you feel, Pamela?"

"Fine, I think." She sat up and wiped the back of her hand across a flushed cheek.

"This settles it," Barton said. "We're going straight back to Charleston." He helped his sister to her feet.

"Charleston?" Pryce asked. "My man and I are headed there, too."

Pamela smiled and Pryce visibly paled beneath the pretty assault. "I'm so glad," she said. "My father will want to thank you for saving me."

"Perhaps the young lady should ride in the carriage with you, my lord," Sam said.

"My lord?" Carrie asked, sounding suitably impressed by the title.

Pryce bowed from the waist. "Permit me to introduce myself as Henry Tracy of Oxford, England, now traveling in America."

"How thrilling!" Pamela seemed completely recovered and head over heels in love. Her eyes were wide, and the pulse in her throat fluttered wildly as introductions were made.

"I am fortunate to have made your acquaintance, Captain Fletcher," Pryce said. "I am looking for the camp of one of your countrymen, General Henry Wise. Perhaps you could instruct me where I might find him?"

"I can help you with that," Barton said. "General Wise is arriving in Charleston today. He will be dining with my family tomorrow evening. It would be an honor if you would join us. And you and Carrie must join us, too, Captain Fletcher."

"I cannot wait to tell Papa and the general what a hero you are, Lord Tracy," Pamela said.

"Shall we go?" Pryce asked, and handed Pamela into his carriage.

Barton, Rance, and Carrie rode behind the vehicle back to Charleston. During the ride, Rance noticed that once again, Carrie looked inordinately pleased with herself.

Chapter Twelve

General Wise established his headquarters in the Kanawha House and his camp at Two-Mile, where the road to Ripley branched away from the valley turnpike. Littlepage Mansion, which Wise had attempted to commandeer as his headquarters, overlooked the Confederate camp from inside a fenced yard filled with trees and shade and playing children.

It was toward that shade that Carrie rode on a steamy day in mid-July. She'd been in the saddle for two days, stopping only long enough to change horses at tavern stables.

Mrs. Littlepage and her son, Charles, were sitting under one of the old oak trees. It had been Mrs. Littlepage's adamant refusal to allow anyone, rebel or Yankee, to take over her house, which had caused General Wise to seek residence at the hotel. She'd become a heroine in Charleston, for no matter how much sympathy the townsfolk might have for the Confederate creed of states' rights, they believed in their personal rights more.

"Heavens, child," she said now as Carrie almost fell out of the saddle. "I've seen dead people that look better than you. Molly! Molly, bring this girl some lemonade."

"General Garnett is dead," Carrie said. The popular general had been in command of the Confederate forces facing General McClellan's troops in the mountains north of Lewisburg.

"In battle?" Charles asked, his voice cracking in his excitement. "Were there lots of cannons?"

Carrie nodded and drank deeply from the glass of lemonade that Molly had brought. "Thank you, Molly," she said. "And yes, Charlie, there were a great lot of cannons."

"Were you there?"

"No, but I heard about it." She had, however, seen the defeated rebels running for their lives. It had been wonderful. The beginning of the end for the Confederacy. Maybe the Washington papers had been right, the war wouldn't last past the summer.

"I saw a Confederate map of the Rich Mountain battlefield, though. General Rosecrans captured it after he defeated Colonel Pegram's forces there." Carrie realized her mistake instantly.

"You were with the Union army?" Mrs. Littlepage asked.

"I was in Clarksburg, where General McClellan has his headquarters. The Federals took almost six hundred prisoners and I wanted to know if any of the men were from Charleston. While I was trying to get a pass, General Rosecrans arrived and showed the captured map around."

Not bad for a last-minute lie, Carrie thought. In reality, she'd been in the Confederate camp when the map was being drawn and had told General Rosecrans about it. After his victory at Rich Mountain, he found it in the abandoned Confederate papers.

Poor Charles looked like he was about to die from excitement at actually being so close to someone who had been so close to a battle.

"It was a good map," Carrie told him. "Showed exactly where every Union cannon emplacement was located. General Rosecrans said it was better than his own map of the camp."

"Were any of our men there?" Mrs. Littlepage asked.

Carrie shook her head. "I only saw a few of the prisoners, though. Most had already been transferred to other camps. Speaking of camps, what happened to General Wise's men?" When she'd left Charleston two weeks ago, Camp Two-Mile had been a beehive of activity. Now it looked abandoned.

"They marched away before dawn this morning," Mrs. Littlepage said. "This is the first peace and quiet I've had since they arrived."

"They went that way," Charles said and pointed west. "And they took their cannon."

"General Cox is bringing his Federal troops up the valley," Mrs. Littlepage said. "Our men at Camp Thompkins marched out to put a stop to their advance."

"They're gonna fight at Scary Creek," Charles said. "I've been hearing thunder all morning, least ways Mother says it's thunder. I think it's the cannon."

"How do you know they're going to Scary?" Carrie asked. The creek was only about thirteen miles due west of Charleston.

"I heard them talking before they left. There's gonna be a fight there, and General Wise's men went to help Captain Patton's men. They didn't leave camp until today so the Yankees wouldn't know they were coming."

Carrie grabbed her horse's reins. "I have to go. Thanks for the lemonade."

"Now you just wait one minute, young lady. Charles, run along." Mrs. Littlepage assumed a maternal expression. "I want to talk to Carolina."

Carrie knew what was coming next. At one time or the other, every woman in town had undertaken the task of mothering her, believing it their duty to try to undo some of the damage Peach and Harris were doing.

"You know I think of you as one of my own, Carolina, and it is with that feeling in mind that I feel I must caution you against this practice of riding alone. It is not only dangerous, it is simply not acceptable. I know that you are a lady and would never allow liberties by a man, but there are those who might think otherwise."

"I appreciate your concern," Carrie said, "but it's hard to abide by all the rules a woman is expected to abide by and still run a business, which you know I'm only doing because it is so difficult for my father to get around." She kissed Mrs. Littlepage's cheek. "I really have to go now. I haven't seen Pops or Gramps in weeks."

"Tell them that I'm thinking of them and hope to see them in church on Sunday."

Carrie mounted her horse and waved goodbye. She didn't go home, though, she headed for Scary Creek.

Charles Littlepage had been right. The thunder he'd heard was cannon, and the cannons were at Scary Creek. Smoke from their discharges marked the place of the battle as it clung like heavy clouds to the sides of the mountains.

Carrie approached from the turnpike. The Camp Two-Mile reinforcements had already arrived. Two Confederate cannons were blazing away, one of them Peacemaker, the gun Dr. Hale had made at his salt furnace. The valley was overrun with their noise, and the noise of musket fire and screaming horses, shouting men and the rattle of sabres being drawn as a mounted charge by Yankee cavalry surged across the empty field west of the creek.

The Confederates were a safer position, having a forest to fight from on their side of the creek. The Yankees seemed unafraid of the open field crossing, though, for they roared across it with a mighty swelling yell, only to be beaten back at the bridge by Confederate fire.

Next the Kanawha Riflemen caught the fever and charged forward.

Carrie's heart leapt into her throat as she recognized George Patton at the head of the charge. She followed his brave advance all the way to the bridge. A volley of Yankee fire obscured her view for a moment. When the smoke had cleared, George was no longer in command. He was on the ground and his second in command, Albert Finney, was salvaging what he could from the charge.

The Union soldiers retreated from the field.

Carrie was so close to the Confederate line, she heard the order for them to fall back and retire from the field, too, which didn't make sense. Apparently one of the Confederate colonels agreed with her, for he rode toward the creek and declared a Confederate victory.

George was carried off the field. Carrie ran to him, but after finding his wound, though serious, was not deadly, she turned her attention to General Wise, who was toasting the colonel's claim of victory with a glass of sherry.

"I have news for you," Carrie said after declining the general's offer to join in the toast. She told him about the Confederate defeat at Rich Mountain, their surrender at Laurel Hill, and General Garnett's death. "The rest of the Confederate forces escaped across the border into Maryland."

General Wise scowled at the news. "Now McClellan will no doubt send his men to aid General Cox in crushing my meager forces. I have written to President Davis asking for the support I need to protect this valley. Now I must go to him in person and demand it." Wise emptied his glass, wiped his mouth, and stood staring toward Scary Creek. "Here I am on the field of my first victory, and instead of planning to advance on the enemy, I must plan my retreat."

"I'll stay with your wounded, sir, and see that they are treated with respect by the Federal troops."

"That's very brave of you, Miss Blackwell." General Wise seemed to be seeing her for the first time. "You're the girl Captain Fletcher of the 1st Virginia Cavalry was raving about."

Carrie stiffened in caution while letting her cheeks color with a slight blush. "I am flattered by the captain's attention."

"Don't be, my dear. He called you a Lincoln

lover."

"My father is the Yankee in my family."

"Are you saying this Fletcher was lying? What motive could he have?"

"Captain Fletcher is an enthusiastic patriot of the cause. Occasionally his suspicions get the better of him."

General Wise laughed. "Well said! And now, if you will forgive me, I must get back to Charleston and prepare for my withdrawal."

It was a long night for Carrie. Already exhausted from the ride from Rich Mountain to Charleston, she had to fight off the effects of her fatigue and attend to the needs of the wounded soldiers in her care. Twenty-six men had received injuries in the battle, four so badly they had been left with her while the rest fled to Charleston with General Wise.

It wasn't just fatigue that made the night seem to last forever. It was the wounded themselves. She carried water from the creek to bath their fevered faces and clean their horrible wounds as best she could, but still they suffered so terribly there were times when she didn't think she could bear it another moment.

She held tightly to her self-control, though, refusing to give in to the urge to run away and leave them to their fate. Instead, she rededicated herself to easing their suffering as best she could, and throughout the night she prayed with them and for them, soothed their fears, and listened to their silent crying.

When dawn finally came, and with it the Union advance, she was so shattered by the horror of the night that she almost cried herself when the Union doctor offered to lend her aid.

"I didn't have anything to give them except water," she told him.

He took from his pocket a handful of morphine papers. "You should always carry a few of these. They won't cure anything, but they will allow you to ease the worst of a man's suffering until you can get help for him."

"They kept begging." She covered her face with her hands trying to hold back the memories of the long night. "They just kept begging."

The doctor paused in his cleaning of the wound of a Charleston boy named Welch whose entire heel had been shot off. "Corporal," he said and waved his assistant to his side. "Take this girl outside and give her a drink of whiskey." The doctor winked at Carrie. "For medicinal purposes."

She let herself be led out of the hospital tent that had been erected around the four men. "No," she said to the offered tin cup of whiskey. "I need to see General Cox."

"The general's mighty busy, miss. If you live around here, I'll see you home."

"Tell your busy general that I have a message

for him from Major Allen."

She waited for the corporal's return by leaning against a tree whose lower limbs had been pruned by yesterday's artillery fire. Instead of the corporal returning, General Cox himself came to find her.

"You poor child, you need some sleep. As for your message, if it's about Rich Mountain, I already know. It came over my telegraph days ago."

"It's about General Wise, sir. He's preparing to vacate Charleston. He thinks McClellan will send you reinforcements now that he's run Garnett's men out of the state. As for sleep, General, I can do that after the war."

Chapter Thirteen

"They sank the *Julia Maffitt,*" Carrie said.

Her father seemed a lot less devastated than she by this catastrophe. He just kept staring at the unlit cigar he was rolling back and forth, back and forth between his fingers.

They were sitting on the back porch of Riverway Cabin to escape the July heat that continued to hold the Kanawha Valley in its vengeful grasp. The view from the porch was wonderful, thanks to Lucy Bream, who had one virtue that outweighed even the most aggravating of her faults. She was a natural landscape artist.

The lilacs that surrounded the cabin were only part of her work. The meadow behind the house had been so transformed by plantings, it looked like a watercolor painting when in bloom, as it was now, with the hundreds of wild violets she had transplanted there from every hollow in the valley. There were also the white lace flowers of wild carrots, the gently waving spikes of cattail plants, and the cool blue beauty of Sweet Williams. Lucy had also changed the forest that surrounded the cabin by planting dogwoods for spring color, maples for fall brilliance, and pine trees to catch the wind in their needles and make it sing.

Although the back porch of the cabin afforded a beautiful view, it also provided a less-than-beautiful smell from the nearby pigpen. Carrie almost wished that she hadn't stopped Pops from lighting his cigar. Anything, even those things he smoked, would smell better than Goliath and Jezebel on a hot day, Delilah having been sacrificed to General Cox's dining table.

"General Wise commissioned the *Julia Maffitt* to tow wheat to his camp in Gauley," Carrie said. "When General Cox's men saw her, they sank her." She was determined to finish the tragic story despite her audience's lack of interest.

"I don't know what you're so upset about," Harris said. "The boat was involved in military action and paid the price for it. I think Cox did the right thing. What about you, Dad?"

Peach was checking Elijah, his favorite hound, for ticks. He stopped picking through the hair on the dog's back and looked at Carrie as though he were going to check her for ticks next. "What I think is that boat somehow got itself mixed up with our girl's growing up."

Carrie jumped to her feet, scattering across the porch floor the strawberries she was supposed to be cleaning for dessert that night. "I think you two need a hobby other than me, that's what I think."

"We didn't ask you what you thought," Peach said. "Pick up those berries before they get crushed and yellow jackets start buzzing around."

"I think what we need to settle her down is a son-in-law," Harris said.

Peach nodded. "That would do it, all right."

"Too bad that Fletcher boy is a rebel. She looked addled in the head when we met up with him that day at the wharf. It's going to take a head addler to keep her under control."

Carrie stopped trying to pick up the dropped berries. "You're just doing this to irritate me. Well, you can stop now because it worked. I'm going into town."

"Hold up," Peach said. "I'm going, too. I want to be there when the first news comes in over that telegraph wire Cox's men are putting in today at the court house. I'll hitch up Luke and John."

Carrie went into the house for her hat. When she came back out, Elijah was eating the strawberries and Harris was searching his pockets.

"I threw away all your matches," she told him.

He glowered at her. "You're going to make some poor man a terrible wife someday."

"Maybe I'll just stay here and aggravate you

and Peach instead of going off and aggravating some stranger."

Elijah was snuffling under the wheelchair trying to get the last berry.

"Get this dog away from me. I'd kick the mangy mutt if I could."

"You can't," Peach said from the carriage, "so stop dreaming about it. If you're coming with me, girl, you'd better run. I'm leaving right now."

Carrie kissed her father's cheek. "Do you want anything in town?"

"A match, but I know you won't bring me one so just go and leave me to suffer in peace."

As she was climbing into the carriage seat beside Peach, Harris yelled, "Lucy Bream, bring me a match!"

"No!" Lucy shouted back from the depths of the house. It was fly season in the valley. The cure was to boil onions, then brush the smelly water on the windows so flies wouldn't light. Lucy had been boiling and brushing all day.

"I'm going to set this dog of Dad's on fire with it!"

"I'll be right there!" Lucy bellowed.

Chapter Fourteen

Kanawha Court House was crowded with spectators. Many believed the telegraph would lift their town out of the wilderness and allow it to be treated with the respect the rest of the civilized world, meaning Richmond, already had. Even Carrie was gloating a little. Rance Fletcher couldn't insult Charleston now, unless he wanted to talk about its lack of a post office, paved streets, gas lighting, and a railroad.

The last wire connected, the telegraph operator keyed an opening sequence of dots and dashes into the machine, which immediately responded with an incoming message. The crowd cheered the event so enthusiastically that the operator couldn't hear. He hushed the cheers and requested the message be repeated.

"There's been a battle," he said.

Peach snickered. "We know there's been a battle, you fool. It was right here at Scary Creek."

The town was proud of what they were calling the Skirmish at Scary, even though the victors had fled to Gauley and probably hadn't stopped running yet. The crowd gave them a cheer of support anyway for having made the telegraph news.

"Four hundred Union dead," the operator said. The crowd fell silent, an uneasy, painful silence that weighed upon the room.

"Eleven hundred wounded, thirteen hundred missing and assumed captured."

Carrie couldn't breath. Eleven men had died at Scary Creek. It had seemed like so many.

"The fight was July 21st at Manassas Junction in eastern Virginia."

"That's just outside of Washington," Annie McFarland said. Her eyes were shadowed by disbelief and shock.

"A complete Confederate victory," the operator said. "Washington was not attacked."

Carrie was drowning in fear. So many men dead. But it wasn't the thought of all those deaths filling her with so much fright. It was the thought of one death, a tobacco farmer with flashing eyes and an unbuttoned cloak, a spy catcher with an attitude, a rebel with gentle hands.

"What about Confederate casualties?" she asked, the words tearing at her throat.

"Nothing on the wire about that."

Peach was the only thing keeping Carrie on her feet. It felt like the ground was pulling at her, and she clung to his supporting arm with desperate fingers.

The telegraph spewed another string of dot

and dashes. "New story, folks. Yesterday the United States Senate passed the Crittenden Resolution."

Carrie's world continued to crumble. The Crittenden Resolution reaffirmed President Lincoln's persistent claim that the war was to maintain the Union, not abolish slavery. Hearing this tragedy so close on the heels of the Manassas defeat was like trying to swallow two doses of castor oil, one right after the other.

"Let's get out of here," Peach said.

He and Carrie stood on Front Street and drew in great breaths of the humid air.

"All those men, Gramps. They died for nothing."

"They died for their country, girl. If you think that's nothing, you shouldn't be risking your own life for that same country."

"But the Crittenden Resolution—"

"Is just a way of keeping this war going until the country is ready to face what has to be done. You and me, we've already faced it and we're willing to give our own lives to see it through. As long as you believe that your life is not more important than the lives of the men who die fighting for what you believe in, they'll always be heroes."

She gave him a hug. "You're the best, Peach."

"Now tell me the rest of what's got you so worried."

Carrie saw again the image of Rance Fletcher

lying dead on a mist-shrouded battlefield. "It's nothing, Gramps." She had picked up the mail before going to the new telegraph room. Now she shuffled through it to disguise the fact that her hands had started shaking again.

"Which means it's something more than you want it to be and you'd rather bite off your tongue than admit it to me or anyone else, including yourself."

There was a letter for her postmarked from Richmond the day after the Manassas battle. It was from Lisset Lewis. Usually Lisset's letters were so long that the envelope bulged with the effort of holding so many pages of stationery. This one was flat and thin and had no hearts drawn on it.

Carrie closed her eyes and tried to pray, but the only words that came were *please don't let him be dead.*

"Why don't you get the carriage, Gramps?"

After Peach left, she opened the envelope and took out the single sheet of lavender-scented stationery.

"Dearest Carolina,

You can stop worrying. The delectable but testy-tempered Rance is completely alive and perfectly well and absolutely as rude as ever. The battle was terrible, but Papa says I must think of the victory, not the cost.

I have a new beau! A terribly handsome and wonderfully romantic Navy lieutenant who right this very minute is waiting to walk me to the post, so I must dash. I promise to write pages and pages later.

Your adored and adoring friend, Lisset"

There was a postscript: "Please come for a visit soon, Carrie. I do so want to show off my darling Andrew."

"Ready, Mosquito?"

Carrie climbed into the carriage and settled herself beside her grandfather.

"You're not worried anymore," he said.

"I wasn't worried to begin with." And it was true. She hadn't been the least bit worried about Rance.

"Then why is my arm bruised from you holding onto it?" Peach was grinning at her.

"Watch the road, old man, or I'll tell everyone in town that your name is Almarene."

"Is not."

"Is too."

"Is not."

He steered the carriage around Widow Hitch's pig, which liked to stand in the middle of the turnpike and snap at horse flies. When Luke and John returned to the middle of the road, and the carriage wheels had settled back into the road ruts, Peach turned to Carrie.

"Well?"

She bit her lower lip. "I forgot whose turn it was."

"So did I."

It wasn't much, but it would do. "I thought you never forgot anything," she said.

"Did this time," he said, and they were off and running again.

"Did not."

"Did too."

"Look!" She pointed at a metallic brown dragonfly hovering over the ditch beside the road. "A banded skimmer."

"Nope, it's a brown darner."

"Is not."

"Is too."

Chapter Fifteen

Rance ducked his head to enter the commander's tent. The rain that had been pooling in the brim of his hat spilled forward, adding a new puddle to the already wet canvas floor of General Robert E. Lee's tent.

"Captain Ransom Fletcher, sir. Sorry about the water."

"Don't worry, Captain. There isn't an inch of this accursed country that's dry. I've never seen such rain."

It was the twentieth straight day of rain. Rance couldn't understand why anyone would want to live in this swamp. For that's what western Virginia was, one big mountainous swamp.

On August 20th, the Yankee-loving residents of this backwater wilderness had voted to secede from both Virginia and the Confederacy. They'd formed their own Union state, calling it Kanawha. Good riddance, had been Rance's opinion. Unfortunately, both the Confederacy and Virginia disagreed with him. They both wanted the region's salt, as well as its people and their richly producing farms.

General Lee had been struggling to wrest the region from Union control for weeks. The incessant rain, the treacherous terrain, and a lack of cooperation from his own staff had brought him nothing but frustration and failure.

"I have been informed, Captain, that your recent duties have given you a familiarity with this area. That is why I requested you be assigned to my staff. This country is not hospitable to telegraph lines. Any wire that the Signal Corp manages to string through the brush and trees is just as quickly washed out by the rains. I am therefore being forced to rely on couriers to communicate with my generals. As you are no doubt aware, these hills are infested with bands of cutthroats, as well as a great number of backwoods loyalists who are more interested in shooting at my couriers than hunting their supper. I am putting you in charge of my communications, Captain. I want reliable contact with my outlying camps, and if to accomplish that you have to exterminate the two-legged vermin plaguing us, so be it."

It wasn't the assignment of command that Rance wanted, but it was certainly better than what he'd been doing, which was searching every warehouse, barn, and outhouse from Charleston to Richmond for Carrie Blackwell's stockpile of salt.

"Your duties, Captain Fletcher, will give you the opportunity to continue searching these hills for the salt which our President is eager for you to find."

Rance bit back a scowl.

Lee handed him a packet of papers wrapped in oilcloth. "I need these delivered to General Floyd before morning. My aide will give you the most recent location of the general's camp. Good night, Captain."

"Good night, sir," Rance said and left the tent.

"There is one more thing, Captain." General Lee followed Rance out into the rain. "There have been occurrences of forged orders appearing in the outlying camps. They are also being supplied with what appears to be intentionally inaccurate information from locals claiming to be sympathetic to our cause. See if you can't unravel this plot to confuse my officers, Captain. They are confused enough without any outside aid."

"I will look into it, General."

Forgery and confusion, Carolina Blackwell's two favorite pastimes. Instead of wasting time looking for the troublemakers responsible for General Lee's failed communications, maybe Rance should just look for Carrie. She was at the bottom of all his other problems. Why should this one be any different?

Chapter Sixteen

Carrie was thirsty, but not so thirsty that she'd drink from any of the streams she passed. A great many skirmishes between Confederate and Union troops had taken place in this part of the Greenbrier Mountains in recent weeks. The water could be contaminated by the decaying bodies of wildlife, horses, maybe even men. So, on her long ride from Summersville to Clarksburg, where General Rosecrans' headquarters were located, Carrie had restricted herself and Malachi to only drinking from wells. Because they was traveling the back country instead of the Weston Turnpike, there were few wells to be found.

After an unbelievable thirty-four days, the rain had ceased its persistent downpour just that morning. It hadn't taken long for a hot September sun to burn away the last of the dark clouds or to turn the wet forest into a steambath. The air was so humid that breathing was difficult, activity almost impossible. Both Carrie and her horse were lagging. Both could do with a cool, refreshing drink of clean, sparkling water. The very thought of it caused Carrie's throat to convulse in anticipation.

When she finally came across a farmhouse, it was all she could do to control herself. But safety came first, so she waited a long fifteen minutes in the woods at the edge of the clearing to be certain it was abandoned, as were most homes in this area because of the fighting. No chimney smoke, no chickens, no children, or horses or dogs or anything. Just a house and a barn and a fallow garden and a well, a lovely well with a bucket dangling provocatively above its inviting depths. She tied Malachi to a tree, giving the mare enough room to munch on leaves while Carrie attended to drawing water.

She stood on tiptoe to lean over the rocky rim of the well to see if it was clear of trash. The rebels had a bad habit of dumping debris, including dead animals, into wells so Union troops couldn't use them. All she could see in this one was darkness. She could smell the water, though, and it had a clean scent, like morning dew on a mountain meadow. She grasped the hand crank and lowered the bucket.

A crashing of brush set off an explosion of fear in her. Along with the sounds of horses approaching, she heard men's voices. She couldn't make out what they were saying, but she could hear the unmistakable sound of their rich Southern drawls.

Normally Carrie wouldn't worry about facing

rebel troops. But not today, not when the telegraph line to Rosecrans' headquarters had mysteriously stopped working at the same time eight thousand Confederate troops had converged near Summersville. A takeover of the Kanawha Valley had to be their objective, and unless reinforcements could be brought down from Clarksburg, the Union troops in Gauley and Charleston wouldn't stand a chance. She didn't have time to waste pretending to be a loyal Southern belle. She had to get to Clarksburg, and she had to get there today.

There wasn't time to reach her horse. Carrie released the well crank and ran to the farmhouse. *Which is the first place they'll look,* she thought, and turned instead for the only other cover in sight. The cellar. The slanted door lifted open without a single squeak leaking from its hinges. She stepped down through the wheelbarrow-sized opening and closed the door above her.

"Hey, Cap'n. There's a roan mare over here with a sidesaddle."

Carrie's heart sank. She should have tied Mally deep in the woods to avoid accidental discovery, but it was so hot that carrying water to the mare had seemed like the last thing she wanted to do. She looked down into the cave-dark depths of the cellar. Hauling water seemed like a lark compared to having to hide down there.

"The rider can't be far off," a voice rank with authority announced. "I want her found. Search the house and barn first, then fan out into the woods."

Carrie took a deep breath and started going down, and down and down and down into what had to be the deepest cellar in the world. She gave her eyes only a second to adjust to the darkness before she began to search for a place to hide. On the back wall was a protruding rock shelf. On it were half a dozen jars filled with what looked like pickled beets. Beneath the stone shelf was enough room for a very small person to hide. She scrunched into it and tried to act small.

They won't find me, they won't find me, she silently chanted, hoping that by forcing herself to believe the impossible, she could make it come true.

Crouched there as she was, her nose almost buried in the dust-covered folds of her skirt, and wanting to sneeze so badly that her entire body ached, Carrie became aware of what felt like a draft of moist air. *Impossible.* Yet there it was, so chill and wet it caused her to shiver, and the shiver caused her to sneeze.

"I heard something," the rank-voiced captain said. It sounded like he was right outside the cellar door.

"Squirrels," someone offered.

"Rats," another suggested.

Carrie shuddered. Rats were second only to snakes on her list of things not to think about in dark, dank, deep places. Bugs were third, and the involuntary thought of them turned her shudder of disgust into a terrified tremble.

The cellar door opened, letting in a welcome shaft of sunlight and dispelling for the moment Carrie's creeping fears. She leaned her head out from under the shelf and saw the towering silhouette of a man outlined against an impossibly blue sky.

"Private Kitchen, bring a lantern. I want to search this cellar."

"Damn rebels," Carrie muttered, the oath causing her to think of her grandfather, whose favorite pastime had become cussing Confederates.

"It's taken almost seventy years, but I finally found my calling in life," he'd told Carrie last month. They were sitting in the spring house, having gone there to escape the heat. While she wiggled bare toes in the mud that surrounded the little cooling spring, Peach had told her a story about his parents' farm.

"We didn't have a spring like this so when Pa dug our well, he dug the cellar right beside it. Just above the water level, he put in a window to let the cool air from the well into the cellar. Mother used the window like a spring house. It was fine for butter and milk, but no fit place for a person to keep comfortable when it was hot. This is much better," he'd said and stuck his feet into the mud beside Carrie's.

This farm didn't have a spring house, either.

Maybe, please maybe, Carrie prayed.

She crawled out from under the shelf and moved the jars of pickled beets to one side. There was the answer to her prayer. An opening into the well.

"Got it, Cap'n."

Carrie was lifting out the wooden shelf above the beet shelf. She glanced up at the cellar opening. The silhouetted man had been joined by a smaller man, who was holding a lantern.

She had only seconds. She gathered her skirt into one hand and with the other, dragged herself across the stone shelf and through the opening. Inside the well was another protruding rock. She stood on it while she replaced the wood shelf. Then she reached for the beets and began placing the jars back in front of the opening.

The men had started into the cellar, the rank-voiced captain descending first, then the other man, who held the lantern aloft so it would spill its light into the gloomy corners below.

One last jar. Carrie's fingers closed around it. She lifted it, positioned it, and set it in place. Then she took what felt like the first breath she'd had in hours.

The rock ledge was narrow and slick, but she

managed to creep slowly along it until she found handholds among the mossy stones in the wall that would help keep her from slipping. Above her was the sky, its beams of sunny brightness angled just enough to encase her in shadow, keeping her safe from an accidental sighting from above. The bucket was still lowered. It was floating on the surface of the water, which lay silent and dark a mere inch below the toes of her boots.

This isn't so bad, she thought, and then her heart stopped. Completely, totally, dead still. For there, directly beneath the opening to the cellar where she'd been kneeling only moments ago, was a snake.

Rance was certain he'd heard a sneeze coming from this cellar. There was no one here, though, so the only answer was he'd imagined it, just like he'd imagined that the mare they'd found looked familiar. Usually he remembered horses better than people. It irritated him that he couldn't place this one.

"Let's go, Kitchen."

"Just a minute, Cap'n. I want to get some of these beets. I'm mighty tired of eatin' nothin' but salted beef."

"No pillaging," Rance reminded him.

"But there ain't nobody livin' here. How can us eatin' them hurt?"

Rance knew he should argue, but he was tired

of salted beef, too.

"One jar, Kitchen, and make it quick."

"Cap'n, do you smell what I'm smellin'?"

Rance went to the back wall of the cellar and sniffed. Lilacs. No doubt about it. He also felt a draft blowing on his face.

He put a finger to his lips to silence Kitchen and motioned him to hold the lantern closer to the beets. The jar lids were coated with fine beads of condensed moisture, but the stone shelf was dry. He leaned over farther to look at the back wall of the cellar and saw the opening he knew would be there, just like the one in the cellar at his plantation.

He ran a hand across his unshaven chin. Now he knew where he'd seen that little mare before and why he hadn't been able to place her. His attention had been too completely taken up by her rider.

"I don't smell anything," he said. "Let's go."

Outside the cellar, he ordered Kitchen to stand guard. "I don't want our lilac-scented friend escaping. Close these doors and sit on them if you have to, but don't let her out." He walked to the edge of the well and glanced down. Most of the interior was cloaked in shadow, but Rance was certain he saw a gleam of yellow hair in the darkness.

Carrie tried to control the fear swelling inside her. She closed her eyes tighter together and tried to convince herself that the snake on the ledge wasn't stalking her. She should look and see what he was doing, she knew she should, but she couldn't because what if he was slinking toward her? She'd already availed herself of the only place there was to stand in the well that wasn't on the ledge with the snake. There wasn't any place left for her to go except up, which was out of the question, not to mention impossible.

"Sergeant Stillson, you can give up the search. Our lady rider has given us the slip."

It was the rank-voiced captain. He'd finally left the cellar, but now it sounded like he was standing right on top of her, which meant he had to be standing right beside the well.

Please don't let him be thirsty, God. I swear I'll never say anything mean about a snake again if only you'll not let that man be thirsty.

"Before we go, Sergeant, I want this well filled with rocks. Start with that big one over there."

"NO!" Carrie screamed, then bit her bottom lip so hard in punishment that she tasted blood.

The patriotic thing to do was keep silent and get stoned to death. But the well water which was soaking up along her stockings felt exactly the way she imagined it would feel to have snakes crawling up her legs. She wasn't brave enough to deal with dying and snakes at the same time, and so she'd screamed. Maybe the rank captain hadn't heard her, and she could still die with her honor intact, if only she could get her fear under control. That seemed a remote possibility considering the way her teeth insisted on clattering together like castanets.

"Is there someone down there?"

Something about his smug tone was familiar to Carrie. She tried to remember where she'd heard it before, but the mariachi band rhythm section in her mouth was making too much noise for her to concentrate.

"I must be hearing things again," Rance said. "All right, Sergeant, you can throw that boulder in."

"Stop!" Carrie cried, sobbing out the word as fear once again won over patriotism. "I'm down in the well."

"How did you get in there?"

"I crawled through an opening in the cellar." She looked up, but all she could see of her questioner was the silhouette of his shoulders and head against the sky. "I'm standing in the bucket. Would you please pull me up?"

"Why don't you go back through the opening?"

Carrie pressed her forehead against the bucket rope and tried to stop her teeth from clattering. "Because," she said, her voice breaking under the stress, "there's a snake down here."

"I see. And you want me to pull you up so the snake won't get you."

Thousands of rebels crawling around in these mountains and I get the one with all the brains.

"Yes, I want you to pull me up so the snake won't get me."

"Haul her up, Sergeant," Rance said. "Give him a hand, Kitchen."

When the bucket finally stopped rising and the first warm flush of sunlight fell on Carrie's face, she opened her eyes, prepared to swear undying love for her rescuer. What she saw was Rance Fletcher grinning at her.

"This must be my lucky day," she said.

"My sentiments exactly," he said.

There were two other men besides Rance, both of them gawking at her like she was a two-headed calf. They lurched unexpectedly into action, one grabbing for the bucket and the other, who had been holding the bucket crank, abandoning his post to grab for her. Through a haze of Confederate-gray arms, Carrie saw her life flash before her eyes.

It was Rance who saved her. He'd intended to keep his distance and let her huddle in humiliation before him. When she began to drop back into the well, he grasped her around the waist, lifting her out of the bucket and into his arms.

"I thought you didn't do heroics," she said.

She was so pale, he'd thought her unconscious. He held her shivering body close against him.

"Only on Saturdays."

"As I said before, Captain, this must be my lucky day."

Only she didn't feel lucky. She felt sick. Carrie had always wondered what being seasick felt like. Her ride up in the bucket had given her a good idea. The possibility of falling back into the well had added so much to the illusion that now all she could do was lay like a sodden blanket in Rance's arms, not caring what happened as long as it didn't involve throwing up. But the longer he stood there looking down at her with that expression that made her feel like a chocolate eclair, the sicker she felt.

"I thought you were Yankees," she said, feeling a sudden need to explain herself.

Her teeth were chattering so hard Rance could barely understand her.

"Kitchen, gather some wood and get a fire going so we can dry her out."

His face was very close to hers. Actually, what she was noticing was that his lips were very close to hers.

"I don't like snakes," she said.

Rance smiled. "I'm not partial to them, either." He carried her into the empty farm house and looked around for a place to sit her.

"There aren't any snakes in here are there?"

"There isn't anything in here except us." He sat her on the raised hearth. Her face and hands had changed from ghostly white to icy blue. "Can you unbutton your way out of that dress or do you need help?"

"Are you asking because you're concerned for my health or because you want to know if I'm carrying Union messages?"

He knelt before her, took her hands in his, and began rubbing them, trying to bring a flush of warmth to them. "You know, Carrie, there is a third possibility."

He had that eclair look on his face again. She pulled her hands away and stood up.

"Tell your kitchen help to forget the wood, I don't need to get dry, I need to get to Clarksburg." *Why don't I just give him a signed confession and be done with it?* "My uncle, Uncle Dutch, he's in Clarksburg, and I need to talk to him, so I'll just be leaving, and you can go back to shooting Yankees. Thank you for getting me out of the well. Good day."

She made it to the door, but before she could open it, he was behind her, holding it closed with both hands. She stared at the peeling paint on the door and tried to pretend she wasn't surrounded by his arms.

"Do you really expect me to believe that you are going to Clarksburg, which just happens to be where the Union army headquarters are located, to talk to an uncle named Dutch?"

"He's sick," she said, inspired by the fact she was feeling quite sick again herself. "It came on him suddenly last night."

"Let me make certain I've got this straight." Rance turned her to face him. He could read nothing in her eyes. Their dark beauty was hidden by shadows, but he didn't need them to know she was lying. He touched a finger to the dimple in her chin. "You are going to Union headquarters to see an uncle named Dutch who took sick last night and somehow got word of his illness to you, in spite of the fact that communications with Clarksburg were severed by Confederate troops just before we whipped the pants off General Cox's forces at Cross Lanes. Is that right?"

"You know, Captain, you remind me of a parrot that belonged to the wife of a traveling preacher who came through Charleston last year. The bird sat on a perch beside the pulpit and at the end of every service, it would squawk, 'Save yourself, save yourself!' It drove my grandfather crazy. Night after night, 'Save yourself, save yourself!'

"On the last night of the revival, before the service started, I saw Peach up beside the pulpit talking to the bird. That night the preacher got to shouting pretty loud and for a pretty long stretch, so he paused to take a breath and wipe the sweat from his face. The bird thought the service was over and shouted, 'Save yourself, save yourself, my husband's home!' Peach just about died laughing. Apparently what he'd told the bird to say was, 'Save yourself, he's about to pass the hat.' "

"Is there a moral to this story?" Rance asked.

"Once a parrot starts to run on at the mouth, sooner or later he'll say something he shouldn't."

"And I said something I shouldn't?"

"I didn't know Cross Lanes had been taken by Confederate forces." If it was true, it was even more imperative that she reach General Rosecrans as quickly as possible.

He lifted his finger to her lips. The bottom one was swollen, and a tiny drop of blood was welling from a cut. "Does this hurt?"

He traced the outline of her lips, pausing beside, then passing the wound her anger had inflicted in the well. "Yes," she said softly, her breath touching his hand. "Am I under arrest, Rance?"

He tugged at her lower lip with his finger, moving the little cut out of the way so he wouldn't hurt her. "I can't let you go, Carrie."

Her eyes were so wide he could see all the way to her heart, which was beating as fast as his own.

"But my uncle—"

"Not now," he said with his lips so close to hers, he could almost taste them. I don't want to hear any more stories about Dutch uncles and shouting preachers, Carrie. I don't want to hear anything at all."

Her mouth was cool and soft, and he covered

it gently with his kiss.

I'm doing this for my country, Carrie told herself, but it wasn't Abraham Lincoln or the Union she was thinking of when Rance's tongue touched hers and her knees gave way beneath her.

A knock on the door caused her to almost jump out of her skin.

"I got the wood, Cap'n."

Ever since he'd seen her standing in the well bucket, her hands clenched around the rope and her eyes as wide as saucers, Rance had wanted to kiss this little Yankee spy. He wasn't about to stop now, no, not just yet.

"Leave it on the porch, Private."

The wood clattered as it fell, sending shock waves through the floor that transferred themselves up through Carrie's shoes and wet stockings. "I'm cold, Captain," she said, trying to distance herself with his title even though her arms refused to yield their hold on him.

"No, you're not," he said and pulled her away from the door and into his arms, lifting her into his kiss and holding her close against dreams he'd thought would never come true.

At first he thought it was just a woman's tremble that caused her to shiver in his arms. But as the heat of their kiss was close to inflaming him beyond control, he realized her shaking had become violent, and he released her lips quickly.

"I'm cold," she said again, and he saw that part of the fire he'd felt in her embrace was from the flush of a threatened fever. He sat her again on the edge of the hearth. In two strides, he reached the door and threw it open.

"Bring that wood in here right this minute," he ordered, then ran out to his horse. Cain shied at his approach, but Rance ignored the stallion's nerves. He jerked his bedroll from behind the saddle, ran back inside, and wrapped Carrie in the woolen warmth of his blankets while Kitchen bent to the task of lighting a fire.

When the flames began to dance, Rance chased the boy outside. "Out of those wet clothes now," he ordered Carrie, and ignoring his own need, left her alone to tend hers.

Carrie's clothes had dried and her trembling had long since stopped before she finally thought of a plan. There wasn't much to it, only that she had to escape. She was lucky to even have thought of that much with her mind so busy remembering Rance's kiss.

I have to reach General Rosecrans. I have to reach General Rosecrans, she chanted silently while she hooked the laces on her boots and buttoned her dress up to her chin and opened the door of the farmhouse.

Rance stood with his back to her. His right shoulder was pressed against a porch post, his weight resting on one leg while the other dug at the wood planking of the top step. The other men were out in the dirt yard. One was checking the load in his pistol, the other was watering the horses. Malachi was with them, looking none the worse for her capture.

"I'm ready," Carrie said. Rance didn't move except to jab his heel deeper into the step. "Where is my prison to be?"

He turned, and they both realized that something had changed between them. What had happened in the farmhouse had been more than just a harmless bit of lovemaking. They hadn't just seen the comet. They had touched it.

"You aren't under arrest," Rance said. He felt like he was on fire. It wasn't only his body, though, that was being consumed by the flames she had set ablaze within him. "You are in the protective custody of the Confederate States of America. Sergeant Stillson and Private Kitchen will escort you to Lewisburg, where you will remain until General Floyd retakes the Kanawha Valley. At that time you will be escorted to Charleston and handed over to your father."

Carrie's emotions made her feel almost as though she were still inside the well. She felt trapped and afraid. The only way she knew to avoid the trouble they'd fallen into was to deny it existed.

She paused as she passed him on the step. "It will take a lot more than a snake to frighten me into your arms the next time, Captain Fletcher."

Rance watched her ride away. "For both our sakes, Miss Blackwell, I hope that never happens," he said and went into the farmhouse to smother the fire.

It was almost dark before her break came. After passing through the roughest country she'd ever seen, every inch of it barren of even the smallest sign of human habitation, the little party of three was startled to come upon another party of three who were washing their socks beside a trickling waterfall.

They looked almost as wild as the country. One wore a Confederate foraging cap, another a Virginia artillery uniform jacket. The third had a sabre lying at his side and was wearing a pair of Confederate cavalry trousers. Those few touches were the only thing military about the three, but there were a lot of Confederate soldiers without proper uniforms. The Confederacy had little money to spend outfitting backwoods soldiers. It was too busy trying to buy them guns.

"Stay here," Stillson told Carrie.

He and Kitchen approached the threesome. Carrie caught only an occasional word, not enough to even figure out where she was. Stillson had told her that he grew up in these hills, which explained their traveling without benefit of roads. The only thing Carrie knew was that they were traveling the opposite direction she wanted to go.

She tried to read Stillson's lips, not an easy task with a moustache like his. It hung down almost to his chin. Her attention kept straying to the three men by the stream. There was something about them that sent a chill of caution through her. Their casual acceptance of the unexpected appearance of three strangers was unusual, as was the almost rude way they spoke to Sergeant Stillson.

Stillson and Kitchen rode back to where she waited beside a thicket of rhododendron. They seemed as undisturbed by the chance meeting as the three men. But Carrie couldn't shake her feeling of unease. As they rode on through the gathering gloom, a silence as uneasy as her nerves settled over the forest. Frogs, crickets, and a hundred other night creatures should have been tuning up their evening songs. The only sound was the crunch of their horses' hooves in the leaf litter of the forest floor.

Carrie suddenly realized what had disturbed her so much about those three men. She'd seen a lot of soldiers in the last four months, and not once had she ever seen one of them wash their own socks. They sewed on buttons, scrubbed cooking pots, gossiped like schoolgirls, and fussed among themselves like old maids. But they didn't do laundry.

A Federal soldier hired a washerwoman to do the menial task, a Confederate soldier found a slave to do it. Only a man with neither of those options did his own washing. In these hills, the person most likely to have neither option was also most likely a bushwacker.

"Ambush!" she cried.

"Yip yip yip aieee!"

The scream came out from the forest to her left, and it sounded like Lucy Bream on a dusting rampage. That alone was enough to spur Carrie into immediate action. Before the "aieee" was finished, she'd wheeled Malachi behind a dogwood tree and pushed the mare to top speed.

Branches and bushes and fear dragged at her as every story she'd ever heard about bushwackers crowded into her mind along with the noise of gunfire, shouts, limbs breaking, the crashing of hoofbeats, and the chatter of her own heart quaking in terror. Even though she was so scared she could hardly stay in the saddle, Carrie didn't lose her wits. Just because they were running for their lives, there was no reason they couldn't do it in the direction of Clarksburg.

Chapter Seventeen

Malachi was blowing like a wheezy church organ. It would be outright cruelty to ask the exhausted horse to take even one more step. There was nothing more despicable than an animal abuser, but with the noise of her pursuers drawing closer, Carrie had no choice but to keep moving.

The mare was having none of it, though. She stopped and refused to take another step.

Carrie slid slowly from the saddle. She was almost as tired as the horse. When her feet hit the ground and then kept going down, she wondered if she were dreaming. Finally she stopped sinking. It was so dark she could barely see her own hands, so she leaned down and stared at the ground. She was standing ankle deep in water. It wasn't a creek or even a puddle. The water seemed to be oozing up from the forest floor itself. She took a tentative step. It was like walking on a sponge.

"No wonder you're so tired, Mally. It's impossible to walk on this stuff."

But Carrie had no choice but to walk on it,

for no matter which direction she turned, she was met by the same gushy ground.

The forest was thinning, the trees and underbrush becoming almost swamplike. Bullrushes spiked the edges of a great clearing, acres and acres of it lying still and flat beneath the moonlit sky.

"I know what this is."

Her father had once told her of there being boggy stretches of land in these mountains known as the glades. Strange plants that grew nowhere else in the hills flourished here, and game was plentiful. "I was in one of the glades hunting one time and the fellow I was with sank completely out of sight," Harris had said. "One minute he and his horse were there beside me, the next they were gone. It was all I could do to get out before I sank, too."

Whoever was chasing Carrie, whether it was Rance's men or the bushwhackers, was so close now she could almost feel their hot, slavering breath on the back of her neck. She couldn't afford to get caught by either of them. Alone, she had a chance in the boggy glade. With Mally, it would be suicide. The horse was too heavy for the raftlike vegetation. She would also be easy to spot in the open glade. There was enough cover for a person to hide, but not a horse.

She unbuckled her saddle and pulled it from Mally, dropping it to the soggy ground before leading the mare back to the forest edge.

"You're on your own, girl. I hope it's not a heavy-handed farmer in need of a plow horse who finds you." She removed Mally's bridle and slapped the flat of her hand on the mare's rump. Mally looked so surprised that Carrie laughed. "Go on," she said and slapped the horse again. This time the mare took the hint and bolted out of sight.

Carrie went back to the saddle and stood on it until it sank out of sight. She pushed the bridle down with it and, when all trace of her presence had been erased, she began to walk.

After an hour of tremulous flight, she decided to risk taking a short break. Her legs were quivering almost as much as the ground. She longed to sit down and never get up again. The only place to sit, however, was on the wet ground.

She realized that it had been a long time since she'd heard anything from her noisy pursuers. Either they had decided she wasn't worth the risk of wading into the glade, or they'd followed Mally. As Carrie stood there in the silence waiting for her exhausted hopes to rise, she realized something else. She was surrounded by beauty.

The sky was dark with night, bright with stars and moonlight. Rushes stirred in unfelt breezes. Everywhere water rippled, trickled, seeped, and sighed. The wind smelled of cranberries, and the air was alive with swallows, bats, owls, and the cry of an eagle. And there were winged insects, fireflies and dragonflies, damselflies and moths hovering and darting and making even such a strange world as this feel familiar and friendly.

"There must be a billion dragonflies here," she said and turned in a slow circle. She stopped half way through the turn. "And at least two billion snakes."

The observation was not accompanied by the usual rush of panicked fear. The only thing she was afraid of right now was not reaching General Rosecrans in time for him to send his troops south to defend the Kanawha Valley from invasion.

No, there was one more thing she was afraid of—Rance Fletcher's kisses. The very thought of them made her so sick with fear that she forgot how wet the ground was and sat down.

Sometime during the night, Carrie stumbled across a river. Actually, she stumbled into it, but it wasn't very deep, and she managed with only minimal trouble to stumble back out again. Twelve feet wide at the most, it meandered through the glade like a drunken hound. Still, along its mudpacked banks, the ground was firmer than the glade itself, so Carrie meandered, too, for what felt like miles.

When she finally reached the northern edge of the great glade, which was marked by a thick forest, she was too tired to even care. She just kept following the river. The branches of the red spruce and black ash trees that cloaked the riverbanks were festooned with lichen that dangled like decorations from a Christmas tree.

Dawn came slowly, lightening the sky and warming the air but doing little to stop Carrie's teeth-chattering chills. The sound of men talking hit her like cannon fire. The sound was coming from downstream. She ran into the woods to look for a thicket of laurel in which to hide. All she found was enough poison ivy to cause the entire Confederate army to fall to its knees in a rash of surrender.

She was still looking for a place to hide when she realized that where there were men, there would be horses. Even better than that, maybe these men were Union soldiers. Maybe they had a field telegraph. Maybe she could run into camp, tell them about the invasion, and while they contacted Clarksburg over their handy wire, Carrie could lay down and sleep for a week.

They could be Confederates. But that wasn't a disaster, either. Rance had been so preoccupied with mauling her, he hadn't bothered to search her, so she still had her Confederate pass. But maybe he'd put out the word that the pass was no good, and she was to be arrested on sight. Maybe even shot on sight. Maybe even dropped into a pit of snakes and abandoned to her fear and fate!

"Maybe I'd better get hold of myself and stop scaring myself to death."

She crept toward the voices. There were two

men and three horses, two with saddles and one with supplies. Both men were dismounted. One was buttoning up his pants. The other had his back to Carrie. She didn't want to know what he was doing. What mattered was that the men and their animals were wearing the same brand, CSA.

"Nothing is ever easy," Carrie muttered.

When she'd first decided to volunteer her services to the Union, her grandfather had said that she would need a lot of nerve and stamina. He had failed to mention that she would need a lot of plans, too.

She needed one now. This one was easy, though. Between her and the men was another patch of autumn-reddened poison ivy leaves.

She crept toward it.

"I done told you twice," Carrie said in imitation of a backwoods accent. After what she'd been through in the last twenty-four hours, she didn't need to do anything to look the part of a poor mountain girl. If anything, she looked too terrible. "Ma's sickly and the baby's mostly dead. They need a doctor and that's where I was goin'."

She scratched at her right arm with vigorous abandon, pushing her sleeve up to expose rash-red skin.

"I went to them Yankees up at the fort, only they said they didn't have no doctor. Said I oughta go to Clarksburg. That's where I'm headed now, only when I got off my mule to wet a rag to cool my fever, old Henry heard you and run off." She gave a convincing shiver and scratched her neck.

"What fort?" Lt. Strickland asked.

The other man had introduced himself as Corporal Rucker. He was staring at Carrie's exposed arm. He switched his gaze to her neck.

"Laurel Hill," she said and saw the lieutenant's eyes sharpen.

"If you're going to Clarksburg, ma'am," Rucker said, "what are you doing here? This is quite a ways south of both there and Laurel Hill."

Carrie looked at him in horror. "That can't be! That captain pointed out which way I should go and I been goin' that way as fast as I could go 'cause he said General Rosecrans was there and he'd get me a doctor for Ma."

"He was wrong about that, too," the lieutenant said. "Rosecrans is moving his troops south along the Weston Turnpike toward Summersville."

Carrie's head snapped up. *He's marching right into a trap!*

She gave a violent shiver to cover her response to his news. "I wonder what's got hold of me? I feel like I've been throwed in hot grease, but I keep gettin' these chills."

"Lieutenant Strickland, could I see you for a minute over here?" Rucker was still staring at

Carrie's rash-covered neck and arm. He looked almost as sick as she was pretending to be.

They held their conference under a chestnut tree. The longer Rucker talked, the harder Strickland stared at Carrie. When they approached her again, it was like they were approaching a black widow spider.

Lieutenant Strickland cleared his throat. "We would like to help you, ma'am, so we're going to give you our packhorse to ride and send you onto Clarksburg."

She jumped to her feet. "Ma was right, you Confederates are true gentlemen. Not at all like them Yankees."

"You said you were at Laurel Hill," Lieutenant Strickland said. "You wouldn't happen to have noticed how many Federal soldiers were there, would you?"

"That I did," she said and inflated the small four-hundred-man force at the fort to a more respectable number. "I'd say there must've been close to 4,000 soldiers there. They was totin' rifles and diggin' those ditches they like to hide in and makin' like they was gettin' ready to fight Robert E. Lee himself."

The interest in Strickland's eyes again sharpened, revealing another interesting secret to Carrie.

"You know," she said, "I figure them Yankees was lyin' when they told me they didn't have no doctor. That many men doin' that much gettin' ready to get shot at surely have a sawbones somewheres nearby. I think they just wanted to be shed of me 'cause I told them that Ma's been tendin' folks sick with the smallpox and that she was actin' a goodly amount like they was actin' before they died."

The men exchanged glances confirming that their fears over her apparent disease had been right. Rucker stripped the packhorse of its burden, and Carrie mounted the animal, not an easy effort considering neither man offered her a hand.

"I'll bring this horse back if you'll just tell me where it is you're gonna be."

"No!" Strickland said and held up his hands as though stopping a charge. "You just keep him, ma'am. After all, we did spook your mule."

She smiled down at their pale faces. "If you're ever up in Slaty Hollow, stop in, and if Ma's still alive, she'll fix you the best plate of hog jowls this side of the Blue Ridge."

Carrie had to keep her hands firmly clenched around the reins to keep from scratching as she rode away. She wanted desperately to look for touch-me-nots, a wildflower that made an excellent poison ivy cure. It was more important that she reach General Rosecrans, though.

Chapter Eighteen

Retreat. Rance found it impossible to believe, but after a five-hour battle at the Carnifex Ferry near Summersville, during which General Floyd's men held at bay a bigger and better-equipped Union army without the loss of a single man, Floyd was retreating. While the Confederate forces marched along the Sunday Road toward Dogwood Gap, Rance rode to the rear to deliver a message to Colonel Thompkin, who was in charge of the rear guard.

As Rance came to the first wagon in the supply train, one of the drivers waved him to stop. "You're Captain Fletcher, aren't you? I recognize that horse. There's a boy hurt in one of the wagons asking for you. He's back about halfway with the doctor."

It was Kitchen. He was stretched out on a bloody blanket in the back of a supply wagon. Dr. Samuel Gleaves of the 45th Virginia briefed Rance on the boy's injuries.

"He rode in about an hour ago. Asked for you, then collapsed. Right shoulder had a bullet pass all the way through it, left leg has one still in it. His injuries are about three-days old. I don't know if I can save the leg, but I think I can keep him alive."

"Three days," Rance repeated. His voice sounded as tight as the knotted pain in his chest. "Is he conscious?"

"In and out," Gleaves said. "I gave him morphine to keep him quiet until we get someplace where I can take a better look at that leg."

Rance climbed into the back of the wagon. Kitchen's face was so pale and drawn, his freckles stood out like a stereoscope image.

"Cap'n." The voice was weak, but it was as full of Alabama as ever.

"What happened, son?"

"Bushwackers, sir. The sergeant's dead."

"The girl, Kitchen, what happened to Carrie?"

"She got away."

Rance closed his eyes in relief.

"They went after her, though. I tried to trail them, but—" His eyes clouded over.

Rance grasped the boy's good left shoulder and squeezed until the eyes cleared. "But what, Private?"

"There was this bog, the biggest flat place I've seen since we come to these mountains. The sergeant told me about it once, but I didn't believe him. I guess I should've."

"Stop rambling, Private. What happened to Carrie?"

"I found her horse near the edge of the bog. She'd stripped off the saddle and bridle to keep from givin' herself away again while she went in on foot. Them bushwackers went after her for a ways, then came back out and doubled back to where they ambushed us. I tried to go in, but it was like tryin' to walk on water, Cap'n. My horse was sinkin' and there weren't no trail to follow anyway. Just weeds and water."

And Carrie.

Why couldn't she be like other women and stay at home where she belonged? The thought had no sooner occurred to Rance before he realized how ridiculous it was. Right this minute, his sisters were probably sitting in the parlor at Tory Plantation, giggling about some silly bit of nonsense while they knitted socks for soldiers. No matter how hard he tried, he couldn't picture Carrie as part of that scene.

He could, however, picture her trying to cross an uncrossable swamp.

"She might make it, Cap'n."

Rance frowned at Kitchen. "What's that?"

"Miss Blackwell, she might make it, sir. Sergeant Stillson said he used to go huntin' in that big bog, that's how come he was to tell me about it. We were talkin' about huntin'. That must mean that somebody can go in there and not get drowned. Only he also said there was a lot of snakes in there, Cap'n."

Rance remembered how frightened Carrie had

looked when she first appeared out of the well, and how her voice had shaken when she told him there was a snake down there.

He leapt from the wagon and mounted Cain.

"You goin' after her, Cap'n?" Kitchen asked.

Rance pushed his right boot into the stirrup and reined the stallion close to the wagon. "Of course, I'm going after her. I'm going to ride through the middle of the Yankee army, across miles of hostile territory and into a snake-infested swamp so I can rescue a bull-headed damsel in distress because I am a Southern gentleman and Southern gentlemen are always doing idiotic things like this. And if you still have that silly grin on your face when I get back, Private Kitchen, you'll spend the rest of this war cleaning up after Virginia horses instead of doing a damn poor job of riding them!"

Chapter Nineteen

Carrie came across General Rosecrans' camp unexpectedly. She'd been riding so long and for so far, she'd thought the terrible ordeal would never end. Every breath she took sounded like a sob, every heartbeat exploded like cannon fire in her chest. Her hands were so swollen from the poison ivy, she could barely hold the packhorse's reins as she rode through the Union camp looking for the tent of its commander.

The object of her search rose like a castle from out of the gloom of twilight, battle flags flying from its canvas ramparts. Carrie brought her steed to a halt and collapsed from his back like a warrior wearing too much armor.

Once she'd been ushered into the castle, her fever-clogged mind realized its mistake. There were no rushes on the floor, just mud. There was no great fire, no long bows, no trestle tables. Just a single lantern and three generals in blue uniforms.

"You have information for me?" General Rosecrans asked. He wasn't the embattled king of her imaginings, either. His face was as kind as she remembered, but he was no longer the humble ruler on the field of his first victory. He was now a victorious and triumphant king.

"A Confederate—" Carrie tried to swallow the dry taste in her throat. "A Confederate force under the command of General Floyd has massed at Carnifex Ferry on the Gauley River, sir. They have defeated General Cox at Cross Lanes and are preparing to march on Charleston."

"That's the important information that could not wait for me to finish my council with my generals? I don't need to know where General Floyd was, I need to know where he is now."

She blinked away the image of being hailed a heroine. "I don't understand."

"This is Carnifex Ferry, Miss Blackwell. General Floyd was here yesterday. Because I didn't know that, I lost one hundred fifty-eight men when my troops chanced across his camp. Those men might be alive today if you had delivered your news in a timely fashion."

Carrie folded her arms in front of her, a weak wall of protection against Rosecrans' anger.

"With God's help, I was able to overcome the odds which beset me. I have rousted the enemy from his entrenchments and have sent him into full retreat, thereby protecting the Kanawha Valley from attack. I am now awaiting word of General Floyd's present location so that I might continue my campaign to rid this country of its Confederate invaders. I hope that the scouts currently searching for General Floyd are not as negligent in reporting their findings as you have been, Miss Blackwell. Now if you will excuse us, my generals and I have a war to fight."

"There is something else," Carrie said. She felt so strange, hot and dizzy and disoriented. She had to struggle to remember what she'd been about to say. "General Lee is planning to attack Laurel Hill."

Rosecrans sighed. "General Lee is not planning to attack anything, Miss Blackwell. He has withdrawn his forces from the Laurel Hill area and is most likely trying as desperately as I am to figure out where General Floyd has gone."

"Why did he withdraw?"

"There is speculation the withdrawal was the result of an overestimation of the size of our garrison at Laurel Hill. There is also the rumor about an outbreak of smallpox in the area. You may believe whichever story you prefer, Miss Blackwell."

"I shall believe them both," she said and left.

One hundred and fifty-eight men. A terrible toll. But she had saved the men at Laurel Hill. Smearing poison ivy on her hands, arms, face and throat had been a good idea. The next time she got such a good idea, though, she would use it more sparingly. If she lived long enough to ever have another idea. The way she felt right now, the possibility was looking very remote.

Chapter Twenty

Rance was wearing a greatcoat, not to ward off the chill which had unexpectedly settled over the Alleghenies, but to prevent his uniform from being recognized and his neck stretched. The turnpike past Summersville was crowded with travelers, most of them glowing with the news of the Federal victory at Carnifex Ferry.

"Thanks to Floyd's folly," Rance muttered. If the Confederate army was going to run every time they were faced with superior forces, the South might as well give up right now.

"We made them rebs tuck their tails between their legs and run like a scared dog," boasted an old codger at a tavern where Rance stopped for directions.

"Follow the Greenbrier River east to Stamping Creek," the innkeeper told him. "At the house where the Grahams used to live, turn west and keep going until you see the place where Big Dan Green got shot for selling bad whiskey. Then go north and you'll find yourself knee-deep in the glade."

"I suppose there are signs to identify these

historical points of interest?" Rance asked sarcastically.

The old codger laughed. "Run along, Pete. I'll take care of this. A body couldn't find the outhouse if you were giving the directions." The tavern keeper left to wait on another customer, and the old man fixed Rance with a look of interested disbelief. "You wouldn't happen to be looking for somebody you lost near that glade, would you?"

"What makes you ask that?"

He swirled a finger in his whiskey. "You're wearing a Confederate uniform in the middle of a nest of Federals. That either means you're crazy, or you're in such a hurry to get someplace, you didn't take time to make yourself presentable. Your next mistake was coming in here at all, then you compounded it by asking how to get to the exact place where two of your kind recently got themselves shot up by some no accounts. Since there was a girl with those rebs and she took off into the glade, it makes sense that you came to find her." He grinned at Rance. "How'd I do?"

"Better than I expected."

"Just because a man doesn't have blackskins picking his crops doesn't mean he can't think his way out of a potato sack. You make that mistake too many times around these parts and there won't be enough left of you to ship home to your mama."

"You were singing the praises of Lincoln when I came in, old daddy. Why aren't you turning me in?"

The old man tipped his glass up and his chair back. "Because my name is Peach Blackwell, and that girl you're looking for is my granddaughter. And even though I don't like the trouble you got her into, I like the fact that you're risking your neck to get her out of it. Now, I think it might be a good idea for you to head on back to your side of the fence before that Union major in the corner over there figures out what it is about you that's bothering him. And there's no need for you to be worrying about Carrie. She's safe."

"She got out of the bog?"

"If she hadn't, I wouldn't be here jawing with you, I'd be out looking for her."

Rance could see a little of Carrie in this old man. She had his easy manner and his way of smiling with his eyes when it was least expected.

"She's all right?"

"Had a bit of a go around with some poison ivy, but she'll survive."

Rance cast a glance at the far corner. The major was still looking at him with a suspicious gleam in his eye. Rance had to get out of there before the gleam turned into gunfire.

"About Carrie, Mr. Blackwell. She's in over her head."

"That girl's a lot taller than you think, Captain. Besides, she's got me looking out for her." Peach gave Rance a sly smile. "Looks like she's got you, too."

"I felt responsible for what happened."

"That's how it starts."

"There's nothing to start, old man." Rance wasn't certain which of them he was trying to convince.

"Keep it that way, Captain. Carrie doesn't need you adding a broken heart to her worries." Peach was watching the major. Now his lips tightened into a thin line. "Get moving right now, Fletcher, and don't slow down until you're deep in Dixie."

"I'll leave her horse outside," Rance said, and was out the door before he realized that Peach Blackwell had known not only his rank, but also his name.

Chapter Twenty-one

The most eagerly anticipated holiday of any year was Valentine's Day. It was a national obsession. Everyone sent valentines to everyone else: friends, family, lovers, spouses, even enemies. There were preprinted valentines, homemade valentines, comic and satirical, even rude and nasty valentines.

In 1862, the already intense emotions evoked by the day of love were heightened even further by the war. People on both sides of the fight were determined to celebrate with a passion.

Carrie spent all of January preparing for the event. She crocheted dozens of delicate hearts, which she stiffened with sugar water, "to make them sweet hearts," she told a giggling Lisset. Cupids, doves, and frills weren't among Carrie's preferences for decorations. As a substitute for those printed paper geegaws, she used wildflowers she'd picked last summer and had pressed between pages of her father's copy of *Romeo and Juliet*.

"Can you think of a place more appropriate

for valentine flowers?" she'd demanded when he'd protested the abuse of his book.

She attached the flowers to the crocheted hearts with a dab of paste. Ribbons were the only other adornment, along with a hand-lettered card attached to the center of each elaborate creation, the sentiments on each card chosen especially for the intended recipient.

Now the grand day had arrived. Along with the task of hand-delivering the valentines to her friends in Richmond, where she was staying at the Spotswood Hotel, Carrie had a task to fulfill that had been assigned her by Major Allen. The order had arrived before dawn in the guise of a valentine. Elizabeth Van Lew, the best of a few Union-loyalists in Richmond, had delivered the card to Carrie.

Hannah had answered the knock. "What is you doin' here?" she had whispered loud enough to be heard on all five of the Spotswood's floors.

Carrie was in bed. Her first reaction had been that the visitor was Rance. Uncertain of whether to dive under the covers or point her pistol at him, she ended up doing neither. When it was Elizabeth who was ushered into the bedroom by Hannah, Carrie didn't know whether to be relieved or disappointed. She opted for surprise.

"One of my couriers brought this from Washington this morning on a special run."

Carrie was almost afraid to take it. "I hope something didn't happen to Pops or Peach." She ripped open the elaborate envelope and laughed. "It's a valentine." A beautiful one with embossed roses and enough Cupids to decorate a dozen cards. " 'Constant and True,' " she read from the front of the card. The back had a personal inscription, which she also read aloud, " 'Carolina, I worry about your safety in Richmond and need immediate reassurance that our paths will soon be joined.' It's signed Major E. J. Allen."

Elizabeth looked confused. "I know he wouldn't risk the life of a courier to deliver a valentine, but where's the message?"

"He wants information on Richmond's fortifications for the invasion of Virginia General McClellan is planning."

"It's that simple?"

"Too simple for you to figure out, and you knew it had to be a message."

She laughed. "I wish my codes were so easy. Sometimes I can't figure them out, and I'm the one encoding them. Do you want to send your reply to Washington with one of my couriers?"

"That's a good idea. This is too important to risk using only my usual method. I'll have Hannah bring you a copy to send, too."

"I should leave before the rest of the hotel guests awaken," Elizabeth said.

Hannah locked the hotel door behind their departing guest. She came back into the bedroom and cocked an eyebrow at Carrie. "Don't you be forgettin' Miss Decca is comin' here to have lunch with you today."

Carrie tapped Major Allen's card on the edge of her dressing table. "I need an excuse to get away from her and a reason to tour the fortifications."

"It's gonna be a warm day. Maybe Miss Decca would like to go on a picnic and a long walk while she tells you all the Greyston gossip, which I just know you is itchin' to hear."

Carrie jumped to her feet and gave Hannah a hug. "You're a genius!"

Seventeen earthwork batteries in a north-facing semicircle that began and ended at the James River. Entrenchments are—Carrie paced off the height—ten feet high and—she stepped off the distance across—twelve feet across.

I'll never be able to code that.

It was an unseasonably pretty day, sunny and warm and perfect for a picnic. And though the implications of her surroundings were depressing, Richmond's fortifications were beautiful. Grass, green and bright as a sparkle in a child's eye, grew thick across the man-made hills. The sky was a startling blue, the kind of blue that takes the breath away, the kind of blue that reminded Carrie of Ransom Fletcher's eyes.

"Midnight blue," Decca had called it, "just like the lace on my dress. Isn't it lovely, darling?"

"Yes," Carrie had replied, "the sky is lovely."

Decca had begun to pout, which was her preferred state of mood when men were present, for then they would concentrate all their energy on raising her spirits. And there were several men at the picnic party. Franklyn Bredon, who was the reason Decca was in Richmond, couldn't make it due to a meeting with President Davis. James was there, though, valentine in hand and charm firmly in place. With him was a South Carolina artillery lieutenant named David Foster whose stalwart face sent Lisset Lewis into the throes of ecstasy.

"I'm in love," she confided to Carrie.

"What happened to Andrew?"

"He's on duty," Lisset said and gave Lieutenant Foster a dazzling smile.

Alice Barton was there, too, and with a beau. His name was Virgil Smith and he was a clerk in the War Department. "His job might not be interesting, but he is," she told everyone. Carrie won Alice's undying gratitude when she confessed to thinking Mr. Smith's job intensely interesting. Her honesty was rewarded with the promise of a tour of the offices of Confederate command.

It had taken quite a bit of effort for Carrie to rid herself of her party while she mapped the fortifications. She'd been forced to set a blistering pace up and down and across and into and over the seventeen batteries that eventually discouraged all but her most determined companion, James. It was only when she'd announced her intent to do the whole thing again that James had finally realized she wasn't doing this just to be alone with him and left her to continue her work.

Now all she needed to do now was convert her findings into code, and she could spend the rest of the day eating potato salad and avoiding James.

On a bluff overlooking the river was an oak tree whose spreading limbs offered her a bower of winter brown foliage under which to compose her letter to Major Allen. Once seated with her sprigged muslin skirts spread around her and her hat discarded on the grass beside her, she leaned her head back against the tree's knobby trunk and tried to remember everything she needed to tell the major.

The canopy above her parted and a face appeared.

"Hello," the face, which was quite handsome, said. It had the blackest, curliest hair she'd ever seen and a moustache that was most dramatic and blue eyes that twinkled and a smile that dimpled when she said, "Hello yourself."

"Have you seen my brother? He's three years old and lost."

"I've seen no one except you, not that I've seen very much of you."

"Easily fixed." The face disappeared. It was

replaced an instant later by a pair of long legs in cavalry boots, a trim body in a Virginia cavalry uniform, and long arms that held onto the tree limb for a dangling moment before letting the entire person drop to the ground beside Carrie.

"Lt. Michael Lester Fletcher of the 4th Virginia Cavalry at your service, ma'am."

"Carolina Grey Blackwell at yours." She offered him her hand, which instead of shaking, he kissed.

"You are very pretty, Carolina Grey Blackwell."

"And you, Lt. Michael Lester Fletcher, are a flirt. Shall I help you find your brother?"

"What an excellent idea! That way I can look at you and for him at the same time. I'm afraid the sprout has me skunked."

He helped Carrie to her feet, retrieved her hat, which she dangled from her arm like a straw basket with a green ribbon handle, and together they set off across the entrenchments to the next stand of trees. Michael stared unabashedly at her, a grin on his face and in his eyes that suddenly looked so familiar to Carrie, she stopped dead in her tracks.

"Are you Rance Fletcher's brother?"

He winced. "Guilty. You're not going to slap me, are you?"

"Why would I do that?"

"It happens all the time. I introduce myself,

women get this glazed look in their eye and then slap me either for something he did or didn't do. Sometimes, it's both."

"You may relax, for I have no intention of slapping you. Your brother isn't worth the effort."

"I am in the presence of greatness! You are the only woman in the entire world who, after having the dubious honor of meeting my big brother, has resisted the temptation of falling victim to his deadly charm." Michael rolled his eyes to heaven and pressed both hands over his chest. "It's a miracle. Be right back, Miss Blackwell." He reached for the lowest branch of the towering pine they'd come to.

"Carrie," she said.

He grinned. "We're going to be great friends, Carrie. I can tell already," he said and climbed like a squirrel into the needle-bright green of the tree. "Chance!" he shouted. "Are you in here, you little troublemaker?" A noisy search of the tree ended with Michael again dropping to earth beside Carrie. "No luck."

"There's someone riding this way." She pointed at the approaching horse. "What a beautiful animal." And it was beautiful, a great black stallion of spirit and breeding who raced up the side of the battery with his head high, tail streaming, and hooves flashing in the sun like polished ebony. She was certain she'd seen the animal somewhere before.

"Speak of the devil," Michael said. "It's big brother himself."

Of course. She caught her tongue between her teeth and held it tight, but whether it was to keep her mouth from babbling something stupid or to prevent her teeth from chattering in response to a sudden chill, she didn't know. What she did know was that even though it had been five months since she'd last seen Rance, the taste of his kisses was still warm and sweet on her lips.

"Found him," Rance said as he pulled Cain to a stop in front of Michael. There was a girl standing a little behind his brother. Rance ignored her while he pried Chance off the saddle so he could drop him in Michael's arms. Cain sidestepped closer to the girl. Rance stiffened as he looked down into those dark eyes.

"Hey, Sug, *hey!*"

Chance's yell caused Rance to realize he was dangling the child from his outstretched arm like a twitching rag.

"Sorry, kid." He lowered Chance into Michael's custody and looked back at Carrie. She was especially beautiful today, her soft skirt belling out around her in the river breeze and her hair so full of light it shone like the sun itself. "I found the rascal trying to put his head in the barrel of one of the cannons."

"Stop kicking, sprout," Michael ordered.

He set the squirming child on the ground,

where he immediately began spinning in a circle with his arms outstretched, windmilling himself over to Carrie.

"Hi, lady! Are you Michael's girlfriend? I don't have a girlfriend, but I got a book about birds! Wow, your face sure is red!"

"Chance, mind your manners." Rance dismounted and pulled the boy to him. "This is a surprise, Carrie. Are you here to gather information for Lincoln or were you looking for me?"

Michael looked horrified. "No wonder I get slapped so much."

Carrie gave Rance a tight smile. "Instead of your present post, President Davis should have commissioned you as court jester."

"You would still be my best joke."

"That's enough, Rance," Michael said. "One more word and I shall be forced to call you out. Carrie and I have just fallen deeply in love and were trying to decide how many children we're going to have when you arrived, weren't we, dearest? I won't have my future wife and the mother of my eagerly anticipated children spoken to in that manner."

"I'm sorry, Michael, but the wedding will have to be postponed until after I've eaten lunch," Carrie said. "I'm much too hungry to pledge my troth right now, so if you gentlemen, and you, Rance, will excuse me, I shall rejoin my party."

"Are you havin' a picnic?" Chance's eyes were

wide with surprise. "We're havin' one, too! Can we take her with us, Sug? She's awful pretty, and Michael's gonna marry her, so it ain't like we're kidnappin' her or nothin'."

"What a jolly idea," Michael said. He dropped to one knee and embraced her right hand. "Please say yes, oh noble and most gracious princess. Mother has enough fried chicken in her basket to satisfy your hunger, and then we can talk about what color we want the nursery to be."

Carrie was laughing so hard, she couldn't catch her breath. "But my mother and friends are expecting me. They've probably already sent out a search party to find me, I've been gone so long."

Michael jumped to his feet. "No problem. Big brother will ride over, tell them that you've been taken hostage and will be returned only after we've eaten every last wing and leg in Mother's bountiful basket."

"Yes, yes, say yes," Chance pleaded. He flung himself at her, clinging to her skirts like a blue-eyed leech while he implored her with dimpled smiles.

She lifted her gaze to Rance. "I'm not so sure it's a good idea."

Chance tore away from her and threw himself at Rance. "I like her, Sug, and I want to keep her. Make her say yes."

Carrie was touched by the tender way Rance

stroked the little boy's hair back from his face. Chance was barely as tall as his great cavalry boots, and he wrapped both arms around Rance's left leg and looked adoringly up at what was obviously his hero.

Rance met Carrie's uncertain gaze. "Mother would love to have you join us. Where is your party?"

She pointed east and told him how to find them.

Rance nodded. "Let's go, Chance." He mounted Cain and leaned down to take the squirming boy from Michael.

"Are we gonna catch us a Yankee, Sug?"

Rance glanced at Carrie. "Alan's already caught us one." He touched his spurs to Cain's sides, sending the stallion leaping into action.

"What did he mean by that?" Michael asked.

"My father is a very vocal supporter of the Union, as is my grandfather. Your brother is convinced that I share their sentiments. Why did he call you Alan?"

"Rance doesn't call anyone by the right name. I'm Alan, Chance's real name is Chase. Our grandmother is named Hummingbird and Rance calls her Birdie. Mother's name is Emma, but she's called either Mother or Mae, depending on whether she's angry with Rance, which she usually is."

They walked as they talked. In the distance, spread out across the sides and top of one of the batteries, was a group of people involved in a strenuous game of tag, as well as a great deal of tickling and laughing.

"That's my family," Michael said. "I'll point them out to you in descending order of ages. First is Ransom, the beast of the group, then me, the lovable one. Next is Jackson, alias Jessie L. He's the one in the Navy uniform, a real sailor, that boy. Mother said he was born with the wind in his sails and no brains in his head.

"There, running across the picnic blanket, that's Roberta Rose, also known as Bobby Rose. She thinks she's quite mature and grown up, but occasionally loses control and acts like the rest of us. The girl in pink is Clarence, who is really Clarcia. She likes Clarence better, and I can't say that I blame her. She was named after a doddering old aunt of Father's who is incredibly wealthy and so mean she makes Rance look like an angel."

They were so close now, Carrie could see their happy faces as they raced and chased and teased each other into fits of giggles.

"There's so many of them," she said, awed by the thought of such a large family.

"That's Patterson, also known as Clarke. He's the scholar of the family, after Rance. The two of them consume books like I eat chocolate. That saucy thing in yellow is called Lilly Blue but was christened Lila. And, of course, you've met Chance, the baby of the family and Rance's own personal pet." Michael tucked Carrie's hand into the crook of his arm and smiled down at her. "So, little wife-to-be, any sisters at home to steal my heart away from you or brothers to beat me up for stealing yours?"

"I had a brother. He died when I was just a baby. Now there's just me."

"It must be delightfully quiet at your house."

"Yes, it's very quiet." She slowed her step as an attack of shyness overcame her. "Are you sure your mother won't mind me joining you? I mean, there's already so many of you and I wouldn't want to impose and I really shouldn't just run off and leave my party since it was my idea we go on a picnic."

Michael was laughing at her, a wonderful, joyous laugh that drew everyone's attention, causing the whole crowd of them to come running to greet him.

"Hold up, don't run us over. This is Carolina Blackwell. I've already told her who you are. Carrie is a friend of Rance's—"

Lilly Blue howled with laughter. "*Rance* has a friend? I don't believe it."

"Quiet, child." The gentle reprimand came from a woman dressed in black mourning.

"Carrie, this is my mother," Michael said.

Emma Fletcher was a beautiful woman, but not the way Decca was beautiful. Emma's beauty was deeper and less selfish. Love seemed to pour out of her with every smile that touched her face.

"I've invited Carrie to share our lunch, Mother, but she's a little nervous, so we must all work very hard to make her feel welcome."

"It's lovely you could join us, Carolina."

"You're very kind to welcome a last-minute guest."

"Rance is on his way with Chance, Mother. The sprout had his head stuck in a cannon, but Rance put a match to the fuse and blew the kid out."

"That boy," Emma said, and Carrie had a feeling she was commenting not just on the child, but also the man. "Come, Carolina, we were just about to eat. Sit with me and tell me how you met my eldest."

The picnic blanket was spread with enough food for a church social. There was a great glazed ham with pickled crab apples, deviled eggs and jars of pickles, a cherry cobbler and jelly cake—"Raspberry," Lilly Blue assured her, "my favorite"—loaves of bread smelling so fresh they must have just been baked minutes ago, butterfly-shaped pats of sweet butter, blueberry muffins and smoked turkey and absolutely gallons of potato salad and a platter of oysters and salmon cakes and an apple pie and pitchers of tea with chunks of real ice clinking inside the crystal pitchers and, as Michael had promised, a whole henhouse of fried chicken.

"And ice cream," Birdie added to Lilly Blue's

listing of goodies. The spry little grandmother was just like a bird, quick and bright and pretty as a flash of jeweled feathers on a summer day.

"At a dance last year in Richmond," Carrie said in answer to the question Emma Fletcher had again asked. "We lost a Langaus."

Bobby Rose looked aghast at Carrie. "Ransom lost a Langaus? I don't believe it."

"He didn't take it well."

"My eldest takes nothing well," Emma said. "How did you meet Michael?"

"I dropped out of a tree on top of her."

"Gracious! I hope you apologized."

"Actually, he asked me to marry him."

"Michael!" Emma cried and the cry was taken up by the rest of the family.

Rance arrived during the second chorus. Chance was in such a hurry to join the laughter, he tripped over Clarke's foot and fell face down in the cherry cobbler. He sat up, surprised and blinking cherry juice out of his eyes.

"What happened?" he asked.

"Nothing that hasn't happened before," Emma said and wiped her youngest's face.

Rance dropped down between Carrie and Michael. He stretched out on the blanket between their plates and propped his head up on a raised hand. With the other, he stole a pickle off her plate.

"Did you find my party?" she asked. She was quite nonplussed by his eating of her food. It seemed such an intimate thing to do.

"They were packing to leave, so I told your mother we would take charge of you this afternoon."

"Mother isn't fond of picnics. Let me guess, she got a grass stain on her dress."

Rance scavenged a chicken breast from her plate. "It was an ant in her shoe or maybe a bee in her bonnet. Some kind of bug someplace it shouldn't be."

"Stop eating off Carolina's plate, Ransom." Emma filled a plate for him. "Here, sit up and behave."

Carrie couldn't help it, she laughed. Rough, tough, big-talking Rance being treated like a three year old was simply too irresistible a picture.

"Yes," she said and shook her finger at him. "You leave my chicken alone."

He had obeyed his mother without a word. He responded to Carrie's jest with a glance that melted her all the way down to the buttons on her shoes.

"Looks like you've met your match, Sug," Michael said.

Birdie had been watching the two of them with quick eyes. "Or your better," she said, eliciting a round of giggles from the feasting Fletchers.

Carrie was having trouble recovering from Rance's searing gaze, the heat of which had nothing to do with anger. Rather than let him see just how affected she was, she tried to think of something lighthearted to say.

"So, Sug, tell me how you got your nickname."

Michael was leaning across Rance to heap potato salad on her plate. "That's my doing. When we were sharing the nursery, our mammy—"

"Carrie and I have talked about Mammy before, haven't we?" Rance's gaze burned into her again.

She refused to blush at his glance or the memory of what they'd discussed, even though the effort of not doing so was so great she almost lost consciousness. "As I remember, we were discussing your lack of manners."

Lilly Blue rolled her eyes. "Must've been a long talk."

Bobby Rose hushed her little sister. "Let Alan finish his story."

"Yes," Michael said with a noble expression. "You should never interrupt a great storyteller like myself. Where was I? Oh yes, the nursery. Mammy was always calling him 'sugar.' She obviously had no idea what the word meant. I thought that was his name, so I began calling him Sug, multisyllable words being beyond my grasp at that early age. He used to beat me up on a regular basis for the infraction. Being the wise person that I am, after about ten years of being brutalized on a daily basis, I decided to only call him Sug behind his back. Chance picked up on it last year, then everyone else got into the act."

Clarence leaned close to Carrie. "He hates it. That's why we do it."

"Driving me crazy is their favorite hobby," Rance said to Carrie. "You have a lot in common with them."

The Fletcher children, which was the way Carrie thought of them even though, except for Lilly Blue and Chance, they were all older than she, ran off to play an enthusiastic game of tag.

"Go with them, Michael," Birdie said.

He jumped to his feet. "Would you like to join us?" he asked Carrie.

The thought of trying to hold her own with that group brought on another attack of shyness. "I don't think so," she said, even though she longed to.

"Then you have to promise that you won't let big brother here steal your heart while I'm away."

"I'll try to resist him."

Michael ran off to join the game. Emma went, too, scooping Chance out of the way of careening bodies and taking him to the carriage for an afternoon nap. The black servants gathered the dishes and leftover food, taking it all away to pack back into the huge baskets. The result of everyone suddenly doing something else was that Carrie found herself alone with Rance and Birdie, who had fallen asleep in the sun.

Carrie couldn't think of anything to say, especially not with Rance once again lying down beside her and watching her like she was a dragonfly under a magnifying glass. She pretended to be fascinated by the game, which had dissolved into an argument.

"You're out!" Lilly Blue was shouting at Clarke. "Tell him he's out, Alan."

"Okay, he's out."

"I am not!"

"Okay, you're not out."

"He is, too, it's my turn now!"

"Is not!"

"Alan, stop looking cross-eyed at us and tell us if he is or isn't out and if it is or isn't my turn!"

He threw up his hands. "I quit. Fight it out among yourselves." He ran over and dropped down beside Carrie. "They intimidate you, don't they?"

She nodded. "I've always wanted to be part of a big family, I've just never been around one before. I almost married a man once just so I could be part of a small one, but I realized in time that having your parents live in the same house doesn't make a family." She looked out at the playing children. "This is what a family should be like. I don't think I ever really knew that until today."

Rance gave a skeptical laugh and sat up.

"This isn't a family." He opened his arms to catch Chance, who had come flying out of the carriage and directly at him. "This is chaos."

"No, it's not," Carrie said. "This is wonderful."

Rance had taken Chance on another ride, "To try and calm the little beast down."

Michael spun a blade of grass between his fingers while he watched Carrie, who was trying not to watch Rance.

"When did you fall in love with him?" Michael asked.

She tore her gaze away from the stallion and his two gallant riders. "I'm not."

Michael lifted a skeptical eyebrow. "When women get that look in their eye, it's either love or heartburn. I suspect that the two ailments strike simultaneously where my big brother is concerned."

She laughed. "I've heard that about him. What did he do to get such a bad reputation?"

"He doesn't trust women, believes they only exist to undermine a man's morals, happiness, and ultimately, his sanity. It's all our father's fault. Rance worshipped him, and Father worshipped Mother. Rance was jealous of Mother. Don't get me wrong, he loves her. Gracious, what Virginia boy doesn't love his mother? But there was this wall between them that I didn't understand until Father died."

"What happened to him?" The question was a mistake. She knew it instantly. "I'm sorry, Michael. I shouldn't have asked."

He threw the grass blade away. "Its a natural question. Father was killed in what our family politely calls a gun-cleaning accident."

"How terrible."

"The terrible part is that it's a lie. Chance, as you no doubt have noticed, is quite a bit younger than the rest of us. He's the result of a wedding anniversary celebration. Mother took it in stride, as she does everything, but Father was mortified. He was quite moral, the kind of man one could never imagine doing anything even remotely sinful. As a result of his well-known moral perfection, Father was frequently asked to give the lesson at church. His favorite sermon, in and out of the pulpit, was a fiery condemnation of the sins of the flesh. Not long after it became obvious to even the most unsuspecting churchgoer that Mother was in the motherly way, Father locked himself in the study one gloomy Sunday afternoon and blew his brains out with a dueling pistol."

Carrie was so shocked that she had to cover her mouth to keep from crying out.

"Rance heard the shot and broke down the door."

"He blamed your mother?"

Michael nodded. "He never said anything, but

Rance can say volumes without ever speaking a word. Father's death changed him. He became obsessed with being a success, I guess because Father used to accuse him of being too wild to ever do anything except get in trouble. And then Chance was born. That changed big brother, too. He'd never been able to reach out to anyone before. But the two of them, well, you've seen how it is between them. They're mad about each other. Rance's attitude softened toward Mother after that, and he let the rest of us push in a little closer, too."

Rance was turning Cain in tight circles, to the delight of the laughing little boy he held safe in his protecting arms.

"You said we were a family, Carrie. If we are, it was Rance who made us one. Before Father died, we were just a lot of people with the same last name. You were right when you said it takes more than having your parents live in the same house to make a family. Mother is wonderful and Father loved us, but Sug made us a family. After he tagged the baby Chance, he gave us all nicknames, and suddenly we were a family."

Michael pulled another blade of grass. He used it to tickle Carrie's chin. "Did you mean it when you said you weren't in love with him?"

"I'm—I don't know, Michael, I guess I'm overwhelmed by him." It was true. She'd never met anyone like him.

"Does that mean our wedding is off?"

She took the blade of grass away from him and used it to tickle his ear. "It's your own fault. All that talk about us having thousands of children has frightened me into spinsterhood."

Michael went back to camp, taking Jessie L. and Clarke with him. Rance gave up trying to calm Chance down and was now trying to ride him to sleep. That left Carrie with the three sisters, Emma, and a snoring Birdie.

"I received valentines from dozens of friends, but only three beaus," Lilly Blue, who was just sixteen, confided to Carrie. "Bobby Rose got dozens, but only opened the one from that boring old band conductor she wants to marry. And Clarence got hundreds. How many did you get?"

"Not quite hundreds."

"I love valentines," Lilly Blue said. She laid her head on Clarence's lap. "Jessie L. refused to tell me how many he got and Michael said his filled an entire train car and Clarke got tons, too. I wonder how many Rance got? Did you send him one, Carrie?"

She'd been writing her letter to Mary Allen and was trying to think of the code word for cannons. She looked up from the letter, startled by Lilly Blue's question. "Heavens, no."

"He must be devastated. I can see he's sweet on you. He never eats off anyone's plate ever, so I think the reason he did it today was so he could sit beside you. He didn't send you one either, did he? He never sends any except to Mother. He makes them himself, which is the very best kind, and he paints the most beautiful flowers on them. He's as good an artist as he is at raising tobacco, and he's very good at that, even though I'd never tell him because he's much too conceited as it is."

"You're talking too much, dear," Emma said. She was putting perfect little stitches into a piece of floral embroidery.

That's it. Carrie remembered suddenly. *A cannon is a cabbage rose.*

"Pay the child no mind," Emma said. "She has less manners than Ransom."

A clatter of hoofbeats announced his return. He dismounted with a yawning but still awake Chance in his arms. He carried the boy over and sat between his mother and Carrie. "He's never going to take a nap."

"Nope, I'm not," Chance said. He burrowed deeper into Rance's arms. "I'm gonna join the cavalry."

Carrie put her letter aside in favor of watching the love between this charming little boy and his seemingly impenetrable big brother.

"They don't take babies," Rance said. "You

have to be a man to be in the cavalry."

"When's that gonna be?"

"Let's see, Father told me I was a man the year he gave me my own pony."

"Then that's what I want on my next birthday."

"Next birthday?" Rance pretended to be shocked. "You had a birthday last year. What makes you think you deserve another one?"

"Mama says I'm gonna have one in April and that I'm gonna be four years old."

"Still not old enough for a pony. You have to be six. That's how old I was, and Alan and Jessie L. and Clarke, too."

Chance's face dissolved into a prelude of tears. "But that's forever!"

"Crying won't help," Rance said. "Six it is, and only then if you take a nap every day, including today."

"Then I can join the cavalry?"

"I promise," Rance said, and Chance leaned his head on his brother's shoulder and fell instantly asleep.

Emma frowned at Rance. "You shouldn't fill his head with such things, Ransom. Not with this war."

"It'll be over long before then, Mae."

"I pray so," Emma said.

"So do I," Carrie added. She brushed a raven curl off Chance's forehead. The little boy had completely entranced her with his sticky-fingered

hugs and lopsided smiles. "He's going to break a lot of hearts when he grows up."

"He's already broken a few," Rance said. His voice was filled with such pain.

She wanted to soothe it away, but instead she turned back to her letter, filling it with secrets which would destroy everything the Fletchers loved. And with every word Carrie wrote, she felt Rance's gaze resting on her. It was warm, just like his kisses, and it was disturbing, just like him.

Chapter Twenty-two

"It's the same as all the others," Rance said. "Listen to this." He read from the letter in his hand. " 'I saw a most excellent hat today, quite a well-made affair with seventeen rows of the most perfect ruffles you can imagine, quite deep and extra wide. They were only on the front of the hat and wrapped around the wearer's head in a semicircle that stretched completely from ear to ear.' Female dribble!" he said and threw the letter on the table.

General Lee picked it up. "It is refreshing to know that there is still a girl so untouched by what is happening today that she can fill page after page with such free-hearted chatter."

"This is not just any girl, General." Franklyn Bredon struck a match and lit his cigar. "This girl can write an iron-clad contract without the aid of a lawyer, and she doubled the output from her father's saltworks while cutting expenses in half. In the two years prior to the war, we estimate she stole fifty Negroes from their masters, including several from me, and bought more than that at auction, then set every one of them free."

"I've also discovered that she supports a school in Canada to teach them to read so they can find work," Rance said. "It's hard to believe a girl capable of all that would even notice a hat as atrocious as this one sounds. She goes on to describe, in detail, the location of every cabbage rose on the thing. 'A perfectly placed array,' she called them. Carolina Blackwell wouldn't notice a cabbage rose if it was pinned to her nose."

General Lee put the letter back on the table. "It is obvious to me, Captain, that this girl's letter is nothing more than it seems, a description of a bonnet and tidbits of gossip. If she does fancy herself a Union spy, and this is a sample of the secrets she is stealing, we have nothing to worry about. Instead of being obsessed with trying to find something that doesn't exist, you should direct your energies to finding what apparently does exist, her stockpiled salt. President Davis has made it clear that the command you want, and which I would like you to have, Captain, will not be considered until that matter is resolved."

After the general left, Rance picked up the letter again. It was exactly the kind of thing Lilly Blue would write or maybe Bobby Rose.

But not Carrie. And yet he'd watched her write it.

"I know there's something here," Rance said. "I can see it every time I look at her."

Franklyn Bredon studied the ash hanging from the end of his cigar. "You don't have to convince me. One look into those devil-dark eyes of Carolina's is enough to convince me she's capable of anything short of cold-blooded murder. I wouldn't even put that past her if there was a good reason for it. When she was running slaves, she never tried to hide them. For the most part, she did it right under everyone's noses. I knew she wasn't a supporter of slavery, but it never occurred to me to question why she was buying them, because she did it right in front of me." Bredon inhaled cigar smoke. "What you have to do, Fletcher, is stop trying to catch her dealing from the bottom of the deck and look closer at the cards she taking off the top. Whatever Carolina's doing that's most obvious is where she'll conceal her secrets." With those words of wisdom, he left, too, trailing the aromatic scent of Tory Plantation tobacco.

Rance opened his portable desk, a boxlike device that opened into a writing surface complete with blotter and writing supplies. He took out paper, pen and ink to make a copy of Carrie's letter.

When he finished, he blotted the copy and

put it in a compartment hidden beneath the ink well. Copies of her other letters, the first dated the day Anderson Hatfield shot off her feather in Charleston, were already in the hidden compartment, the originals having been obtained, like this one, by Franklyn Bredon's extensive network of postal agents in both the Confederacy and the Union.

Rance returned Carrie's letter to its envelope and called for Task to take it to the flag of truce boat anchored in the James River. "Give it to Herbert Spencer, Task."

"This letter done got a postmark, Master Rance."

"Spencer knows what to do with it. Here, don't forget this." Rance gave Task a pass authorizing him to be out at night. Negroes found on the streets at night without a pass were taken to jail, where their owners, or guardians if they were free, had to claim them in the morning.

After Task left, Rance tipped his chair back onto two legs, crossed his arms over his chest, and thought about the day he'd kissed Carrie. She'd invaded not just his memories, but also his desires to the point where he'd been unable to stir even a spark of interest in another woman since the day he'd tasted her lips.

Seeing her today had intensified his desire for her. The easy sound of her laughter, the sparkle of sunlight on her hair, even the shy way she had watched his family with such obvious envy and delight. It had all had the effect of pouring kerosene on a bonfire, and Rance knew it would take a lot more than kisses to extinguish his blaze.

He wanted more, and he was determined to get it. After all, his job was to break her. What better way than to make her face not just what he wanted, but what he knew she wanted, too.

Chapter Twenty-three

Breathing was like drowning. The rain was so heavy, pelting and pouring out of the sky onto Carrie's bowed head and shoulders, it felt like she was being blasted by liquid musket fire. And the mud was as terrible as the rain. Every step was torture. It sucked at her shoes, her skirt, and her stamina until she was so exhausted she was tempted to just quit, to lie down and let the mud bury her and the rain wash away all trace of her.

She kept struggling forward, though, even after she'd forgotten where she was going and why. The only purpose to living was to struggle, and she faced the battle straight on, not giving an inch to her enemy.

"I'm going batty," she muttered and stopped to let Malachi rest. The little mare was limping, not an easy feat in this much muck.

They had been walking uphill for what felt like hours. Carrie knew it was an illusion, for they were still on the peninsula, much too far east of Richmond to encounter anything except the smallest of inclines.

Carrie had been tired even before this latest rain struck. Storms had been divesting themselves of rain over the peninsula all day. Streams were swollen into rivers, rivers had turned into raging seas. Bridges had been washed out, roads had dissolved into ruinous mud, and to make matters worse, General McClellan was acting like a baulking mule. He'd been invading Virginia for two months now and was barely sixty miles away from his original landing point at Fort Monroe.

It had taken him all of April just to get his superbly trained army of a hundred thousand past the ten thousand Confederates entrenched at Yorktown. The problem hadn't been the rebels. It had been McClellan, who believed he had been facing ninety thousand more Confederates than had actually been there.

Now here it was the 30th of May and McClellan was still cowering before his inflated opinion of Confederate troop strength. The Union frontline was so close to Richmond, they could hear the church bells in the city. Seven Pines, the junction was called, and General Erasmus Keyes had his troops strung out along that front line from White Oak Swamp to the Chickahominy River.

The Confederate troops facing Keyes were under the leadership of Gen. Joseph Johnston, who for days had been plotting and planning his attack, which would begin tomorrow.

Carrie had taken word of Johnston's plan to General McClellan, but the Union commander's lack of positive response to her news had caused her to take matters into her own hands.

Johnston's plan was to advance his troops down the three roads that led from Richmond and converged at Seven Pines, where he would attack Keyes. It was a simple plan, and therefore simple to interrupt. Hannah had forged a new set of orders for General Longstreet, who was to have taken his division down the Nine-Mile Road. His new orders were to march cross-country to the Williamsburg Road. That was where General Hill was to deploy his division. With any luck, not only would Longstreet be in the wrong place, he would also be in Hill's way.

Once Carrie had taken care of Longstreet, she'd ridden to General Keyes' camp to start a rumor that the rebels would attack tomorrow morning. With that done, she'd headed back to Richmond to await the results of her meddling.

But the rain, the eternal rain, had added its drenching insult to the injury Mally had incurred right after leaving the Union camp. Now it looked as though instead of being safe in Richmond when the shooting started, Carrie was going to be right in the middle of it.

"Come on, Mally, we won't find any shelter by standing here."

The steady downpour and the storm-dark night closed in around them as they again struggled forward. Carrie could no longer tell which direction she was going and whether they were still on the road. After Mally's injury, Carrie had intended to go along the Williamsburg Road to the Hughes Tavern. She was certain they had walked a lot farther than a mile, yet there had been no sign of the tavern, or a building of any kind.

Carrie was so used to seeing and hearing nothing but rain, she didn't believe it at first when she heard something that sounded like hoofbeats, or to be more exact, hoofmucks. She stopped and looked around. It wasn't her imagination, though. There was a horse approaching. It wasn't going in the same direction as she was, but she didn't know where she was going anyway, so it didn't really matter.

"Hey, over here!" she shouted.

The horse stopped alongside her. Carrie looked up into the face of the rider and was so surprised, she laughed. "Captain Fletcher, what a pleasant surprise. It's nice to see a friendly face on a night like this. My horse went lame."

There was a terrible scowl of displeasure on his wet face that her greeting seemed to make worse instead of better.

"Let me amend that," she said. "It's nice to see an unfriendly face on a night like this."

Her attempt to inject some levity into the

soggy situation failed. Rance's scowl remained intact.

"Fine. I didn't want you to offer me a ride, anyway. I love being wet and lost and walking through mud up to my elbows. I've waited my entire life to have this much fun, and I'm glad a clod-stomping tobacco farmer doesn't want to rescue me because *I don't need it!*"

He reached down, grabbed her by the upper arm with a grip that would have bent metal, and dragged her and her anchor-heavy skirts across his leg and onto the back of his horse, where he dumped her.

Carrie was knocked breathless by the heroic act. "I always thought you had a secret desire to sweep me off my feet."

He jerked around to face her. She resisted the urge to cower back from him, since there wasn't any back to cower into.

"So now I know I was wrong," she said.

"What are you doing here?" he growled.

"Just out for a ride. How about you? Giving a peninsula girl the chance to swoon at your charm?"

Rance couldn't decide whether to push her off Cain into the mud or just strangle her.

Her hat was flattened across the top of her head like a wet rag, its feather was stuck to her forehead like a scar. Her lashes were so heavy with rain she could barely keep her eyes open, and there was a dollop of mud on her nose.

She looked miserable, tired, and cold. But still her lips, those wet, soft, beautiful lips, were smiling at him, and her eyes were dancing with laughter.

"Not a word," he said. "I don't want to hear one single word out of you."

"The last time you told me that, you followed it with a kiss. That time I was dripping with well water. There must be something terribly irresistible about me when I'm wet."

"You are a nuisance, Carolina Blackwell. You are a pest and a nuisance, and the sooner I find someplace to dump you, the happier I'll be." He faced forward in the saddle, then jerked around to face her again. "And you can be damn well certain I'm not going to kiss you this time. Do you understand?"

"Yas, massa, dis pusson unnerstans" She put a finger on her lips to subdue an urge to laugh at his glowering face.

Rance whirled back around so fast, he almost knocked himself out of the saddle. He spurred Cain into a gallop, and the stallion surged forward.

Riding on the back of a wet horse wasn't easy. Riding sideways on the back of a wet horse was as close to impossible as Carrie ever wanted to come. Riding sideways on the back of a wet horse who had just leapt into motion and was running like a racehorse, changed the close-to-impossible to completely impossible. She felt like she'd been launched backwards out of a cannon. Only she didn't fall, she just stayed suspended in the blast thanks to the hand Rance had locked around her right wrist.

"Stop gasping like a fish and hold onto me," he ordered.

Carrie obeyed, but it only made her feel slightly less out of control. "You have to slow down! Malachi can't run like this!" she shouted over the roar of the blood pounding in her ears.

Rance brought the stallion under quick control, slowing him to a walk.

"Thank you," Carrie said and was rewarded with a threatening glare. "I know, shut up. I will, but first I want to thank you for slowing this beast down. I almost lost Malachi once because of you. It was a miracle that Peach found her last year. I believe a person is allocated only so many miracles in life and I don't want to waste this one just because you're made at me, even though I don't know why you are. There, I'm finished. Now I'll be so quiet you won't even know I'm here."

Carolina Blackwell could be deaf, dumb, mute, and invisible, and Rance would still know she was there. The pressure of her hands on his waist, the warmth of her breath on the side of his face, even the weight of her wet skirts against his leg was such an exquisite torture that it was all he could do to keep his hands and lips off her. He had even begun to consider the logistics of taking her right here on horseback.

Carrie was aware of his change in mood, but didn't concern herself with it. She was too busy trying to keep as much distance between his back and her breasts as the rump of his horse would allow, which wasn't much, to care what his mood was, just as long as it wasn't murderous. After all, getting rescued wasn't half as important as surviving the rescue.

Chapter Twenty-four

The barn seemed to materialize out of the rain and darkness and their need. One second it wasn't there, the next it was, looming up at them so suddenly, they were both startled. It was dry inside, though, so neither of them cared where it had come from, only that it was there.

Rance found a lantern with a bit of kerosene in it. He lit the wick with a match, lowered the sooty globe over the flame, and hung the lantern from a nail to let it dispel the worst of the gloomy shadows.

"I'll look for a house," he said and left Carrie alone with the horses. When he returned, she'd put both animals in stalls and was unsaddling Malachi, which was the worst name for a horse he'd ever heard.

"Nothing out there but a blackened chimney and a few charred timbers," he said.

"That explains why the barn is empty."

Rance unsaddled Cain and rubbed him down with a burlap sack. The hay in the barn was old, but not moldy. He gathered enough for bedding for the stallion and carried some across the barn to Carrie's horse.

She was trying to look at the mare's lame foot and was knocked against the side of the stall for her trouble.

"Let me." He opened the stall door and edged in beside the nervous mare.

"Do you think we could have a fire?" Carrie was shivering. The chill of the night and the rain had settled so deep into her bones, even her fingernails had goosebumps.

"Too risky. You should dry off, though. Take this." He gave her Cain's saddle blanket.

She retreated to an empty stall near the lantern. Instead of taking off her wet clothes, though, she watched Rance. He was whistling, low and soft, to sooth the mare's fear. The song was familiar. It was "The Evergreen Waltz," the same song they had danced to the night they met. And while he whistled, he rubbed a burlap sack across the mare's neck and back, gentle and slow, again and again.

Carrie knew she was in danger, danger at being in the hands of the enemy, danger in that enemy being Rance. And there was danger in the way her heart was beating too fast, faster than the rain on the roof, so fast she couldn't think or breathe. All she could do was watch him.

He bent to lift Mally's foot. When he raised

up, he glanced across the barn and caught her watching him. For a moment that lasted forever, they looked at each other. Then she whirled around and stared at the shadows surrounding her.

She should run. She should escape.

The whistling had started again. She lifted a hand to her throat. Her pulse was racing. Her hand dropped to the front of her coat, and while her heart trembled, she began to undress.

He came to tell her that it had been a rock in her mare's hoof. One look at her, one touch of his gaze on her unbound hair, and all thoughts were chased from his mind except those of her. Of those, there were many. Haunting thoughts, whispering thoughts, dark and dangerous and secret thoughts.

She was beauty. The turn of her head, the curve of her shoulder, the soft glow of her skin. And her hair, glorious hair, long, gentle, thick waves of hair falling free across her face and shoulders and back, hair that glowed like river-washed gold in the soft glow of the lantern light.

She untied the ribbons of her chemise, pulled it down over one shoulder, the other, slipped it down to her waist. Her hair embraced the skin he longed to touch. Just once, gently, a single caress to prove she was more than his fantasy.

When had the wanting started?

When had it not been there?

The first time he looked into her laughing eyes, the wanting had been there then. Listening to her describe her father's crippling accident. Watching her tonight as she blinked raindrops from her lashes.

And now, as she stepped out of the last barrier of silk and lace and wrapped her loveliness in the rough fiber of the saddle blanket, Rance knew that no matter what happened tonight, he would regret it in the morning.

Carrie shivered at the touch of the scratchy blanket on her bare skin. She turned, and looked into his eyes.

How long had he been standing there?

He was leaning against the stall door. She disliked men who leaned. It was arrogant and it was conceited. And when Rance did it, she felt as though she could die from wanting him so much.

"Did you like the show?" she asked.

He stopped leaning and walked toward her, his boots heavy on the floor, his eyes dark as the need that filled her. He pushed his hands into her hair and pulled it to him, then let it go so it would fall across her breasts and shoulders. Before the last curl fell, the fingers of his right hand closed around it.

"I found a rock wedged under your mare's shoe."

She was so aware of his touch on her hair that she felt brittle and breakable.

"Thank you for taking care of her."

"What were you doing behind Union lines, Carrie?"

"I was lost."

"What are you doing on the peninsula?"

She jerked her head to the side, pulling her hair away from him. "If I'd known this was going to turn into an interrogation, I'd have stayed out in the rain."

He traced the outline of her lips with the tip of a finger. He paused at the place on her lower lip where she'd bit herself in the well.

"No scar," he said.

His touch was destroying her. "No visible ones."

His finger left her lips, trailed down to her throat where her pulse fluttered. "Why do you always smell of lilacs?"

She was having trouble concentrating on what he'd said. "Lucy Bream says it's because I was born at the very moment the spring lilacs all burst into bloom."

His eyes softened. "Is that true?"

"It was the middle of winter, there was six feet of snow on the ground and more falling.

He moved his caress onto her collarbone, then lower.

I can't let him know what he's doing to me.

"My father went to get Dr. Patrick and

couldn't get back. Lucy Bream and Kye delivered me. Mother was so angry, when Pops finally did get back, she wouldn't let him near me."

"Is that why she left him?"

His finger began to trace along the top edge of the blanket just above her breasts. Her will to ignore him disappeared, and she began backing away. First one step, then another, each step back bringing him one step closer until she was trapped between him and the rough wood of the barn wall.

Carrie's eyes closed. "No."

His single-fingered caress moved up onto her left shoulder and down her arm, freezing and burning her, making her tremble, making her so afraid that she couldn't think of anything except the sheer ecstasy of his touch.

This is suicide, Rance thought, but he couldn't not touch her. His hands were like moths drawn to her flame.

She covered the front of the blanket with her hands. Rance pulled them away.

He bent to taste her lips, claiming the sweetness of them with a kiss so gentle, he could feel her tremble at the first touch of his tongue. He slanted his mouth across hers and drank deeply of her softness. Fingers locked with hers, he raised their hands up and turned them so the backs of his hands touched the sides of her face.

And he kissed her. Over and over, deeper and longer until his lungs hungered for breath and his body ached for more than kisses. And still he kissed her, trying to quench the thirst that had been raging within him for too long.

Carrie was lost in those kisses. The taste of his mouth, his teeth on her lips, his tongue filling her and his heat caressing her and his body pressing her tightly against her dreams until she couldn't remember anything except the smell of him and the touch of him and the hot, hard feel of him as he fulfilled her every fantasy and brought new ones raging to life.

Everything she had ever been taught told her that this was wrong. The war had brought about a softening of the strict rules of courtship etiquette. But what was happening now wasn't a slight bending of social rules, it was a fire raging out of control, it was a violation of law and morals. It was everything that was wrong and nothing that was right.

Only it didn't feel wrong. It didn't feel sinful or immoral, and it wasn't a violation, it was a celebration, a sharing, a giving and taking, an explosion of feeling and emotion and fire that felt so very, terribly right that it was frightening.

His kisses came faster, harder, deeper, desperate.

She gasped at the heat of them, she trembled at the strength of them, she moaned beneath the desperate depth of them. And she clung to him, their fingers still entwined, his strength her only support, his body her only desire.

A breath, a shattering, aching breath drawn with their lips still touching, their faces wet with more than rain.

He broke away from her, trying to make it look casual, as though not touching her was easy. But in that loss of touch, he lost himself, too.

"It won't work," she said, her voice almost a whisper. "You can't break me like this, Rance."

"Don't be so sure," he said and reaching out his hand, took hold of the front of her blanket and pulled her to him.

Her eyes betrayed nothing. He wondered at his own.

He bent to her, touching his lips to hers, hesitating, then kissing her again.

Not deep. Not demanding. Not with fire and need and desire.

With tenderness.

Gentleness.

Simple, exquisite sweetness.

This time when he broke away, Carrie had to hold her breath to silence the sobs that filled her chest.

"How about now?" he asked.

She knew he was as affected as she. It was there in the hooded look of his eyes, the hard swelling of his lips, the scent of his body that burned in her nostrils like the hot smell of fire.

"I'm still standing," she said.

His mouth twisted into a sneering smile. "Do you want me to show you how little that means, Carrie?"

Her knees almost gave way. She couldn't resist him, but she wouldn't surrender. That left her only one course of action. Offer him what she could not deny.

"You've had your turn, Captain. Now it's mine."

She put her hands on his chest and stroked them up the front of his jacket, wet and cold, brass buttons gleaming dully in the lantern light, his heart beating hard against her palms. The muscles in his jaw hardened beneath her touch. She ran her fingertips across his lips, and the light in his eyes went black.

"Why were you behind Union lines, Rance?"

She put her hands on his shoulders, trailed her fingers across his collar and into the tangled waves of his hair.

"No answer? Let's see if your technique works better on you than it did on me," and she tried to draw his head down to her.

Rance refused to yield to her touch. "This isn't a chess game, Carrie. You can't attack without getting hurt."

"Does that apply to what you were doing to me? Did you get hurt when you kissed me, Rance? Are you hiding scars, too?"

He tore away from her and walked out of the

stall. "This is just a game to you. It's not to me. I don't play at war. I don't play at anything."

She followed him, stopping a few steps away. She felt like she'd just run a long race. Her lungs ached for air, and her lips, they ached, too. All of her ached, but most of all her heart.

I don't play at anything.

Did she dare believe that he meant that? Did she dare believe that his caresses and his kisses were more than just tools meant to take her apart one emotion at a time, the way a mechanic takes apart an engine one tiny piece at a time, until there was nothing left to resist him?

Right and wrong. She didn't know the difference anymore. With the rain beating on the roof and the night pressing close around them, right and wrong no longer mattered. The want and the need and the way touching him made her feel were all that mattered, because at this moment, those things were her entire world.

"I'm not playing either, Rance."

He turned to look at her over his shoulder. Then he spun on his heel and came toward her. He swept her up into his arms and carried her into the shadows.

Chapter Twenty-five

He placed her on a bed of hay, and covered her with his soul. "Rance," she whispered, and he lifted his face from her hair to kiss away the shiver in her voice.

His hands. Carrie trembled at the thought of his hands touching her skin. She wanted it so, she wanted him. But how could she make love to a man she didn't love? And she didn't love him. She didn't.

He drank her kisses. She drowned in his.

He pressed her deeper into the hay as he tasted and touched and sought more and more from her lips and mouth.

Carrie turned her head away. A breath, desperate and pleading, burned into her. "Your buttons," she said when he tried to reclaim her lips.

His face was shadowed, his eyes dark and hard with a hunger that fed her own. He raised himself up onto one knee to rid himself of his Confederate jacket before he stripped to the waist.

She reached for him, her fingers brushing across the tight muscles of his stomach, her palms caressing up across his chest, his shoulders, and neck. He curled an arm beneath her and lifted her to him.

"I want you, Carrie. Since that first night, I've wanted you."

"You wanted to hang me."

"I wanted to save you."

She touched his face. "And who will save me from you?"

He kissed her forehead, the tip of her nose, and the corners of her mouth. "You don't want to be saved from me." He pressed his lips against her right ear, his breath sending shivers of desire racing through her. "Do you, Carrie?"

She caught his lips with hers and touched her tongue to the tips of his teeth. "Not tonight," she whispered, and he held her tight against him, destroying her anew with a kiss that blazed hot and wild.

His confession had blazed across her heart like a comet. It scorched and branded and set her on fire. And his touch, that burned too, as he pressed his hand against her left leg where the saddle blanket fell open from her ankle to her knee.

He bent her backwards with his passion, pressing her into the hay, stroking his hand higher beneath the blanket's folds, sampling the silk of her leg, reaching for and finding and touching the curve of her thigh, her waist, then higher. His first touch on her breast caused her to arch into the caress of his hand, which cupped to greet her softness. His thumb brushed against her nipple, and she cried out.

"Did I hurt you, Carrie?"

She pressed her face against his neck. "I've never—" Her voice failed. She turned into his arms, soothing her fear in his embrace.

He kissed her ear, her neck, and shoulder. "I know that, baby. Just hold onto me and we'll see it through together."

His hair, long and wavy and dark as midnight, fell across her lips and throat as he lowered his head to her chest. She stared at the ceiling of the barn where the rain danced like music and shadows watched. He unwrapped the saddle blanket from around her, exposing her to the chill air and to his eyes.

She shivered and clung tightly to him as he placed kisses across her skin, his right hand warming her with caresses while his left cradled her head, stroking her hair, making her feel more than just pleasure.

Rance worked slowly toward the peak of her breast, blowing on, then taking between his lips, the hard tip of her nipple. She trembled at his touch, then arched into his sucking kiss. His play became more fevered, more demanding, and her hands moved down his back, hesitated, and then into the waist of his pants.

Her left leg lifted, pushed between his, finding his hardness and pressing against it, causing him to moan against her breast.

Back up her hands came, around to his chest, onto his own nipples, brushing them with hesitant fingertips, then again with confidence.

And all the while she touched and pleased him, he teased and tormented and pleased her, building her passion, feeding her desire so that when his own hand began to explore, she did not pull away. Instead she arched into his caress, the skin of her stomach shivering with delight, the curve of her hips quivering with pleasure.

His hand dipped between her knees, went higher, almost touching, teasing, then reaching for and finding and pressing against the spot that he'd set on fire. She gasped and cried out, clutching at him with desperate fingers, but not trying to escape as he began to trace his fingers through the moist heat of her pleasure.

She surprised him then by reaching for his own need, twisting the fabric of his trousers with questing fingers.

"Let me take them off."

"No," she whispered. "Let me."

He raised up onto his knees. She lay unashamed before him, more beautiful than beauty itself, more bewitching than a fantasy, more innocent than a dream.

Carrie felt the caress of his gaze on her naked flesh, but was not ashamed. She unbuckled his belt, opened the buttons on his pants, then hesitated, her courage failing.

He lifted her hands to his lips, kissed her palms, then placed them on his naked waist while he finished the task of undressing. The boots took time. The pants went faster, and as he shed them, he turned so she could not see him.

Knowing that he recognized and respected her fear, made her ache inside with more than passion.

And then he was hers again, warming her with caresses, inflaming her with kisses, embracing her with the hard strength of his need. Carrie tried to pleasure him, too, but he was like a man possessed, and refused to succumb to her attempts to touch him.

"I want to make this special for you, baby. Let me do this."

She tangled her hands in his hair and drank the sweet wine of his kiss. "Hurry," she said, and he smiled against her lips. Then he bowed his head to kiss her stomach. He lifted her hips from the blanket and with his hands cupped around her bottom, lowered his kiss between her legs. She arched and gasped, and he held her tighter, holding her still to enjoy the torture of his lips and tongue.

"Please, Rance, oh, please!" she cried, clutching at his shoulders when her body began to tighten with spasms of pleasure.

He raised up and stared down at her for a long moment where the only sound was the falling rain and her quavering attempts to breath.

"Are you certain, Carrie?"

She suddenly felt shy, the way she had with his family, and her gaze met his with hesitation. "Are you?"

He smiled. "Yes, I'm very certain."

Her shyness fled. "So am I," she said and putting her hands on his chest, drew him down to her with her touch.

He spread her legs with his knee, braced his hands beside her head, and entered her. A tearing pain, then immediate pleasure.

"And now, my sweet Carolina, just hold on."

She raised her hands to his, wrapped her fingers around his wrists, and smiled at him with her eyes.

He pulled almost completely out of her, then thrust in again, and again, lifting her higher, making her hotter. Again and again, faster and deeper and faster and stronger, higher and higher and faster and faster until she forgot everything except the feel of him and the weight of him and the pleasure of him, her hands tightening around his wrists, their faces touching, their lips brushing and reaching and kissing, crying out, trying to breathe, trying to give and take and feel and be, and higher and tighter and faster and tighter and higher and tighter—and having it all, just for a moment, the span of one heartbeat, two, three, then falling, into and onto and over each other, holding and breathing and crying and touching, always touching, but never talking, never saying what they both wanted to say, what they both knew now to be true, what they both were afraid would not end with the night.

Chapter Twenty-six

He kept her safe and warm in the shelter of his arms, letting her drift slowly back to reality. His own reality had been altered, changed forever by these moments with her, and he regretted that change.

They were enemies.

It was his duty to distrust her and spy on her and wrest from her a secret that would help the country he'd sworn to die defending.

But instead of breaking her, he had destroyed himself.

Her head was on his shoulder. She turned her face against his neck and kissed him.

Rance pressed his lips to her forehead and inhaled the spring-sweet smell of her. "Kye was your brother, wasn't he?"

Carrie laughed and looked up at him. "What a strange question."

"Not so strange. You said someone named Kye helped deliver you, which means I owe him my gratitude. At the picnic, you said your brother had died."

"I told Michael that." She tugged at the hair on his chest. "Have you two been talking about me behind my back?"

"Only slightly less than constantly. You have become Alan's favorite subject. What happened, Carrie?"

"Kye was eight the summer after I was born. Mother thought he was too young to be around the dock workers loading our salt, but Pops disagreed and took Kye along anyway. There was a barge ferry that crossed the Kanawha downstream from the landing. When the valley heat got too much for Mother, she would take me to the ferry and ride back and forth on the river all day. One day, something bumped against the side of the barge. She looked to see what it was, and it was Kye."

Rance remembered finding his father in the study. The gun, the blood; it had been terrible. But compared to what Decca Blackwell had experienced, Nelson Fletcher's death had been civilized.

"How do you know this, Carrie?"

"Peach told me. My parents never talk about it. It's almost like Kye never existed, except for his name in the family Bible. His birth is recorded, but not his death. I think Mother looks at it and pretends that he's still alive. She left Charleston the day he died. She took me and her mammy, who was my mammy by then, and left for South Carolina. I got sick on the stage and when it got to Gauley, Mother sent me back to Charleston while she kept on going south."

Rance was horrified. "She just abandoned you?"

"You've met her. She's not exactly a tower of strength. I was twelve before I ever saw her. I'd asked Pops if he'd buy me, let's see, how did I phrase it? 'One of those things boys have that I don't.' He packed me off to a girls' school in Richmond the next day. But instead of taking me to the school, Peach took me to see Mother." She looked up at Rance, then punched him in the ribs. "Stop laughing! It's a terrible, tragic story. What would you do if Lilly Blue asked you for one of these?" Carrie wrapped her fingers around his manhood.

"I'd beat her until she really was blue." He scooped Carrie into his arms and pulled her on top of him. "To punish you for your crime, however, I shall use a technique which your father told me was quite effective."

"You're going to make me eat apples?"

"Not exactly," he said and captured her mouth with his.

She pushed away from him and sat up, straddling him with her legs. "No fair. I told you my tale, now I want to hear yours. Why didn't you attend your brother's graduation from West Point?"

Rance stroked his hands down along her arms, onto her waist and up to her breasts, cupping one in each hand. "I'll let you decide." He rubbed his palms across her nipples, and she arched into his caress. "We can talk about Alan, or we can do this."

She leaned down and kissed him, a long, lingering kiss that set his body and heart on fire. Then she slid her lips across his face, licking and nipping her way to his ear. "I think I'd like my punishment now," she whispered, and sent chills racing through him.

He rolled her over onto her back and lifted himself above her. "Remember, my sweet, this is for your own good."

When their passion was spent, Rance wrapped his arms close around her and pressed his face into the glory of her hair.

"I'm jealous," he said.

"Of what?"

"Of James Bredon. It was he that you almost married, wasn't it?"

First her brother. Now James. Next, just what *were* you doing on the Peninsula?

She had convinced herself that all she wanted

was one night. It was a lie. What she really wanted was for this to be real. What was it Peach was always saying? Anything that seemed too good to be true was just what it seemed. He'd also said that it wasn't her brains Rance would try to outsmart.

Good old Peach. She should pay more attention to the things he said.

She pushed Rance away from her. "Tell me, Captain, how many climaxes do I get before you start asking the real questions, like who my contact is and what is the key to my secret code?"

"Do you really think that's the reason I'm doing this? You're a hardhearted Yankee woman, Carolina Blackwell."

"That's not an answer."

"No, but this is."

He crushed her mouth beneath his, raiding and plundering, invading her with his tongue, biting her lips with his teeth, and draining her desire to resist with his desire for her passion.

"This is for you," he said, and entered her suddenly and with such power, she shuddered beneath him. "Just you and me, Carrie. Not the South, not the war, not anything but us." He thrust again and again. His hands were in her hair, and he dragged her lips to his while his body kept surging into her. "Say it, Carrie! Damn you, say it!" He thrust so deeply into her, her body had to arch to accept all of him.

"Please," she begged, biting the word into his arm and filling her mouth with the taste of his hot, wet skin. She was sobbing with pleasure, dry, racking sobs that ripped out of her in painful gasps.

He put his legs outside hers, pushed her thighs tight together and kept thrusting, again and again, causing her to twist and cry out.

"Say it!"

Her body was convulsing, every muscle was racked with spasms of pleasure and pain and ecstasy and passion.

"It's for us," she said, the words so faint, they were like a single drop of rain in a thunderstorm.

Rance covered her mouth with his and kissed away the tremble in her lips. He was still inside her, and as he kissed her, they both climaxed, softly, gently, quietly, her breath sobbing out of her and filling him with the taste of her heart.

The lantern had long since gone out. The barn was dark and the air was cold and Carrie wished the night would never end. She wanted to stay here forever with this man who made her feel ecstasy and anger and pleasure and—

Her heart closed tightly inside her.

"What did he do, baby? What did James do to lose you?"

The smell of fear rose harsh and rank in her

nostrils. The sound of the whip, cruel and angry and terrible. She didn't want to hear it. She didn't want to see it flash through the air. She didn't want to feel her legs refusing to run, and she didn't want to remember that she hadn't tried to stop him.

"I—I watched him beat a man to death."

For a long moment, the barn was silent. Rance cradled her face in his hands.

"Tell me what happened, Carrie."

"It was a slave. He'd tried to run away."

"I know you don't want to hear this, Carrie, but it's a master's right, even his duty, to put a slave to death for such a serious offense."

"All that man wanted was the same thing you claim you went to war for, Rance. He wanted to be free." She turned her face into the blanket. "Even after he was dead, James kept whipping him. It was terrible, and he enjoyed it. The blood and the screams, James liked it. And when he saw that I was there, he came over and he—he tried to—" She closed her eyes and tried not to remember. "It was his own slaves that stopped him. They had just watched him beat one of them to death, but they were still willing to risk their own lives to save me." She rolled away from Rance. She felt small and alone and so tired, so very tired. "So I started risking mine to save them."

When first Rance reached for her, she resisted him. But when he pulled her into his arms and curled his body around hers, she didn't fight him. She just lay there and tried not to remember.

Chapter Twenty-seven

Carrie jolted awake with such suddenness, she almost groaned. At first she thought what she was remembering was just a dream. But when she opened her eyes, her surroundings proved otherwise. Not that she looked around. She just lay there on her side and stared at the wall. Sunlight, bright and golden, filtered through knots and cracks in the old wood.

All the secrets, all the trust, all the tenderness of last night had disappeared with the rain and the darkness. She couldn't face those things in the light.

What if it had all been a lie? What if he laughed at her? And even if he didn't, how could she watch him put that gray uniform on after what she'd told him last night?

Carefully, slowly, quieter than a wandering thought in church, she rolled to her right, slipping off the blanket and out of the hay.

This had to be the coldest morning in Virginia's history. Covered in nothing but shivers, she crept to the stall where she'd undressed.

There was only one thing worse than taking off wet clothes. Putting them back on.

She fumbled with strings and laces and buttons. And all the time she struggled to dress, she thought about last night, when she'd turned and found Rance leaning against the stall door, watching her undress.

He is the enemy of my country.

In his arms, she'd found everything she wanted, everything she could ever want.

I can't let him know. Not now, not ever. Once he knows that he is my weakness, he'll be able to stop me. I can't let that happen.

It took absolutely forever to dress, and she only put on half of what she'd taken off. The rest she wadded into a damp bundle, which she carried under her arm as she ran to Malachi's stall.

Her sidesaddle had too many clanking buckles and too much creaking leather. She left it where it hung and led Mally outside, keeping her hand firmly over the mare's nose and mouth to prevent her from making any sound that might awaken Rance.

It took two tries to mount. She had to climb onto the top rail of a fence, then try not to fall off the fence while she tried to maneuver over onto Mally's slippery back. All that was easy, though, compared to actually riding away from the man who had shown her the true meaning of—

"Heartache," Carrie said, refusing to let herself finish the thought any other way. Besides, what was the difference? For her, the word she wouldn't say and the one she had said meant the same thing.

The first thing Rance thought when he woke was, *I did it for my country.* It was a lie and he knew it, but he thought it anyway. He even expanded on it. *I did it to break her.* It hadn't worked, but he didn't let himself think about that. Instead he thought about getting out of there before he got in any deeper.

He rolled to his left, slipping off the blanket and out of the hay. He felt exposed and vulnerable. He refused to let his gaze wander past the heap of his clothes. He gathered them and went to Cain's stall to dress.

With him went the memories of last night, memories of her hands unbuckling his belt, her fingers undoing the buttons on his pants, the shy quiver of her lips when her courage failed and she'd been unable to go further.

The saddle would be too noisy. He left it and led the stallion out of the barn with his hand firmly planted over the animal's nose and mouth.

If she wakes up, she'll expect me to find a preacher and give her my name before I've even had a cup of coffee.

He didn't want coffee. He wanted her.

Last night was just a way to pass the time, a means to an end.

He flung himself onto Cain's back. But he couldn't make himself leave. He just sat there, not looking at the barn.

This is for you. Just you and me, Carrie. Not the South, not the war, not anything but us.

"Damn—"

Rance couldn't make himself say "bitch." Last night it had been so easy. Last night. Images of Carrie laughing, Carrie kissing him, Carrie refusing to cry even when she told him what that bastard Bredon had tried to do to her.

The stallion was impatient. He reared, pawed the cold air and jolted back onto all fours. But still Rance didn't leave.

"Damn woman."

He could call her that, for that's what she was. A woman.

He forced himself to ride away before he could take that thought any further.

Chapter Twenty-eight

Carrie was almost as disgusted with herself as she was with General McClellan. The man was a menace, which would be great if it was the Confederacy he was menacing.

In the month since the incident in the barn with Rance, McClellan had been inventing new ways to not advance those final six miles to Richmond. June was almost over and instead of taking Richmond, Little Mac had finally given up and was running for his life. Even that wasn't going smoothly. He'd been retreating for five days now and was still within six miles of Richmond. Instead of running away from the city, he was running around it.

Fortunately for his beleaguered troops, he'd finally managed to maneuver close enough to the James River to attempt an escape, not that he would make it without help.

Carrie had been attempting to provide that help when an upstart Confederate sergeant stumbled across her behind General Lee's headquarters. Now she was locked in a small room in a small tavern near a small crossroads where a gigantic battle was being fought.

The ground shook with the reverberation of cannon. The room's only window rattled so terribly, she was afraid to go near it even though she wanted to see what was happening. The sky was black with smoke, the air filled with the roaring wind of musketry.

Occasionally as she paced her bedroom prison, she saw a flash of fire light up the sky as an artillery shell burst overhead. Some of those flashes seemed to be right over the Glendale tavern where she was being held, causing her to fear not only what was going to happen to her if the Confederates ever got around to interrogating her, but also that she wouldn't live long enough to use the lies she'd been rehearsing.

Her agonized wait came to an end when she heard a heavy fall of footsteps outside her door and the rattle of a key in the lock.

"It's about time," she said, having decided it would be better to take the offensive right from the beginning. "It's quite horrible enough to be humiliated by being falsely arrested, but to be abandoned in the middle of a battlefield is inexcusable."

Not bad, she thought, *all that and the fool hasn't even gotten the door open yet.*

He opened it now and Carrie, who was ready to start on her next tirade, almost swallowed her tongue when he stepped into the room.

"What were you saying about being abandoned?" Rance asked.

Fifty thousand Confederate soldiers within a stone's throw and they'd picked this one to question her. And naturally, the first words out of his mouth were about being abandoned.

He was probably mad enough to spit bullets when he woke up and found me gone that morning. And now, to have me right where he's wanted me ever since this war started—he's probably so happy he could howl.

She forced herself to act as cold as the morning she'd run off from him. "I thought Sergeant Busybody had forgotten about me."

The nosey little rebel arrester appeared at Rance's heels, like the trained hound he was. "It's Sergeant Busbell, ma'am."

Rance had been told a woman had been arrested on suspicion of spying. It never occurred to him that it might be Carrie. Somewhere along the way, he'd managed to convince himself that she was too clever to be caught by anyone except him. His surprise at seeing her here was doubled by how casually she faced him, as though she didn't care one whit that he'd abandoned her that morning at the barn.

"What were you doing behind Confederate headquarters, Carrie?"

"The last time we had this conversation, you wanted to know what I was doing behind Union lines. The answer is still the same. I was lost." A particularly loud explosion rocked the tavern and Carrie's nerves. "Why don't you ask Sergeant Whoever here what he was doing back there? Aren't enlisted men supposed to be on the frontline instead of skulking around headquarters?"

"Sergeant, wait outside." Rance closed the door on Busbell, who had turned crimson at her accusation. "This would go a lot easier for you if you cooperate, Carrie."

"How? By signing a confession or unlacing my corset?"

"You have a dirty mind."

"You should know, you dirtied it."

"This has nothing to do with us."

She gave a short laugh. "I was right, this is a mirror of our last conversation. Why don't we stop beating around the haystack, Captain? You have no evidence against me. There's not a single thing you can do except let me go."

"I can hold you under suspicion of espionage."

"And I can charge you with interrogating a female prisoner without a witness."

Rance wrenched the door open. "Busbell, get back in here!"

"I was referring to your interrogation in the barn last month."

He slammed the door in Busbell's face. "You weren't under arrest last month."

"Did you or did you not drag me forcibly onto your horse after I told you I'd rather walk?"

He looked like a locomotive running on too much steam.

"I want to know *right this minute* what you were doing behind Confederate headquarters!"

"I was looking for the hospital so I could deliver the drugs I smuggled into Virginia yesterday."

Rance's fists were clenched so tightly, he couldn't feel anything from the elbows down. "Sergeant, get in here *now!*"

The door opened a crack.

"Go to the hospital tent and order the head nurse to accompany you here immediately. I want Miss Blackwell searched from the skin out for concealed drugs."

"That won't be necessary," Carrie said quickly. "I'm certain the hospital needs all its nurses right now. I'll just give you the drugs."

The cornstalk mattress rustled as she put her right foot on the edge of the bed and began pulling up the hem of her riding skirt. She expected Rance to stop her before it reached her ankle. He didn't.

Poor Sergeant Busbell was staring at the floor in front of him and looking every bit as mortified as Carrie was beginning to feel as the skirt kept going up inch by excruciating inch.

It was almost to her knees now. Rance still

didn't stop her. He just stood there with his arms crossed over his chest, looking as though his rivets were about to pop. But not from anger. An unmistakable flush of arousal was moving upward from the collar of his uniform.

By the time the hem of her skirt reached her garter, he looked ready to attack. Carrie was feeling a bit woozy, too. It took two tries to extract the papers of morphine from the little pocket she'd sewn behind the pink ribbon on the garter.

"There's more in my other garter," she said, her voice shaking under the assault of Rance's heavy-lidded gaze.

"I want them," he said, and she almost fainted.

This time, she tore the ribbon off, but when she was finally finished, she had ten packets of proof that not even Ransom Fletcher could deny. She put them in his outstretched hand with fingers that were visibly shaking.

"Why didn't you give them to a hospital in Richmond?" he asked.

"I wanted them to be used for soldiers who really needed them." She glared at Busbell. "Not cowards trying to avoid battle."

"I had orders to see that the general's privy got cleaned!"

"Innocent men don't need excuses."

"That's enough," Rance said. "Sergeant, take these to the hospital. As for you, Miss Blackwell—" He backed her against the wall. Her eyes went wide and her lips locked together in a tight line. "You wouldn't happen to have any maps from General Lee's headquarters stashed in your bodice, would you? We seem to be a few short."

She took a shallow breath to prevent her paper-padded chemise from crackling. "I hope their loss hasn't caused any difficulties."

"It has, but we're winning anyway, which is why I'm not going to search you for them."

"Is that the good news or the bad?" she asked, trying to lighten the mood a bit.

"You managed to wiggle out of trouble this time, Carrie. The next time won't be so easy."

"There won't be a next time," she promised.

"No? Why's that?" He traced a finger across her bottom lip. "You're not afraid of what I might do to you, are you?"

She grinned. "I know exactly what you'd like to do to me, Ransom Fletcher." She edged out from under his line of attack and closer to the door. "But you'll have to catch me first, and I rarely make the same mistake twice."

Chapter Twenty-nine

The state named Kanawha was short-lived. Virginia sentimentalists voted it a new name, West Virginia.

"Sounds like a blasted direction," Harris grumbled. "I can hear those Richmond snobs now, 'West Virginia's where we keep our poor folks.' They're probably laughing their heads off at us for not letting go of their apron strings."

"Kanawha was prettier," Carrie said, "but only if the person saying it lives here. No one else can figure out how to pronounce it. I've heard Canah-wah, Ken-ah-waha, Ka-gnaw-hee and about a million other horrible concoctions."

"They'd never make it all the way through 'Kanawha Salines, Kanawha, located on the Kanawha River in Kanawha County' without getting a cramp in their tongue," Peach said.

"The name isn't important, only which side we're on," Carrie said. "And there's no doubt we're on the right one now."

Two months ago, when President Lincoln presented his cabinet with the first draft of an Emancipation Proclamation on July 22nd, she had been in Washington. She'd worked so hard for this and though the proclamation had not been presented to Congress yet, the hardest part, the first step, had been taken. That day, as she gazed up at the Stars and Stripes waving in the Potomac River breeze, her heart had taken such a lurch of pride, she'd come close to crying.

It had reminded her that the United States of America came first with her, not the state where she lived. That's why the name change from Kanawha to West Virginia didn't upset her. What did upset her was while she and Peach and her father were having this conversation, the Confederate army was attacking Charleston.

The Blackwells, along with Lucy Bream and everyone else in town, had taken to the hills. Cox's Hill, to be exact. The graveyard on the side of the hill above the town provided a perfect place to watch the action without being in the middle of it. A few stray shots had sent the onlookers scattering for cover, but for the most part, they had an uninterrupted view of the action.

The Confederate troops were on the south side of the Kanawha and they were shelling the Union troops on the north side. One of the

Federal cannons was in the yard of the Ruffner House on Front Street. In an attempt to destroy it, the Confederate gunners mowed down a six-inch-thick locust tree in the yard.

"I liked that tree," Peach said. His disappointment was quickly tempered by the sudden roar of a cannon being fired over the heads of the townsfolk from behind them.

"Glory geezers!" Lucy shouted and threw herself face down on the ground, which happened to be someone's grave. That showed the true extent of her terror. Lucy was more afraid of dead people than she was of killing animals with Biblical names. Peach had taken advantage of her superstitious fear of the dead by putting a skull in the storeroom to protect his stash of corn whiskey. It worked so well, Lucy was putting their supplies in the largest music room so she wouldn't have to go near the storeroom.

"That's a Confederate gun," Harris said.

"Good," Peach said. "If I'm going to die, I want it to be by rebel fire. That way I'll have a good story to tell when I knock on the Pearly Gates."

"Hah!" Lucy said from her prone position on the grave. "You'll never see no Pearly Gates 'cept in your dreams. Aieee!" she screamed as another blast was fired over their heads.

"Look," Carrie said. "General Lightburn's men are setting fire to the town."

Until now, the Union troops had been fighting merely as cover for their orderly retreat. "Probably took lessons from McClellan," Harris had muttered when General Lightburn's intentions to flee had become obvious to the onlookers.

But before the last troops in the retreat headed for the suspension bridge over Elk River, they were setting fire to the town. Black smoke billowed from the Bank of Virginia, the Kanawha House, Brook's Store, the Southern Methodist Church, the Mercer Academy, and several warehouses.

"I hope one of those isn't ours," Harris said. "There's nothing in it except a few pounds of Confederate salt."

"And twenty-eight years of sweat and worry!"

Carrie grinned at him. "Sorry, Pops, but you know the rule, if it isn't on the inventory, it doesn't exist."

"I should've kept you in the parlor doing embroidery where a woman belongs."

"It never would have worked, Pops. That's where you keep the brandy."

Except for the fire, the onlookers from Cox's Hill thought it a very organized battle. Lightburn got away with millions of dollars worth of supplies, some of which belonged to the town and not the Union. And Generals Echol and Williams, who had masterminded the Confederate takeover, accomplished their goal without hitting anything except a tree.

A Union straggler hastened down the turnpike in his army's wake, trying to get to the bridge before his companions burned it, too. Confederate troops were wading across the Kanawha at a tree-clogged shoal. When they reached the northern shore, they were faced with a breastwork of timber barring their entrance into town.

A few of the Cox's Hill onlookers went to help them tear it down. Others went to try and get the fires under control. Most just drifted around discussing the battle and what they were having for dinner that night.

The socializers were sent into a frenzy of excitement by a Confederate cavalry officer riding up the carriage road toward the graveyard. Several girls oohed and aahed at his approach. "A major!" "And a very dashing one!" "How exciting!"

Carrie craned her neck to see the "dashing" major. The black stallion he rode was all she needed to see for her insides to twist into a solid lump that made her feel as though she had swallowed a cannonball. Rance pulled Cain to a prancing stop in front of the Blackwells. It had been three months since his and Carrie's encounter at Glendale. He didn't even try to disguise his pleasure at seeing her again and grinned down at her like a schoolboy with his first crush.

She was looking exceptionally pretty in a rose-colored dress decorated with white lace that looked like a decoration of sugar icing piped onto a cake. Her lips and cheeks glowed with bright color, her hair was arranged like a crown woven from cornsilk, and her eyes, those dark, beautiful, mischievous cat's eyes, were laughing up at him.

"What heroic acts did you perform to get promoted?" she asked him. "Molesting innocent girls in the name of glory?"

Peach Blackwell's eyes weren't laughing, though. He was looking from Carrie to Rance with a disapproving glare. "Are you going to shoot us, Major, or can we go home, if we still have a home. Those gunners of yours probably mistook our house for a tree and turned it into matchsticks."

"I'm here to accompany your granddaughter to her warehouse, which I am to have emptied for immediate shipment to Richmond."

"If it isn't engulfed in flames, you won't find much to empty," Carrie said. "News of the imminent rebel arrival caused our workers to flee north last week. They took most of our salt with them."

Rance dismounted and gave his stallion's reins to Carrie so he could help Harris Blackwell maneuver his chair off the steep hill.

"And how did your workers learn of the Confederate plan to liberate Charleston from Union occupation, Miss Blackwell?"

"I wouldn't know, Major Fletcher. Maybe a spy told them."

"But that's just a guess, right?"

She assumed a look of innocent surprise. "What else could it be?"

Harris smacked his hands down on the arms of his wheelchair. "Enough! And that means both of you!"

"Yes, Pops."

"General Lee would be incensed at you addressing one of his officers in that fashion, Mr. Blackwell."

Harris twisted in his chair to glare at Rance. "You can tell Lee that I said for him to mind his own business. Now stop gawking at my daughter and start rolling this thing faster. If that Lucy Bream gets to the house before us, she'll probably burn the place down just to spite me and then blame it on you rebels."

Rance left on the second day of the Confederate occupation to accompany the first shipment of salt to Richmond. More shipments followed that one, one almost every day as every crystal of salt in the valley was sent south. While his troops busied themselves with sodium confiscations, General Loring, the Confederate commander of Charleston, spent his time terrorizing the Union sympathizers in town.

Many of the Federalists fled town in what was called "The Exodus from Kanawha." The river was clogged with flatboats, bateaux, skiffs, rafts, and anything else that would float. Loring encouraged the panic, swearing to hang every loyalist who stayed and stripping them of possessions to prove his threat was real.

Harris Blackwell was one of the few who seemed unperturbed by Loring's reign of terror. Some people expressed admiration for his bravery, but others accredited it to Harris having had the foresight to put all his property in his rebel daughter's name the day before Loring's arrival in the valley.

Two Charleston girls had fiancés in the Confederate troops occupying Charleston. Both men decided to take advantage of being in their hometown by marrying their sweethearts during the occupation. On October 19th, R. Q. Laidley took Lydia Whittaker to wife, and the following day, Plus Rand married Annie Norvell. A dance was held to celebrate both weddings and to say good-bye to the brides, who were being sent by carriage to Lewisburg to await the end of the war.

The supper for the gala was held at the beautiful brick house of the Rands. Then the celebration went down the street to the Whittaker home, where the entire first floor had been cleared of furniture so the young people could dance.

Carrie wore a white silk underdress with an overdress of white crêpe. The gown fluttered around her while she danced, making it appear as though she were about to take flight. Yards of delicate violet lace ruffles trimmed the overdress. Her sash was also violet and so heavily fringed, it elicited gasps from Callie Quarrier and Annie Ruffner.

Carrie's *parne* of silk flowers had been imported from Paris before the war, but like her dress, she'd never worn it in Charleston before, so it, too, felt new. It was made of blue periwinkles, white lilacs, and orange blossoms. The pretty arrangement wreathed her hair, was pinned in a corsage at her waist and sprinkled in sprays across her delicate skirts. She'd even pinned a tiny spray to her right garter, having learned at the Seven Days Battle that a lady never knew what part of her costume might be viewed in war.

The band was playing "The Dixie Polka" and Carrie was dancing with bridegroom Plus Rand when Rance arrived. His presence in Charleston was a surprise to her, and his appearance took her breath away. He was freshly shaven, and his long hair had been carefully groomed, as best its wild manner would allow. He was wearing a dress uniform that sparkled with gold braid and polished brass. She also noticed that he was not wearing his riding boots.

A waltz was scheduled next, after a short break by the band. Carrie made small talk with Cornie Welch and Madison Laidley while Rance made the rounds of the room. Cornie couldn't keep her eyes off him.

"He's coming this way," she whispered to Carrie. "Maybe he's going to ask one of us to dance. Oh, I'm so glad we're not using dance cards tonight."

"I danced with him in Richmond two years ago and my feet are still hurting."

"Good evening, ladies, Mr. Laidley." Rance winked at Carrie when saying 'ladies.' Now he gave her his best smile while taking in every delicious detail of her breathtaking appearance. "I understand a waltz is scheduled next."

There was no doubt in her mind that he was going to ask her to dance. The thought of being in his arms again made her feel dizzy, even if it was at the risk of having her feet tromped.

"Since when do you concern yourself with programs?" she asked, answering his unspoken request with her eyes.

"Since my brother-in-law-to-be stopped waving batons and started waving a sabre, Miss Blackwell. Would you do me the honor of being my partner for this dance," he turned to the very pretty Cornie, "Miss Welch?"

"Oh, yes," she said and allowed herself to be drawn onto the floor.

Carrie's face burned. "He'll break all poor Cornie's toes."

Madison looked unconvinced. "He seems to be doing rather well."

She stared in disbelief. Rance was guiding Cornie across the floor in the most artfully executed waltz Carrie had ever seen performed. As the night wore on, her disbelief grew. He danced perfect polkas, stunning lancers, expert quadrilles, energetic reels, and even added an Irish jig to his repertoire while partnering every female at the dance from the youngest to the oldest.

Everyone except Carrie.

"Thank heavens," she muttered after every slight.

By the time the clock in the Whittaker parlor struck three, the band and the dancers were staggering with exhaustion but equally unwilling to call an end to the fun. Carrie slipped away from her friends when the band struck up "The Askew Quickstep" and ran upstairs to fetch her wrap from the bedroom that was being used as a cloakroom.

She was coming back down the stairs when she heard the first notes of "The Evergreen

Waltz." She came to a sudden halt, assaulted by the memory of the last time she had heard this song, memories of the rain, the smell of horses, the night. And Rance.

"I believe this is our dance."

He stepped out of the shadows beside the stairs and stood with one hand on the bannister as he looked up at her.

"I have to leave," she said.

"It's a little late to be posting a letter, isn't it?"

It was the first time she'd known for certain that it was he intercepting her letters. Although they all eventually reached their destination in Washington, almost all of them showed signs of having been opened prior to arrival.

"I was on my way home."

She tried to move past him, but he stopped her, catching her hand in his and holding her motionless with an embrace of her fingers as light as a whisper. Even though she was unable to pull away, she kept her eyes lowered, unwillingly to let him see the emotion she couldn't hide.

He drew her down the last step and into his arms. "Dance with me, Carolina."

The touch of his hand on her waist was shattering. She was drowning in the rich leather smell of him, in memories and the music.

"I don't want to do this, Rance."

"Yes, you do. We both do."

He was right. She wanted it so much.

"Just one dance, baby. Nothing more."

She backed away. "I—I can't." She fled out the side door and into the night.

The air was cold and clear, the valley so quiet she could hear the Kanawha River flowing past. She ran through empty streets toward Cox's Hill, passing dark stores and burned buildings and sleeping houses.

Crinolines, a ball gown, and dancing slippers did not comprise the perfect climbing clothes. It took forever for her to reach the top of the hill. The peak was dusted in snow that glittered like crystal in the fragile silver glow from the sliver of moon that shimmered in the sky.

There was a small clearing at the top where boulders gleamed in the darkness. Carrie made her way among the tumbled rocks until she came to the largest. She leaned against it, wrapped her cloak close around her, and waited.

Below her, Charleston lay in dark silence. She could see the Whittaker House, where the wedding party had finally ended. The lights were being extinguished one by one, until the only light that remained came from a boat on the river.

Not even a whisper of wind disturbed the quiet. Minutes ticked away, counted only by her own heartbeats. Once she shifted her weight and heard a mouse scurrying away through the frosty snow. A dog barked in the distance. The night stretched on.

Rance was so cold, he couldn't feel his face. The copse of trees where he was standing his chilling vigil looked as though they'd been dipped in water and frozen. Snow sparkled along the ice-cloaked branches like drifts of diamonds. And the air was as chilling as the forest. Every breath he drew burned into his lungs like shattered glass.

Carrie had to be freezing. She showed no effects of the cold, though, but stood quiet as a statue, her face lifted toward the lightening sky and her breath frosting the still air. The longer she stood there, the more convinced he was that she had to be there to meet someone.

Rumors of the Union's plan to retake the Kanawha Valley had been flying thick and fast in Richmond, which reinforced Rance's belief that if he could outlast the cold, tonight he would see everything he needed to put an end to her dangerous game once and for all.

Dawn came slowly, bringing with it a sky so blue, it almost hurt to look at it. The sun delayed its appearance for as long as possible. And then suddenly there it was, rising like a golden fireball over the eastern mountain range and sending long bright streamers of warm light sweeping across the quiet valley.

With the first touch of that welcomed warmth, the wind, which had been stirring in the snow-encrusted grasses, lifted into the trees. The cold limbs trembled, and the most incredible sound Rance had ever heard filled the air. One by one the trees were touched by morning, each limb adding its voice to the music while releasing from their embrace veils and streamers of dancing snow that filled the sky and the forest, lending a magical fairytale quality to the sunlight song.

Rance forgot his clandestine mission to watch the magic that had suddenly burst to life around him.

It ended as suddenly and as unexpectedly as it began. The last snow crystal danced through the air, the last rime-coated tree steamed its melted moisture into the warming air, and the forest fell silent.

"Beautiful, wasn't it?"

Carrie's voice was as lovely as the snow music.

"I've never seen or heard anything like it," Rance said.

"It's very rare. In fact, I've never seen it in Charleston at all."

Reality reasserted itself. "If you didn't come up here for this, Carrie, why are you here?"

"To watch the sun come up. And you?"

"Same thing."

"I thought maybe you followed me to see if I was meeting a Union contact."

Her eyes were smiling at him and as he walked toward her he wanted to touch her, to caress that lily-soft skin and to trace his fingers across the soft curves of her lips. Instead of touching her the way he wanted, he brushed a golden strand of hair from her cheek.

"You're a suspicious woman, Carolina Blackwell."

"My father says suspicion is like a cold, it's very contagious and makes you sound terrible. If I sound terrible, Major Fletcher, it's because I've caught your cold. Perhaps we should continue this health discussion elsewhere. The ground is starting to thaw beneath us and if we don't get off the hill soon, we'll be up to our ears in mud."

"We should definitely go, then. If you go home with mud on anything other than the soles of your slippers, your grandfather wouldn't give me time to say my prayers, much less explain about a freak thaw."

"You are a wise man." She slipped her arm through his. "For support," she said, and her chin dimpled.

He covered her hand with his. "Of course," he said and led her out of the forest and onto the carriage road.

Just before they turned the first curve in the road, Carrie glanced back at the boulder she'd been leaning against. A crack ran down its face. The crack was empty, the letter she'd placed in the narrow opening taken by the Union courier who had come and gone while the morning air danced with snow.

General Loring's occupation of Charleston ended on October 29, 1862. During the six weeks he was there, in addition to the exportation of seven hundred barrels of salt to Richmond and his campaign to rid the town of all its Union supporters, he started a newspaper called *The Guerilla,* which spent more column space praising him than reporting news.

He also erected a flagpole on the banks of the Kanawha within sight of Burning Spring, one of Carrie's favorite places in the valley. Just before his reign in Charleston ended, he ordered his men to cut the flagpole down and bury it in a long trench to await his eventual return to power.

The day Union troops reclaimed control of the town, the first thing they did was dig up the hidden flagpole. Carrie and Peach had taken a lunch to Burning Spring and were there when the Union flag was raised.

"Someone must have told them where to find that flagpole," Peach said.

Old Glory caught its first armful of wind and snapped to attention. "Must have," she said and blinked to clear the river glare from her eyes.

Chapter Thirty

On February 13, 1863, instead of anticipating Valentine's Day, the residents of Charleston were preparing for an execution. Private John MacIntyre of the 13th West Virginia Infantry had been tried by a Federal court martial and found guilty of desertion. He'd been sentenced to death by a firing squad, and the day before Valentine's Day was to be Private MacIntyre's last day on earth.

The windows on the second floor of the Blackwell warehouse looked down on the meadow where the execution was to take place. Carrie and James Henry Jones were working on the second floor, transferring salt from storage kegs to burlap sacks. By unspoken mutual consent, they were performing the tedious task on the opposite side of the warehouse from the windows overlooking the meadow.

Rance was there, too. He'd arrived that morning, "to accompany tomorrow's salt shipment," he'd claimed. Carrie didn't believe him.

First, she hadn't planned a salt shipment. Second, it was, after all, the day before Valentine's Day. Just because Rance never sent valentines didn't mean he couldn't deliver one, even if all it consisted of was an unexpected visit.

He didn't avoid the tragedy taking place below. He stood right in front of the window, hands braced on either side of the window frame, and watched the execution scene unfold through a wash of cold sunlight.

Carrie glanced at his back, at the dark hair secured by a leather string at the nape of his neck, and the firm, square set of his shoulders. He was the most hardheaded person she had ever met. Here he was deep in Federal-occupied territory, and he was wearing his Confederate uniform and standing in full view of several hundred Union soldiers.

"They're too busy killing each other to even notice me," he said when Carrie asked if he had any sense at all.

"What does the Confederacy do with soldiers who try to murder their commanding officers before they desert?"

"We don't have enough bullets to shoot Yankees, much less our own men."

"You don't punish them?" James Henry asked.

"We hang them," Rance said, and while the words still dangled in the quiet warehouse, added, "We hang spies, too."

Carrie dropped her gaze to the salt that James Henry was pouring into the burlap sack she was holding open. "Lighter to haul," had been the teamster's reason for the change in packaging. The sacks were also easier to disguise under a load of hay and grain, which was his preferred smuggling cover. "I can hide the salt and feed my mules at the same time."

A military band was playing the death march. The sound was almost as depressing as the people lining the streets. Carrie had seen them on the way to the warehouse that morning. Their faces wore expressions of shock and concern for what was about to take place. But all of them, every man, every woman, every innocent child, were determined not to miss a single moment.

"MacIntyre's coming," Rance said.

Beneath the drone of the music, Carrie could hear the measured tread of the soldiers escorting their companion to his place of death. She held the edges of the sack with tight fists while James Henry finished filling the last few inches. He had to pull the sack out of her hands to close it, wielding his stitching needle with quick flicks of his fingers and wrist.

"Last one," he said and threw the sack over his shoulder to carry to the wheelbarrow. His wooden leg thumped on the floor like a drumbeat accompaniment to the terrible music below.

"They're sitting him in his coffin," Rance said.

Carrie stared at him. He turned to meet her gaze.

"I'll take this down to the wagon," James Henry said. His only comment about the execution had been, "A man ought to die in a war on a battlefield, not in a field with an audience." The sudden silence that descended as the death march ended caused his step to falter, but not stop as he wheeled the salt down the ramp.

"I want you to see this, Carrie," Rance said.

She backed away when he reached out to her. He refused to let her escape, though, and with his hands on her shoulders, forced her to stand in front of him before the window.

MacIntyre was being arranged in a pine coffin with his legs straight out before him. He sat erect, his back and face stiff as he stared at the uneven line of the firing squad. She saw the flash of sunlight reflecting off a rifle barrel, saw the impatient faces of the people crowded along the edges of the meadow.

Carrie tried to pull away from Rance. "This is inhuman."

He refused to release her. "I want you to see what the word *execution* really means. Look at it, Carrie."

She didn't want to obey him. It was a sin to stare at this poor boy's fear and humiliation. Her eyes refused to close, though, and she saw the provost marshal kneel beside MacIntyre. He put his hand on the boy's shoulder, spoke a few words, then stood up and walked away. The muscles in John MacIntyre's face shivered.

"You're the one who should be worried about being executed," she said. "You're the one wearing a Confederate target on his sleeve."

The rifles were lifted, aimed, steadied.

A volley of thunderous fire rocked the building. MacIntyre's body shuddered as it was thrown backwards into the pine box.

Carrie's eyes finally closed, but it was too late. The scene played over and over in her mind like a nightmare that wouldn't stop.

"Quick and clean," Rance said. "Hanging is harder. It's an ugly way to die. The rope is rough and they knot it so tightly around your neck that you can't breath. They tie your hands behind you, your arms are bound to your sides, your feet are tied together. They put a black cloth over your head so you can't see the sun or smell the wind.

"You're choking from the rope and you're choking from the fear and you don't know when they're going to spring the trap beneath you, so you stand there trussed and terrified, drowning in the sound of your own heartbeats.

"Every sound you hear might be your last. You wait and you wait and when you think you can't bear another second of waiting, the trap drops out from beneath you and you fall, but just far enough to make your lungs heave in your chest before the rope snaps tight and your body jerks to a stop and your neck breaks.

"You scream and scream but no one hears you, because no sound comes out. And your body keeps twitching and jerking and struggling and you keep screaming those silent screams until slowly your life drains way into the darkness of that mask."

Carrie'd had enough. "What are you doing here?" She turned to face him. "It's not the salt shipment. We both know it's James Henry stealing those missing pounds."

"If you know that, why don't you fire him?"

"The same reason you don't stop him, there's not another man between here and Richmond who would take the risks James Henry takes every time he leaves here with a wagon. Now let's get back to your reason for being here."

"I told you the truth, Carrie. I'm here for the salt."

"If that's the story you want to believe, fine, I'll pretend I believe it, too. But tell me something, if that salt is why you're here, why didn't you just take it and leave? Why did you make me watch that boy die?"

"It upset you, didn't it?"

"Yes, it upset me. He sat in his own coffin and waited for them to kill him. My God, how could they do that to him? I don't want to die like that."

"Then why are you risking your life to spy for Lincoln?"

She wasn't about to be trapped into a confession that easily no matter how upset she was. "If I did support the Union, which I don't, the decision to risk my life to help the country I believe in would be easy." She turned away from him and looked back out the window. Her eyes were burning. "The hard part would be knowing that while I'm fighting for my country, I'd be fighting against you."

He wrapped his arms around her and kissed her hair. After a few moments, she covered his hands with hers and leaned her head back against his chest.

"What are we going to do?" he asked softly.

She took a shaky breath. "The only thing we can do, we're going to go downstairs and help John Henry load the salt. After all, that's why you're here."

Chapter Thirty-one

On June 20th, West Virginia was officially admitted to the Union. Carrie was in Pennsylvania and missed the celebration Charleston had planned, not that she would have felt like celebrating even if she had been there. The war had robbed her of all feelings of celebration. She'd turned off all her emotions and hidden them away. They'd become a luxury she couldn't afford.

Emotions meant caring about the dead and mangled bodies of Confederate soldiers whose pockets she searched for unmailed letters that might offer a clue to their army's next move. Emotions meant caring that the entire Confederate army was marching and fighting in bare feet and that same army was starving and that so much blood had soaked into Southern soil, it was no longer just the clay of South Carolina that was red.

No, emotions were dangerous, and Carrie had purged herself of everything except her flint-sharp desire to help the Union win, and with that victory, earn the right to freedom for all Americans.

Gettysburg was a perfect example of why she didn't want to feel anything. General Robert E. Lee had brought his troops to Pennsylvania to invade the North, but he brought them to Gettysburg to find shoes.

The first shots were fired on July 1st. On the 2nd, the name of Seminary Ridge was added to Carrie's battle-rich vocabulary. Then Little Round Top and Big Round Top, Devil's Den and the Peach Orchard and the Wheatfield and Cemetery Hill and Cemetery Ridge.

On the 3rd of July, when a thundering volley of Union artillery began to rake through the shouting, charging ranks of General George Pickett's men, Carrie left Gettysburg. She left Pennsylvania, too. There would be no letter-to-home secrets to uncover in the pockets of these Confederate dead. There would be no glory on that field to add to the luster of the Union flag. There would be nothing when this battle was ended.

So she went home, taking first a train, then hiring a horse and traveling day and night without pause, changing tired horses for fresh ones, paying turnpike tolls and ferry fees and riding until she forgot everything except her need to be with her father and her grandfather while she tried not to think that somewhere behind her among the dying might be the man whose smile she wanted to be her only reason for living, but wasn't.

The sound of the telegraph became the only sound in Charleston. It clattered all day, every day, bringing into the lives of the little town's anxious citizens the names of the Gettysburg dead and wounded. It also brought news of skirmishes along the eastern borders of West Virginia as retreating Confederate troops made their way south. And the telegraph brought Carrie an order to report to Washington to be briefed on a new mission.

She didn't obey the order. She went instead to Burning Spring to watch dragonflies flit and clouds drift and to wonder how long it would be before her sharp-edged memories of July's opening days would be dulled by the rust of passing time.

She was sitting beside the little creek that trickled from the gas-rich spring. With skirts lifted to her knees, she dipped her feet in the trickling water. A brown-bodied dragonfly called the Prince was chasing little sticks she threw across the meadow. It was a peculiar thing for a dragonfly to do, and a very charming habit of the Prince. Her grandfather had told her that the only way to catch one was to net it while it chased a stick. She didn't want to catch it, though. She just wanted to throw sticks.

The dragonfly was beginning to tire of the game. He was darting after only the more unusual stick tosses, like one Carrie had made into the tall grass surrounding the spring. She broke another piece from the maple tree twig she'd found in the grass and tossed it at a passing bluebird. The Prince ignored it.

Rance watched from the shadows at the edge of the forest. It was a scene as magical as the snow music. She looked like a farm girl in a simple cotton dress, her unbound hair dancing in the wind, its bright beauty glowing like summer sunlight, and her bare legs flashing as she kicked rainbow-colored droplets of water at the crazy bug chasing sticks like a faithful hound.

The scene was made even more unreal by the images of Gettysburg that refused to be blinked away like unshed tears. And yet this girl, this sweet, fairy-tale child, was involved up to her neck in the war responsible for those horrors.

He pressed a hand over the inside pocket of his uniform jacket. It held one of her gossip-filled letters, this one posted three days before General Lee's forces confronted Union pickets at the little Pennsylvania crossroads called Gettysburg, a confrontation that would have been a complete surprise if not for Carrie's letter.

Even though Rance was still unable to break the code she used to pass information, he did know that the letters were always addressed to either Washington or the city where the Army of the Potomac was headquartered.

Because General Lee had been operating in Pennsylvania under the assumption that the Union army was still in Virginia, it had caused quite a stir when this intercepted letter was discovered to be addressed to Frederick, Maryland, a short twenty-five miles southeast of Lee's invading forces. As a result, the battle at Gettysburg, though terrible in its wrath, had not been a surprise.

Although the letter in Rance's pocket would not convict Carrie of espionage, it was enough to have her permanently barred from the Confederacy. If not for its ever-increasing need for salt.

Her stockpile of white gold had finally become more important than treason.

But salt wasn't why Rance was here. This time he was here for something that Gettysburg had caused him to need more than all the salt in the world. This time, he was here for Carrie.

There was only one piece of the maple twig left. She had to make this throw the best. She turned around and raised herself up onto her knees to toss the stick in the direction of the chestnut tree at the far edge of the meadow. The Prince followed it, a bright streak of metallic brown that disappeared into the shade.

That's when she saw him. His uniform was dirty, his face unshaven. And his eyes, never had she seen anyone's eyes stripped so bare of defenses. With the mask gone, she saw his hunger, and she saw that it matched hers.

She ran across the meadow to him, crying out when a stone struck her stream-wet toes. She didn't stop, though, she kept running and threw herself into his arms, burying her face against his neck and clinging to him while she tried to forget everything in the whole world except that he was alive.

He wrapped her in his arms and drank in the feel of her. "Your father told me where to find you."

She pulled back and smiled into his eyes. "Did you have to break both his arms or just one?"

"Both."

"Why are you here? I hope you haven't come down with that suspicious cold again."

He silenced her with a kiss. "This," he said against her lips. "This is why I'm here, baby."

He was bearing her down to the ground.

"No, not here, Rance. Let's go out in the sun. Since Gettysburg, I haven't been able to get enough sun. I want to feel it and you at the same time."

"You were at Gettysburg?"

She turned her face into his shoulder. "Until Pickett's Charge. I couldn't watch it."

He swept her up into his arms and carried her from the forest shade into the July sun. He laid her on the grass beside the dappling stream and lay beside her, kissing away the tremble that shivered through her lips. He closed her eyes with kisses, whispered kisses into her ear. He undressed her with fingers as tender as kisses. He touched her with caresses as warm as kisses. And he loved her, with his hands and his body, and his heart.

The sun, the lovely, warm, healing sun. It was inside Carrie. He put it there, placing it deep within her with his gentle loving, keeping it hot and wonderful with his passion.

His lips on hers and his hands on her breasts, they were like the song of the meadow and the mountains. They covered her and warmed her, they fed her need and made her safe within their embrace.

Deeper into her he moved, stroking full and

hard, reaching and driving, filling her with his need. She moved with him, lifting herself to accept him, giving to him and taking him deeper, sharing his desire, creating for him the first peace he'd ever known.

The heartbeat rhythm of their loving intensified, strengthened, became swollen and desperate, hot and deep and fast and full, thrusting and reaching, grasping and crying aloud.

"Carrie." Rance dropped his mouth to hers, whispering her name against her gasping lips.

"I was afraid," she said and arched her neck backwards, taking his kiss on her throat while she fought for breath. "I couldn't watch because I was afraid you were in that charge." She met his burning gaze. "And I knew I would die if I lost you."

He grasped her hair and pulled her face to the side. He touched his lips to the soft curve of her ear. "Always, Carrie," he whispered. "I will always be a part of you. No charge can take that away. No battle, no war, not even death will ever separate us."

She turned to look at him. There were tears in his eyes, those beautiful, wonderful eyes of perfect blue. And there was something else, something that filled her heart with so much happiness, it was like a physical pain.

She caught his lips with hers. His pledge

turned into a kiss, his body resumed the beat of their passion and as they kissed, he lifted her up into the dream neither of them dared believe would really come true.

Later, when the shadow of the chestnut tree had crept across their sunburned legs and arms, Carrie rolled onto her side and wrapped a curling strand of his hair around the little finger on her right hand.

"This meadow used to belong to George Washington," she said.

He cocked an eyebrow at her. *"The* George Washington?"

"The one and only." She kissed his chin and began tracing patterns in his chest hair. "The spring is filled with gas. Sometimes lightning, and sometimes little boys, set it on fire and it looks like the water itself is burning. President Washington, who wasn't president yet, deeded the spring to the public forever as a natural wonder."

Rance was watching the play of light in her eyes. He felt cleansed. He felt whole again. He hadn't thought that possible after Gettysburg.

"We lost seven thousand men in Pickett's Charge, Carrie. They crossed a mile of open field. Little Round Top fired down on them. Cemetery Ridge fired down on them. Cemetery Hill fired down on them. Ziegler's Grove fired on them." He closed his eyes. "This has to end."

She pressed her face against the side of his neck. "The South can't win, Rance."

He rolled away from her. "We won't surrender. We'll never surrender."

She reached around him and cupped his face in her hand, forcing him to turn back and face her. "What you mean is that you won't surrender."

He pulled her head down onto his shoulder and kissed her forehead. A hummingbird hummed its wings beside her ear. She sat up to watch the tiny bird flit across the meadow in search of nectar.

"Look," she said and pointed at the spring. Hovering in the air above it was a brown and blue dragonfly with yellowish wings.

"It's a bug," Rance said.

"It's a devil's darning needle. They sew shut the mouth, ears, and eyes of naughty children."

He grinned at her. "He's probably looking for us because what we've been doing is very naughty."

"Lisset Lewis told me that when she was working in one of the Richmond hospitals as a volunteer, she fainted when a wounded soldier kissed her throat. Now she wears a scarf around her neck and refuses to go anywhere near the hospital. She'd probably go into a permanent swoon if she knew about us." Carrie kissed Rance's grin. "But never mind about not-very-naughty Lisset, the dragonfly I showed you was a particular kind of darner, a Janus darner. It was named after the Roman god of beginnings and endings. Peach says that seeing one when you're in doubt about your future is good luck."

Rance caught her to him, holding her so close he could feel her heart beating against his bare chest. "We're going to need all the luck we can get, baby." He released her. "I have to go. I should have been in Richmond a week ago."

"You came here instead?"

He smiled at her disbelieving face. "I would rather be here than anywhere else in the whole world, Carrie, because this is where you are."

He stood and brushed the grass from his naked body. Carrie watched every move he made, memorizing the way he looked and the way she felt, frightened that this might be the last time she ever saw him.

I have to tell him.

He was buttoning his trousers. With him partially dressed, she felt suddenly exposed and rushed to dress while he put on his jacket and boots.

He fastened his pistol belt, then stopped to watch her searching the meadow for her shoes.

"Come to Richmond with me, Carrie."

She was sitting beside the spring. She glanced at him, then down at the worn slippers in her hands. "I have to go to Washington."

He ran to her and pulled her to her feet. He shook her so hard, her teeth hurt. "You have to stop this, Carrie. For me, for us."

" 'We hold these truths to be self-evident,' " she said, " 'that all men are created equal, that they are endowed by their Creator with certain unalienable Rights, that among these are Life, Liberty, and the pursuit of Happiness.' "

He'd stopped shaking her and was looking at her as though she were demented. "I'm trying to save your life and you're quoting the Declaration of Independence?"

"It's why I can't quit, Rance. I believe in those words. If I let what I want become more important than them, it would be like saying that the men who have died to give those words meaning sacrificed their lives for nothing. I can't do that."

She felt him drawing away from her. Not just physically. It was his heart that was retreating.

He touched a finger to her chin.

"Good-bye, baby."

He was walking away. But the only words that came to her lips were the the same ones she'd just quoted to him. Great words. Historic words. Words of freedom and equality. But those weren't the words that would bring Rance back to her. Before she could say the three that might, he was gone.

Chapter Thirty-two

February 14, 1864. Valentine's Day, the third one of the war.

Yesterday, Carrie was in Richmond. But last night when the southbound train pulled out of the station, she was on it. She didn't want to listen to her friends tell her who sent them cards. She didn't want to waltz with recovering soldiers at the hospital balls. She didn't want to roll bandages or knit socks or sew shirts or do any of the dozens of other patriotic things the women in Richmond would be doing on Valentine's Day.

She wanted to be as far away from all that patriotism as she could get, so before the day could begin, and with it her disappointment at not receiving the valentine she knew she wouldn't receive, she'd taken the train to South Carolina, Greyston Plantation, and her mother. Now, instead of being disappointed, she could pretend she was too far away for the longed-for card to find her. It was a lie, but recently lies were the only reality she could face.

Greyston was beautiful. The Combahee River lazed its way past lush green lawns shaded by ancient forests of willow and water oak. Early spring flowers scented the air. The sky was clear, the breeze was lazy and warm, and it was hard to believe that just beyond the reach of her hand, there was a war.

The plantations on the river had plenty of food. Women still dressed in hoops and hats just to stroll on the terrace. They talked of hairstyles and the novels they were reading and the colt that was born in the barn last night.

But life wasn't as perfect as it seemed.

The dresses they wore were not the latest styles imported from Paris. They were prewar fashions that had been patched and mended and turned. The hairstyles they discussed weren't the latest rage of England, they were from old issues of *Godey's Lady's Book* that had been rescued from attics so the reader could pretend she was still in touch with the world beyond the blockade. The novels being discussed were the same ones they had been reading in 1860 before secession became more important than fiction. And the colt that had been born was from the swayback mare used for plowing, not the son of the champion racehorse their daddies once owned.

No, life at the South Carolina river plantations wasn't the perfect picture Decca Blackwell wanted to pretend it was, but it was as close as it would ever again be to the way she had thought life would be forever.

Carrie walked along the river bank with a parasol in her hand and her skirts swinging wide about her, and she wondered what it was she had really come here for. Was it to flee Richmond? Was it to see her mother? Or was it to enjoy, even for only a moment, the life that she'd been working to destroy?

"Look, darling, it's for you!"

Decca held up the envelope that Jessup, one of the house slaves, had handed her. "Dis jus come, Miss Decca. One of dem cabalry soldiers wid a feder in him cap jus brung it," Jessup had said, then backed away, leaving the two white woman to continue their stroll while he went back to his duties.

"Open it, darling, it looks like a valentine, most likely from some terribly handsome man whose heart you have stolen."

Carrie held the envelope between two fingers and extended at arm's length. There wasn't a postmark nor an address. Just her name.

James Bredon. It had to be from him. Decca had probably sent a messenger to the Bredon plantation before Carrie was out of the carriage this morning. Now that she had been delivered a token of James' undying affection, he would be arriving himself at any moment to ingratiate himself to Decca and to Grandmother Grey, both of whom thought he was the answer to their matrimonial prayers.

"If you won't open it, darling, I will."

"I came here to escape valentines, Mother."

"Don't be silly. No one wants to escape valentines, not even your father. He sends me one every year."

Carrie was so stunned, she tripped and would have fallen if her mother had not been holding so possessively to her arm. By the time she recovered her balance, Decca had the envelope open and was extracting its contents.

"I was right! It *is* a valentine."

"Pops sends you a card every year?" The enormity of that revelation was equaled only by Decca's actually telling Carrie about it.

"Look how beautiful." She turned the valentine to show Carrie.

"I want to see it, Mother."

"I'm showing it to you, darling."

Carrie waved the card away. "Not that, Pops' valentine to you. I want to see it."

Decca gave a reproachful click of her tongue. "Now, Carolina Grey, you know that sort of thing is private between a husband and wife." She frowned. "It's not signed."

"It can't be from Pops, then. If he had the nerve to send one, he'd sign it."

"Of course, Harris signed it, darling. He always signs them. Stop going on about your father's card and pay attention. It's *your* valentine that isn't signed."

Carrie was so shocked by her father sending her mother a valentine, not just this year but every year, that when she did look at the card Decca was holding in front of her face, at first what she saw didn't register. But within seconds, the significance of the heart-shaped card's decoration and sentiment caused her own heart to swell with tears of joy.

She took the card with trembling hands and drank in the sight of the blue lilac blossoms painted on the delicate paper-lace heart. The floral spray was frosted with sugar-crystal snow and beneath the fragile watercolor blossoms was printed one word. *Always.*

"How tragic that your admirer was too shy to sign his name, darling. It really is quite a lovely card."

"You're wrong, Mother." Carrie touched a fingertip to the word *Always.* "He did sign it."

Chapter Thirty-three

Richmond was filled with a sense of unease. Ulysses S. Grant, the scruffy general who in March had been made commander of the Armies of the United States, had sworn not to stop marching until he marched into Richmond. It was a familiar threat, one which all the other Union supreme commanders had made, but there was something about Grant that made it sound more like a promise.

Carrie had met Grant once. She'd been eight years old and was dressed in a pair of boy's overalls that Peach had given her to wear when she went fishing.

They'd gone to the upper Kanawha area where Grant's aunt, Mrs. William Tompkins, lived. Peach had stopped to chat a spell with her and her visiting nephew while Carrie hunted for worms in Mrs. Tompkins' flowerbed. She remembered Grant waving to her as she and

Peach set off for the river, each carrying their own willow branch poles, Carrie's longer than she was tall. She even remembered the rainbow trout she caught that day and how Peach had cleaned the fish and cooked it on a rock he'd heated in their campfire.

That had been so long ago. She wondered if Peach remembered that day, and she wondered if General Grant knew that the letters his headquarters received addressed to Mary Allen were from the little girl who all those summers ago had filled his left boot with fishing worms.

To combat their uneasy fear of General Grant, Richmond residents threw themselves into social events. Elegant dinners and elaborate fashions might be a thing of the past, but fun was free. It was that fever of fun that drew Decca to Richmond to celebrate her birthday on the third of May.

The party was in the center court of the Spotswood Hotel. Guests spilled over into the public saloons that fronted on the private square around which the hotel was built. They packed themselves on staircases, behind potted palms, in the hotel lobby, and in every other inch of space that could be found to be packed into.

Decca wore Confederate gray. It was an old dress. It hurt Carrie to see her silly, frivolous, fashion-vain mother trying to make the reworked gown look new with the crimson ribbons she'd given Decca as a birthday present.

The ribbons had been smuggled into Virginia as Carrie's corset laces. She wished she could have brought a new gown across the lines, but that would have made people suspicious of her. After all, if she could bring across a ball dress, she could bring medicine, too. Only there was no longer any medicine to bring. The Union had plenty of supplies, but they were more closely guarded than its president.

Even if she'd been able to smuggle a dress into the Confederacy as a gift for her mother, patriotic Decca would probably have refused to wear it. The war had changed even her.

Carrie resisted the temptation to wear Union blue. She held it up against her in front of the mirror. It was a lovely gown whose skirt trailed like a train behind her. It was too risky, though. The cold of suspicion had reached epidemic proportions in the South.

So she wore a red dress, the same red dress she hadn't worn the night of Richmond's secession celebration. Before she left her suite at the Spotswood to join the party downstairs, she picked up the oilcloth packet that lay on the table beside her bed. Inside its protecting folds was her most precious possession. She held it against her heart for a moment, then gently put it down and went downstairs to betray her friends and its sender.

* * *

Rance was only there to deliver a message from General Lee to President Davis. The first floor of the hotel was so crowded, he had to push around the walls of the rooms as he moved from one to the other, trying to work his way back out of the hotel.

It was while he was moving from the center square into the lobby that he saw her. He stood transfixed in the doorway. She was like a flicker of fire. Her hair was radiant, her eyes shimmered like dark diamonds, her smile was dazzling.

And in the center of her pretty chin was a dimple.

It was a party. Everyone lied at parties. "I honestly don't remember seeing you in that dress before." "I know your son isn't a coward even though he is still paying a substitute to fight for him." "Of course I admire your daughter for having the courage to slip through the blockade and go to England to wait out the war in luxury rather than share the deprivations of her family and country."

What was one more lie among so many?

One too many if the liar was Carrie.

She was with her mother, Maj. Heros von Borcke, and Mary Chesnut. While Decca Blackwell entranced the Prussian, Carrie was telling lies to Mrs. Chesnut. Carrie had even put her hand on Mrs. Chesnut's arm in a gesture of intimate reassurance.

Rance moved closer.

"I most certainly do want to hear about Lucy Haxall's wedding," Carrie said. "I am tired of talking about the war all the time. Weddings are so much more fun."

Maybe General Lee was right, Rance was getting a bit obsessive with his suspicions about Carrie. She wasn't plotting espionage, just telling party lies, a little white one to make a woman feel less silly because she preferred to talk about a wedding rather than the war.

"Was there a crowd at the church?" Carrie asked.

"It was completely jammed," Mrs. Chesnut said. "A woman took a fit in the gallery. If she had not been revived, the poor thing would have had to be handed out over the heads of the public like the buckets of water that were passed in to revive her."

"That was probably Olivia Cardell's mother," Carrie said. "Olivia has canceled her wedding with Fred Thomas, and Mrs. Cardell is so upset, she probably had a fit from thinking that it should be them getting married."

Mrs. Chesnut covered Carrie's hand with her own. "I heard about that. It's because of his leg. It was at Chattanooga that he lost it, you know. I just know that is the reason that girl is having second thoughts about marrying him."

Carrie's dimple disappeared. "It's love that matters in a marriage, not the number of shoes a man wears. Half the men in the Confederacy are missing one body part or the other. Lisset Lewis was telling me just yesterday that she plans to purposely marry a man with a missing limb just to show how proud she is of the reason he lost it. The only one she doesn't want him to be without is his head."

Mrs. Chesnut dissolved into laughter, which caused Decca to stop flirting with Major von Borcke and insist that Carrie repeat whatever she'd just said.

That day at Burning Spring when Carrie refused to give up her dangerous pursuit of treason against his country, Rance had sworn to keep his distance from her. It was better this way. Better for both of them.

But resolutions were always easier to keep if temptation was out of reach. Being this close to her and not going to her, not touching her and claiming her as his in front of this entire room of people, it was the hardest thing he'd ever done. Their lives were complicated enough as it was, though, and he knew if he ever held her in his arms again, he'd never again be able to let her go the way he had that day in Charleston.

So, while she repeated the silly story about

marrying a man with a missing head, Rance left, going back out into the night where not even the brightest star in the heavens was a match for the light in Carrie's eyes.

Chapter Thirty-four

The morning sun, which was just beginning to creep through the curtains and onto Carrie's face, was cruel, but not as cruel as the noise in the hall outside her hotel suite. She pulled the covers up over her head, but she could still hear the maniac raging.

Last night had been torture. After spending hours listening to dull gossip and dancing with dull men, she'd finally managed to sneak away from her mother's party. She'd written her letter to Mary Allen, then slipped out of the hotel to take the letter to Elizabeth Van Lew to be delivered to General Grant's winter headquarters on the Rapidan River.

Today was the day he began his march to Richmond. That's why last night's party had been so important. It was her last chance to gather enough gossip to encode the information he needed to know. Such as the size of General Lee's army and how few cannon the Army of Virginia had in its artillery arsenal.

As a result of being up so late, she'd been determined to sleep until at least noon today. The maniac in the hall apparently had other plans for her, for even though she had no interest in what he was saying, she did hear him say her name.

The door to her bedroom burst open. Through it came Hannah, who was trying to keep out the maniac, who was not about to be kept out. Carrie recognized him instantly.

"It's all right, Hannah, it's Michael Fletcher."

He looked wild and tousled, not at all the perfect example of West Point manhood he'd been the day they met.

"Carrie, thank God. I've been looking everywhere. It's Rance, you've got to come."

He's not dead. He can't be.

Michael threw off her bedcovers and pulled her out of bed.

"He's gone mad, smashing his fists at everything and everyone. No one can get near him."

"He—he's not dead?"

He yanked a dress from the wardrobe and thrust it into her shaking hands. "Not yet, but if someone doesn't stop him soon, I don't know what he might do."

She pulled the dress on over her nightgown. "Get my shoes, Hannah. What happened, Michael?"

"Chance is dead."

Her heart stopped. Little blue-eyed Chance with the lopsided smile and the sticky-fingered hugs. Chance, whom Rance loved so much he would rather die than let any harm come to his baby brother.

"He ran away from home and right into the middle of a cavalry skirmish. He was wearing a miniature version of Rance's uniform. The Federal soldiers didn't see that it was miniature, though. They just saw it was gray."

She saw Chance snuggling into Rance's arms and announcing he was going to join the cavalry.

"Oh, Michael." She stared up at him. The Valentine picnic. When was it? 1862. Two years ago. Chance would have been four that April. "Last month was his birthday," she said. "He was six, wasn't he?" Michael nodded. "And when a Fletcher turns six, he gets a pony and that means he's a man."

"It's a tradition started after our ancient ancestors moved here from Tory Island, Ireland, where we couldn't afford a horse."

"And when you're a man, you're old enough to join the cavalry. Rance told him that at the picnic."

Michael's face went suddenly white. "Dear God. No wonder he's gone mad."

He was battering a brick wall with bloodied fists and emitting cries of tormented anger with every pounding blow of flesh against stone.

A crowd had gathered. Carrie flung herself

from the carriage as an artillery officer stepped forward to stop Rance. He turned on the colonel, knocking him back with a quick flurry of punches delivered as blindly as his blows to the wall. The colonel tried in vain to defend himself against the punishing onslaught. Rance beat him to the ground and stood over him, threatening anyone else to take the fallen officer's place. No one came forward.

Carrie fought to get through the pressing crowd. "Let her by," Michael ordered. He battled ahead of her to clear a path through the spectators to Rance's pain.

"Stop it!" she cried as she broke clear of the crowd. "Please, Rance!"

She tried to fling herself at him, but the battered colonel held her back.

"He'll kill you, ma'am."

"Let me go!" She struggled against his binding arms.

"He won't touch her," Michael said.

She wasn't certain how it happened, but suddenly she was free and the colonel was saying it was her own funeral and the crowd was loud with talk. She ran to Rance, flinging herself between his fists and the wall.

His face was black with rage, his eyes hollow with misery, his mouth contorted with pain. She caught his battered right hand in hers to stop him from further self-abuse.

"It's me, Rance! Look at me, it's Carrie!"

He ripped free of her grasp and roared at her in blind fury, the sound like that of the death scream of a mountain lion. She gasped at the realization he was going to hit her.

Michael threw his weight against Rance's shoulder, staggering him but not stopping him. "Look at her, Sug, it's Carrie, big brother!"

Rance's fist remained clenched and poised to strike, but his eyes seemed to be trying to focus.

"Get that girl out of there," the colonel ordered. A surge of men advanced toward them.

"No!" she cried. "Just stay back." She put her hands on Rance's tormented face. "Michael told me what happened, Rance. I'm sorry."

He just seemed to shatter. All the anger, all the rage, all the terrible fury melted at the touch of her hands.

"Chance is dead, baby."

She put her arms around him. "I know, Rance."

He wrapped her in a desperate embrace. "It's my fault, Carrie. I killed him."

She pulled back and cupped his face in her hands again. "Don't say that, don't even think it."

"I told him—"

"He was just a baby then, Rance. You didn't know the war would last this long, no one did."

"I sent him the pony that he ran away on, Carrie. I should've realized he'd use it to come to me." He buried his face against her neck.

His tears burned her skin.

"It's not your fault," she said again, knowing how empty the words were but also knowing there was nothing she could say that would ease the pain of his guilt.

The crowd was gone, the battered colonel apologized to, the blood on Rance's hands dry. Carrie and Michael were still with him, all three of them sitting on the ground and leaning back against the brick wall.

Rance had been looking at the right sleeve of her dress where it was buttoned at her wrist. He reached over and tugged on a flannel ruffle spilling out from beneath the cuff.

"What's this?"

She looked at it for a moment before she realized what it was. "My nightgown." She tucked the telltale ruffle out of sight. "I was in bed when Michael found me."

"You wear *flannel* nightgowns?"

She was so relieved to see a brief spark of light in his eyes, she wanted to crawl into his arms and never come out. "That's a very personal question. I don't think I'll answer it."

"Not nearly as personal as admitting Alan was in your bedroom."

"I think I'm in trouble," Michael said. "Maybe I'd better leave you two to fight this out."

Rance held up his bruised hands. "I've done

enough fighting today to last a lifetime." He tried to curl his hands into fists. They were so swollen, he could barely move his fingers.

"Major Fletcher!"

Sergeant Kitchen was riding toward him. Three years of war had finally turned the Alabama boy into a good rider, even with his stiff left leg.

"Orders from General Lee."

Rance stood up to take them from him. "I have to report to headquarters in Orange.

"What about Chance's funeral?" Michael asked. "Mother will expect you home no matter how many messages you get from the commander."

"I'll leave for Tory after I meet with General Lee. Carrie, will you come with me? I'd like you to be there with me."

"There's no place else on earth I'd rather be," she said, and he drew strength from the smile that lit her eyes.

"Alan, take her to the hotel, then go to General Wickham and get yourself a pass to go home." He pulled Carrie to her feet. "Can you be ready in half an hour?"

"I can try."

"Leave that nightgown here in Richmond, Carrie."

"What will I sleep in?"

He ran a hand across her unbound hair. "How about my arms?"

"I'll be ready in fifteen minutes," she said and was rewarded with the closest thing to a smile his grief would allow.

Chapter Thirty-five

It was late afternoon before they arrived at the Confederate army's winter headquarters. The little town of Orange was not far from Chancellorsville, where Lee had won a brilliant victory exactly one year ago today. The memory of that victory was as palpable as the camp itself. Carrie could feel it haunting her as she followed Rance through the tent city.

He ushered her into one of the larger tents, where a middle-aged black man sat on an upended crate polishing Rance's sabre. "Task, this is Miss Blackwell. She'll be staying here while I'm with General Lee."

"Master Rance, you got a telegram waitin' here."

Rance turned away from Task. "I know what it says. Carrie, would you read it to him after I've left?"

She put her hand on his arm. He covered it with his own, but couldn't look at her. Then he left her to handle what should be his responsibility.

It was hard for her to meet the question in Task's eyes. She tried to find the words to tell him about Chance. She finally just read the telegram to him.

"He was a good boy, little Chance was." He seemed at a loss. "I got things to tend to if we's goin' home." He left Carrie alone.

She tried to sit quietly and wait for Rance. It wasn't long before she was on her feet again, pacing around the tent and looking at his things. His shaving brush tickled her nose when she tried to smell the scent of his cologne on its bristles. Beside the brush was a cake of shaving soap and his razor, along with a lethal-looking leather strap.

A copy of *Harper's Weekly* lay beside his cot. Carrie smiled. It was easier to get a New York paper in the Confederacy than in Charleston.

Task had left Rance's sabre on the table against the back wall of the tent. She traced a finger along the scrolling handle, imagining it in Rance's hand. Her gaze fell on his portable desk. She was running her hand down the smooth wood on the front of the box to the lock when the jangling of spurs alerted her to Rance's approach.

She was sitting on the edge of the bed when he entered. He went straight to the portable desk. His hand rested on the lid for a moment before opening it and dropping into it the papers he held. Carrie noticed the top paper was a military order.

He closed the desk and turned to her. "Task will be taking you back to Richmond."

"What about Chance's funeral?"

"We're not going."

"But don't you want—"

"We don't always get what we want in war, Carrie."

Something had happened. It hurt her that he couldn't tell her. She was trapped again in the well with a snake of distrust coiled between her and escape.

"No," she said quietly, "We don't always get what we want in war, do we? They should carve that in Latin on heavy stone tablets and make every politician in the world carry it around with them." She stood and moved to the opening of the tent, where she paused to look back at him. "It looks like we've reached another impasse, Major Fletcher."

"Maybe they should carve that in Latin on heavy stone tablets."

She put a hand over her heart. "They already have."

Chapter Thirty-six

Carrie and Task were riding south on a small road toward Trevilians, where she was to take the train back to Richmond while he returned to Orange. That Rance had sent her on a route that was well away from even the most remote Confederate camp was significant. Whatever had happened to cause him to miss Chance's funeral was big, too big for her to ignore. Still, she couldn't stop herself from hoping, though, that Task was nothing like Lucy Bream, even while she prayed he was.

The road they were on cut through the edge of the Wilderness. The forest was like a menacing shadow hovering on both sides of them, smothering sounds and smells and reason. Last year after the Chancellorsville battle, the Wilderness had been unwilling to give up its dead. There were almost daily reports of people stumbling across skeletons among the thick brushy undergrowth.

Carrie didn't have time to chance a macabre discovery. She had to look for one.

"I know a shortcut through here," she said. She reined Malachi into a sharp left into the dense forest.

"This ain't no shortcut, Miss Carrie. We should stay on the road. That's what Master Rance wants us to do. He didn't say nothin' about us takin' no shortcut, not that this here is one, 'cause it ain't."

His arguments went unheeded. Carrie kept Malachi in front of him and her attention on the ground, where she sought a glimmer of white among the forest litter.

She was lucky. It didn't take long to find what she sought. A tidal wave of guilt accompanied the discovery. She ignored it, along with the rest of her already staggering burden of similar emotions, and leapt from the saddle.

"Look," she said. She had to force herself to brush aside the grave of leaves that covered the dull white skull. She shuddered as she touched it, thinking of the poor soul it had belonged to who had died here, alone and afraid, his life seeping slowly away while the war moved on without him.

"Lord a'mighty, Miss Carrie, you put that thing down!" Task was almost as white as the skull. "That ain't nothin' for a lady to be touchin'! Put that down and let's get out of this

place and back on that road where Master Rance wants us to be!"

"He's not my master, and he shouldn't be yours." Carrie turned the skull over and looked into the dark eye sockets. "I think we should give this poor soul a decent burial. Help me gather his bones, Task."

"The good Lord put them bones there 'cause that's where He wants them."

"Nonsense. The war put them here and it's our duty to bury them. I'm taking them." She wrapped them in her jacket.

"We's goin' back out on the road," Task said. He didn't wait for Carrie to finish wrapping up the skeleton before he was riding back the way they'd come.

When she reached the road, where he was waiting, he refused to look at the bundle in her arms. He just started riding south again. Before they'd gone a half-mile, they came across a house surrounded by blooming dogwood trees.

Carrie pulled Malachi to a stop. "That's my Aunt Ethel's house. She's my Uncle Dutch's widow. Instead of going to Richmond, I'll stay with her and bury our friend here in her graveyard."

"Master Rance said I's to take you to the train."

Carrie tried a different tack. "If you insist, Task, I'll go, even though I'd rather stay here with my aunt. There are probably a lot more skeletons between here and Trevilians. We can gather those up, too, for burial. I'll need your jacket to carry them in, Task."

He told her that he hoped she had a good visit with her aunt and without another word, headed back to Orange.

"Poor man," Carrie said. She waited until he was out of sight before she turned her back on the house, which she'd never seen before in her life, and followed him.

Carrie was standing behind a bush that smelled like an outhouse. Such were the hazards of creeping around the outskirts of army camps. This bush was close to the camp and apparently attracted a lot of company. Because it was so close, it was also the best location from which to watch Rance's tent.

After what seemed like hours of holding a handkerchief over her nose and mouth with one hand and her skirts off the ground with the other, the tent flap opened and Task emerged. He was carrying Rance's dress boots and a polishing rag. He started to sit in the chair outside the tent.

"Lord a'mighty!"

The boots went one way, the rag another and a wide-eyed Task went a third, his heels lifted so high in flight, he was almost kicking himself.

Carrie dashed from behind the latrine bush and took a quick breath of fresh air before running across the open ground to Rance's tent. She nodded her thanks to the skeleton piled in the chair where Task had meant to sit, then slipped inside the tent. The portable desk was closed but not locked. The military order was on top. She read it as she lifted it.

The contents were worth the wait behind the bush.

Today's advance of the Union army across the Rapidan River was based on the belief that General Lee was unaware of Grant's plan to get as close to Richmond as possible before facing the Confederate army. This order revealed that Lee knew about Grant's plan two days ago. It also outlined his plans to intercept the Federal troops, not weeks from now in the fortifications of Richmond, but right here in the hellish environs of the Wilderness—tomorrow morning.

The cost of a surprise battle to the Union troops would be terrible. Carrie's knees went weak thinking about the horror of it. She grasped the edge of the table, almost knocking Rance's sabre to the ground. She straightened it before looking to see if his desk held any other bad news.

What she found was her latest letter to Mary Allen.

I should just hand them over to him instead of bothering with couriers, she thought. There wasn't any need to worry about him breaking her code. If he hadn't figured it out in three years, there was no reason to think he would now. All its capture meant was she had another good reason to reach General Grant tonight.

"I's tellin' you this is the very same dead man that Miss Carrie say she was gonna bury!"

It was Task, and from the sound of the angry footsteps accompanying him, Carrie knew his master was with him.

She put the order back into the desk, closed it, and grasped Rance's sabre. With a single stroke of its glittering blade, she sliced through the back of the tent and was running for the woods before Rance's spurs stopped jangling.

Rance fingered the strand of golden hair clinging to the sides of the new back door to his tent. "You said she mentioned an Aunt Ethel. She didn't say anything about a Dutch uncle, did she?"

"She say she was gonna bury that dead man in the ground right beside her uncle."

Rance put a hand on Task's shoulder. "She tricked you, old man. Take care of that skeleton while I see what she was up to in here."

"I ain't touchin' that thing, not even if you

skin me alive, Master Rance."

It was exactly what he'd considered doing when Task told him that he'd left Carrie a few miles from Orange.

"Get an orderly to get rid of it then, but get it out of my chair."

"I's gonna do that, I's surely gonna do that, and I's never gonna sit in that chair again as long as I live. Nope, not me."

Rance waited until Task was gone before checking his desk. The orders from Lee were still there. Carrie's letter was still there, too. That had to be what she came back for. She must've seen him put it in here. It was sheer luck that she hadn't had enough time to open the desk and see those orders.

Rance slit the letter open with his knife. "Let's see what was so important that you felt it was necessary to frighten a man half to death to come back here, Miss Blackwell."

Chapter Thirty-seven

Carrie's horse had been captured. There was a possibility that Malachi had pulled her reins loose by herself and then just wandered off. Capture seemed a more likely scenario to Carrie, though, since she was in imminent danger of suffering the same fate.

She didn't have time to steal a Confederate horse. Rance probably had half the army looking for her right now. So she walked. That lasted about three steps before her nerves got the better of her and she began to run. After all, it was getting dark and there was a lot of ground to cover, and there were Confederate pickets wandering around most of it. The fact that there might also be skeletons and ghosts wandering around had nothing to do with her decision to dash full speed through a forest where she couldn't see a foot in front of her.

Carrie had never been afraid of bugs in her

life, except for the creepy crawly kind that lurked inside houses and cellars and other dank places that she didn't like. Outdoor bugs didn't bother her. Until tonight. Fireflies looked like eyes blinking at her and mosquitos were like spirits chasing her and when she ran headlong into a hovering moth, it was all she could do to keep from screaming.

Guilt. That's what Peach would blame for all this irrational behavior manifesting itself here in this dark forest. Somewhere inside her had been an uncrossable line. Tonight she had crossed it. She had violated her oath not to involve anyone in her schemes by taking advantage of poor Task, and she'd echoed that sin by taking advantage of her relationship with Rance by using her knowledge of his possession of secret Confederate orders to aid her country.

She could think of at least a dozen excuses to rationalize her actions, but as she'd told Sergeant Busbell, innocent people didn't make excuses.

She broke out of the forest beside a river. She'd been running north, which meant this was the Rapidan. General Grant's army would be downstream from here. She headed down river, searching the river bank for hidden boats. It shouldn't be too hard to find one. Couriers, spies, slaves, even regular everyday people kept boats hidden along almost every river in Virginia.

She found what she needed under what looked like a jumble of flood debris. Once she'd pulled the boat into the open, though, she wondered if perhaps it might be part of the debris. She pushed it into the Rapidan. The boat had several impressive leaks, but didn't immediately sink, so she piled into it and pulled most of the flood debris on top of her. Now it was up to the current.

She hadn't been drifting for very long when she heard voices. She peered out from beneath the debris and saw a small campfire near the water's edge. The flames spread yellow light across the faces of Negroes as they cast fishing lines across the river's rippled surface.

On and on she floated, drifting between sleep and consciousness. Consciousness brought thoughts of the information she'd learned and its importance to the Union. Without it, hundreds of men, maybe even thousands, would die tomorrow. She tried to keep her mind on those thoughts. The gentle movement of the water, the close confines of the boat, and her own exhaustion caused fingers of sleep to massage away her sense of duty, though, and turned her thoughts to Rance.

"No, I won't think about him," she said as she was startled awake by a stinging sound. She heard the sound again, along with the splatter of water against the hull of her boat and a ripping sound in the brush over her head.

"Someone's firing at me!" she screamed in a silent whisper.

Rance sat back in his chair. Carrie's latest letter lay open on his desk blotter. Copies of all her other letters were spread across the table. He was tired of trying to make sense of them. Franklyn Bredon had warned him not to underestimate her. The sly old politician had overestimated her, though, then infected Rance with his suspicions.

"Like a bad cold."

There couldn't be anything more to these letters than just what they seemed. The coincidence of the addresses corresponding to Union army headquarters was probably just to drive him crazy. In fact, that was most likely the purpose of the letters themselves. Practically the first words out of his mouth the night they met had accused her of gossiping about him with the Lewis girl. This was just the kind of trick Carrie would take great delight in playing on him.

"I'll wring her little neck," Rance muttered.

The more he thought about it, the more likely it seemed that it was a joke. She hadn't even bothered to write accurate gossip. The letter his men had taken off that courier last night had a glaring error. In it, Carrie described the same wedding Mary Chesnut had described to her. Not only did Carrie claim to have been at the nuptials herself, she misrepresented the number of guests as being only a few and even invented a reason for their absence.

Why would she make up lies when there was a more interesting true fact to relate, the woman who had the fit?

Unless the truth didn't fit the information she needed to send.

Rance picked up the letter again.

"Hardly anyone was there. To say there were even sixty-two souls to witness the happy event would be generous. The remainder of the invited guests deserted Lucy in her hour of need, preferring to stay at home rather than face another foodless wedding."

"Task!"

The Negro came running into the tent. If there was any gossip worth knowing, Task would know it. He would walk a hundred miles in bare feet just to get the latest tidbit of news.

"Last week there was a wedding in Richmond, Task. Do you know anything about it?"

"Miss Lucy Haxall and Cap'n Coffey got married."

"Did they serve supper to the guests?"

"Cap'n Coffey's daddy brung every bit of

food on his plantation to that weddin'. His poor slaves is probably starvin' right now."

Rance laughed. "His poor slaves are probably eating better than this whole army."

That was it.

He felt stunned. Three years of trying every mathematical combination he could think of to assign a meaning to Carrie's meaningless words, and not once in all that time had he ever paid attention to the words themselves.

"Thank you, Task."

"What you is thankin' me for, I's sure don't know," he said and left.

Rance looked at the paragraph describing Lucy Haxall's wedding again.

"To say there were even sixty-two souls to witness the happy event would be generous."

There would be sixty-two thousand Confederate soldiers facing General Grant tomorrow.

"The remainder of the invited guests deserted Lucy in her hour of need, preferring to stay at home rather than face another foodless wedding."

The reason there were only sixty-two thousand men was because of desertions due to the Confederacy's inability to feed its soldiers.

Weddings had been a reoccurring theme in Carrie's letters. Rance sorted through them.

In the letter mailed to Frederick, Maryland before Gettysburg: "There were more blood relations at Annie Stapps' wedding than I even knew existed. Peach said he counted seventy-five for sure, and not a single one wearing shoes."

There were seventy-seven thousand Confederate troops at Gettysburg, and they were there because there had been a shoe factory at Gettysburg whose products were so desperately needed, General Lee had chanced a battle rather than let his men continue to march barefoot.

What you have to do, Fletcher, is stop trying to catch her dealing from the bottom of the deck and look closer at the cards she's taking off the top. Whatever Carolina's doing that's most obvious is where she'll conceal her secrets.

Franklyn Bredon had been right. Rance had been too busy trying to see what was hidden under the gossip to look at the gossip itself. He'd often recognized names, and based on that assumption alone had believed the rest to be—What had he called it the day of the valentine picnic? Female dribble.

He pulled that letter from the stack on the table.

"I saw a most excellent hat today, quite a well-made affair with seventeen rows of the most perfect ruffles you can imagine, quite deep and extra wide. They were only on the front of the hat and wrapped around the wearer's head in a semicircle that stretched completely from ear to ear."

"Richmond's fortifications," he said and laughed. It was so obvious, Chance would have figured it out.

His laughter died.

He couldn't believe Chance was really dead. It was as though Rance had lost his very soul. But because of that loss, he'd discovered the true depth of his need for Carrie. He dropped the letter back on the desk. Now he'd lost her, too.

A glimpse through the cover of debris on Carrie's floating tomb showed no lights on shore. The shots were still pelting into the boat and debris, though. She was too terrified to even call out, not that anything short of cannon fire could have been heard above the noise being made by her attackers.

Despite her terror, she tried to think of who it could be out there shooting at her. The shots were coming from the southern shore, where the main force of General Grant's army should now be. Pickets often shot at things when they were bored, especially if their commanders thought the rebels were too busy running for Richmond to overhear a little target practice at a hunk of floating debris.

Her suspicions that she was approaching the Union camp soon proved right when the night began to brighten. She looked out to see dozens of campfires on both sides of the river. The assault on her boat had pushed it close to the northern shore. It seemed as equally inhabited as the south, so she didn't try to cross the river. She pushed off her covering of debris and climbed out of the boat to drag it and herself onto shore.

With dripping skirts lifted and her heart once again filled with hope, she kept to the shadows as she approached the camp. The sight of Union blue uniforms and the American flag filled her with relief. She stumbled out of the darkness into the welcome warmth of her country's army.

Corporal Simpson Bird took her to the field telegraph station on the outskirts of the camp. The telegraph station consisted of a tent fly supported by rifles whose bayonets had been thrust into the ground. A telegraph relay machine set on a cracker box. The operator was tapping on the machine's key with vigorous energy.

"I have a message that must be sent to General Grant immediately."

"Put it with the rest," the operator said. He indicated a pile of at least a dozen other messages. “I’ll get to it as soon as I can.”

“It’s important.”

The operator looked at her. His eyes were bloodshot, and he looked as tired as Carrie felt. He patted the pile of messages waiting to be sent. “Same story,” he said. “I send them as I get them, ma’am. I’m sorry.”

“It also needs to be sent in cipher,” she said. One of the Confederate army’s favorite hobbies was tapping into Union telegraph wires. Anything that wasn’t sent in cipher was everybody’s business. “I need paper and ink.”

He pointed at a lump of blankets that apparently served as his bed in the back of the makeshift tent. “Don’t spill the ink,” he said. “It’s all I have.”

Carrie put the paper on her damp lap, dipped the operator’s pen in the almost empty bottle of ink, and wrote:

> “General Lee learned of Union advance two days ago. He plans to refight his Chancellorsville victory on May 5th. Ewell and Hill moving east on Orange Turnpike and Orange Plank Road. Longstreet marching from Gordonsville to the Wilderness.
>
> Mary Allen”

She closed the bottle of ink, put it and the

pen back on the rumpled blankets, and placed her message with the rest awaiting transmission.

"Thank you," she said to the operator. He was too busy tapping at his machine to even hear her.

Chapter Thirty-eight

The fighting began the next day when Union troops moving south from the Rapidan were surprised by General Ewell's troops on the Orange Turnpike. The battle was desperate and fierce.

In a forest so thick a man could not see his friend beside him or his enemy in front of him, bullets and cannon hacked and gnawed at trees and soldiers like a deadly scythe of fire and lead.

In a clearing near the crossroads where the first confrontation occurred, breastworks of hastily dug earth and felled trees offered a bit of protection to the soldiers. But still they, along with their companions in the forest, died.

The day was warm. The smell of blood and flesh, of gunpowder and fear was so thick that it became as terrifying as the battle itself. The men's faces were caked with dirt and powder grime. Rivulets of sweat and tears cut paths through their dark masks. They turned away from the fallen, looking always forward into the face of the enemy. Hunger and thirst gnawed at their insides, and they lay for hours in the sun of the meadow and the shadow of the forest, shooting and shooting and shooting.

For two days, Carrie stayed on the fringes of the battle. She hauled water to the tent hospitals, she lifted the corner of blankets that gave hammock-support to wounded who could not walk. She wrote letters for the dying and closed the eyes of the dead. She slit uniform sleeves and pants legs so surgeons could remove shattered limbs. She tossed arms and legs on the scrap pile while her stomach heaved, and her eyes stung with the pain of all that she saw.

And all around her, she heard men saying the same thing over and over. "If only we'd known." "We should've known." "I wish we'd known."

What happened to her warning to General Grant? Why hadn't he known the Confederates were running to confront him, not to escape him?

* * *

Silence did not come with darkness on the second day of the fighting. The Wilderness was burning. Cannon fire had set the dry brush on fire. Now the flames sounded like a distant roar as they spread unchecked through the dense forest.

The Wilderness Tavern lay at the crossroads where the first shots of the battle had been fired. The tavern had become Union headquarters, and into and out of its yard rode generals and messengers.

Carrie approached the lantern-lit tavern on foot. From out of the night came the sound of bugles. Their sweet voices seemed to be coming from everywhere, like a Heavenly Host whose music washed away the pain and exhaustion of the day as the regulation calls were played by buglers posted in various locations throughout the forest to confuse Confederate sharpshooters to their location, and to the location of the Union troops.

An unkempt man riding a prancing bay came into the tavern yard. Carrie instantly recognized the horse's famous rider.

"General Grant," she said.

He dismounted and handed his reins over to a private. "Take good care of Cincinnati for me, son." He turned his gaze on Carrie.

"I've come to see you, sir."

"Hell of a time for a visit." He stripped off

his riding gloves as he walked into the tavern's smoky salon. "Bring me that map, Henry. Now, young lady, what are you doing in the middle of a battlefield?"

"I sent you a telegram, General."

He unfolded the map on a table and scowled at its featureless expanse. "Where the hell are we?"

Carrie put a finger on the map. "Here, General. About my telegram, I sent it the night before the fighting began to give you General Lee's plan of attack."

The air around Carrie suddenly darkened as every man in the tavern crowded close to her.

"How did you know he was going to attack?" Grant asked.

"I was in his camp at Orange and saw his orders outlining the direction his generals would advance toward you." She traced the routes on the map—the Orange Plank Road, the Orange Turnpike, and Longstreet's march north. "I found one of your field telegraph stations and sent you word of the attack."

A staff officer handed General Grant a stack of papers, which he rifled through.

"I signed it Mary Allen," Carrie said and Henry, the hander of the map, stared at her.

"You're the Mary Allen woman? I decode your letters. Did you know that when I get them, most have already been opened and resealed?" She nodded. "Why do they let you stay if they suspect you?"

That was a question which had been a war-long mystery to Carrie. "At first it was the salt I was selling them. Last year the Union closed my furnaces in West Virginia, but President Davis kept renewing my pass to come and go from the Confederacy as I pleased. So I kept sending you letters, which reminds me. They still have my last one. It gave General Lee's army at Orange as sixty-two thousand men, they've had a lot of desertions because of hunger. There are only two-hundred forty-four guns in his artillery and there have been no significant improvements in Richmond's fortifications since my last report."

"There's no telegram from you here," Grant said.

The staff officer was rummaging through the contents of a leather case. "Here," he said and pulled a sheet of pink telegram paper from his case. "It came in uncoded and was put in the Rebel Fodder File."

Uncoded. The word thudded inside Carrie like a ricocheting bullet.

"They listen in on our telegraph lines," the officer was saying. "So anything that isn't in code, we dismiss. We send each other false information that's uncoded just to confuse the rebs."

"The operator was tired," Carrie said. "I should've stayed with him until it was sent." *But I was tired, too,* she thought, and added another excuse to her growing list of unforgivable sins.

"I'm sorry I didn't see this," Grant said. "It wouldn't have stopped the battle, but it could have saved a lot of lives if it had been sent in cipher."

"Including mine," she said.

Grant met her gaze. "They'll know this was from you?"

"One of them will."

She went to the window. The buglers were playing evening taps. The music was sweet and beautiful, and as it spilled through the darkness, it carried with it a note of regret that matched the way Carrie felt.

General Grant came to stand beside her. A fiery orange glow lit the sky over the burning forest. Wounded men could be dying in those flames, and she was upset that her cover had been irrevocably exposed.

"What will you do now?" Grant asked.

"Help from behind your lines instead of from behind theirs." *And never see Rance Fletcher again.* She didn't need to say those words to know they were true, just as she didn't need to say, *not even after the war.* There were too many stone tablets between them to ever believe they could break through them all. "What will you do now, General? You can't defeat Robert E. Lee in this forest. That's why he attacked you here, he knew his smaller force could stop your larger one."

The routine of the war had been for both sides to fall back, regroup, and wait for the next confrontation to occur.

"I'm going forward," Grant said. The room fell suddenly silent. He turned to face his staff. "The days of falling back are over, gentlemen. Tell your men that tomorrow morning, we march to Spotsylvania." A hum of disbelieving discussion filled the tavern. Grant watched the activity for a moment before turning back to the window. "Do you still go fishing, Miss Blackwell?"

The smile in his eyes caused her to smile, too. "When I can find an empty boot for my worms," she said.

"When this is over, maybe we can go together."

It had been a long time since Carrie met anyone who believed it would ever end.

"I'd like that," she said.

Chapter Thirty-nine

She attached herself to the ambulances that traveled in the wake of General Grant's army. While he marched forward to Spotsylvania, she searched the Wilderness for wounded.

"Miss, miss, miss."

The voice seemed to be following her. No matter which way she went through the forest, it was always behind her.

"Miss, miss, miss."

Finally she found it. The body from which the cry was coming was trapped under a cannon-felled tree.

Carrie's stomach cramped with horror as she knelt beside the charnel-house remains of what had once been a man. The heavy tree lay across his lap. Apparently his legs were doubled beneath him, for the bottom of one leg of his butternut-stained trousers could be seen sticking out from beneath the tree beside his right hip.

He wore no shoe, and his foot was so swollen and black with death it was almost unrecognizable.

"I'm gonna die, ain't I, miss?"

His accent was as country as an accent can get, and he looked at her with the pain-encrusted eyes of a farmboy.

"Swallow this," Carrie said and tried to give him one of her precious papers of morphine.

"You ain't one of them Union ladies come to kill wounded Confederates are you, miss?"

"Where did you hear that?"

"In camp this winter. Two men that escaped from a prisoner camp said the Union was tired of wastin' their time treatin' wounded prisoners so they was just killin' them."

"That's nonsense," Carrie said. "And besides, my name is Carolina Grey. Does that sound very Union to you?"

The boy's eyes widened. "Is that really your name?"

"My mother was a prophet," she said and lifted the morphine to his lips again. Once he'd swallowed the drug, she followed it with a drink of water from the canteen she'd scavenged from the body of a Union soldier.

"Would you do me a favor, miss? I was afraid I'd die before somebody come and I could ask them to do me a favor."

She pushed the hair back from his forehead.

His skin was cold and clammy. "Why don't you tell me your name first, and then tell me what you want me to do."

"My name's Daniel Wilson, miss, and I'm from the Cumberland Mountains over near Kentucky."

He tried to reach inside his blouse. His chest was dark with blood. He had a letter pinned inside his blouse. Carrie helped him unpin it.

"My sergeant wrote this for me. It's for my wife. I didn't send it 'cause I had a likeness took down in Richmond, and I wanted to send it to Abbie with the letter. Maybe, miss, maybe you could write on there that if she sent a dollar to that operator, his name was Dean, maybe he'd send my likeness to her. Abbie ain't got no picture of me at all. I sure would like her to have one."

He coughed and blood stained the sleeve he used to wipe his mouth.

"You know, miss, I don't feel nearly so bad as I did. The only thing that wasn't hurtin' before was my legs. I ain't been able to feel them since this old tree fell on me. I guess they got broke under there." His eyes took on an unfocused, glazed expression. "You'll send my letter for me, won't you, miss? And would you tell Abbie that I got hurt but not to come because she shouldn't be leaving our babies to come tend me. I sure wish I could see her again. I ain't seen her since the war started." A smile touched his lips. "I guess them babies ain't babies no more, but she shouldn't be leavin' them anyways. You'll tell Abbie about my likeness, won't you, miss? I sure would like her to have it."

"I'll see that she gets it, Daniel." Carrie took the letter from his cold hand. "You just sleep now."

"Thank you, miss. You've been real kind." He closed his eyes, and fell silently into death.

Chapter Forty

Rance stood with hat pulled low and eyes narrowed as he watched the surging tide of the battle. Jeb Stuart's mounted cavaliers were clashing with the Union cavalry to put a stop to General Philip Sheridan's raid on Richmond. While the cavalry was fighting here at the Yellow Tavern, Lee and Grant were facing off further north at Spotsylvania Court House.

Rance dropped his angry gaze to the map he held. There had to be something that would help, some angle he could recommend to Stuart, some small piece of hope he could offer the battling hero.

"Are you Colonel Fletcher?"

"Who's asking?"

"Private Stanton, sir. There's a prisoner at the tavern. I was sent to find you."

It was a strange place to take a captured

soldier. Usually they were herded to the rear and held there until Rance could question them.

He folded the useless map and stuck it in his back pocket. General Stuart had sent word a half-hour ago that Rance was to meet him here to discuss strategies for turning Sheridan back. Something must have gone wrong or Stuart would have been here.

Rance picked up Cain's reins. "Take the prisoner to the rear, Private Stanton. I don't have time to deal with him now."

Stanton shifted his weight from one foot to the other. "That's just it, Colonel. It's not a him, it's a her."

The private's words caused the hair on the back of Rance's neck to crawl.

"She almost took Sergeant Kitchen's head off when he said he had to search her. Said she'd strip naked on her own before she'd let him touch the hem of her skirt with her wearin' it."

Rance's lips twitched into a reluctant smile. "What did Kitchen do?"

"Got out of there quicker than a possum out of a fallin' tree and told me to come get you."

Sergeant Kitchen's face was so red he appeared to be on fire. "I delivered them dispatches to President Davis' house like I was supposed to, Colonel, and was ridin' north out of Richmond along the creek. When I passed the place where all the picture makers got their tents set up, I saw her comin' out of one of them."

"What was she doing in a photographer's tent?"

"I asked, but she didn't answer, so I put a guard on him and brought her up here." Kitchen swallowed hard. "I told her I had to search her and she—she—"

"I heard," Rance said.

"I was only gonna look in her bag, Colonel, but she didn't give me time to explain before she was undoin' buttons, so I lit out of there and no matter what you say, I ain't goin' back in." He turned and looked at the door he'd been guarding. "What're you gonna do, Colonel?"

"My duty," Rance said and opened the door.

Carrie stood at the window, her back to the room and her gaze fixed outside. The sounds of the fighting were like a distant groan, the noise of the battle shuttered by the dusty windowpane and her own fear.

When she'd been caught during the Seven Days Battle, she'd never doubted that she would be able to talk her way out of trouble. This time was different. That uncoded telegram had sealed her fate.

Every second she was forced to wait made the fear worse. She tried to calm herself by reasoning that no matter how frightened she was, it could be nothing compared to the fear a slave felt when waiting for the first lash of the whip.

It was in Richmond that Patrick Henry had proclaimed, "Give me liberty or give me death." What would he have thought of this war? Would he have been as willing to die to free other men as he had been to free himself?

She had once visited St. John's Church, where he made that famous speech. It was after she led her first runaway slaves north. She thought she would feel something, a lingering bit of Patrick Henry's bravery and strength, perhaps. All she had found was an empty church.

The door behind her squeaked as it opened.

"I emptied my reticule and my pockets onto the table," she said. "If you still want to search me—" Her voice faded. It wasn't Sergeant Kitchen this time.

The floor seemed to be falling out from

under her. She stared sightlessly out the window, unable to breathe. A long silence, too long, pressed against her. The air in the room had all disappeared, destroyed by everything that wasn't being said.

She couldn't let him know that her heart was breaking. "It looks like history is repeating itself," she said, and turned to face him. "A different battle, a different tavern, but the same players in the same play."

He looked so tired. There were dark scars of exhaustion under his eyes. And in them, the look of a man caught in the middle of a situation he could not control.

She had done this to him. She regretted nothing she had done for the Union, and she regretted everything she had done to this man.

"I know about the telegram," she said, "so I know this time the scene will have a different ending."

Rance could see the effort it was taking for her to hold herself together.

Her gaze fell to the letters in his hands. He wanted to hide them. He couldn't, though. All he could do was watch the smile that lit the dark beauty of her eyes.

"How did you finally do it?"

"Lucy Haxall's wedding."

"And now you're wearing colonel's bars."

"I tried to refuse them."

She turned away. Daniel Wilson's letter and likeness lay on the table beside her oilcloth packet. She reached for the blood-stained letter, and handed it and the likeness to Rance.

"I know you have no reason to trust me, but these have nothing to do with me or the Union, just a promise I made to a man who was dying. Would you send them for me?"

Rance looked down into the unsmiling face of a Confederate private etched into the tintype likeness. "Is this why you went back to Richmond?"

"I made a promise."

"To an enemy soldier."

"It was still a promise."

The face blurred. "Of all the foolish things you have done, Carrie, this is the worst."

"Will you send it?"

He looked up at her. The sunlight streaming through the window turned her hair into a golden halo of light. He wanted to touch her, to soothe away the fear that paled her face and washed the life from her eyes.

"Yes," he said, and for a moment, the eyes smiled again, then she turned away and never saw the arms he reached out to her.

Outside, the battle still raged. It was like a storm that threatened but never broke.

That was how she felt. Emotions that threatened to break but never did, words that wanted to be spoken but could never make it past her heart. And now it was too late. There was nothing she could say now that wouldn't sound like an attempt to wiggle her way out of trouble again.

She wrapped her arms around herself. "Now what?"

He opened the door. "Sergeant, take Miss Blackwell downstairs."

She kept her arms crossed in front of her as she walked to the door. She hesitated beside the table. "May I take my things?"

"I'll bring them down in a minute. I have to go over them first."

He saw her gaze flick to the oilcloth packet. She looked quickly away. "Please, Rance." Her lower lip trembled. "They're personal."

"It's my job, Carrie."

Her chin lifted. "I understand," she said and joined Sergeant Kitchen in the hall.

After she'd been led away, Rance looked at the oilcloth. The string that bound it was tied with a lovingly prepared bow. He untied it, and when the protecting cloth fell away, his heart stopped. It was his valentine.

She stood in the shadows behind the front door of the tavern. Rance had come downstairs and signaled Sergeant Kitchen to join him on the other side of the room. They talked for a minute, then both of them came across to where she waited.

"Are you ready?" Rance asked, and Carrie's heart rose into her throat so that she could not breathe.

"Yes." She couldn't look at him.

He held out her reticule. She grasped the tasseled string handle in shaking fingers. She held it tightly, refusing to give into the desire to see if it still held her most precious possession. Instead she put her other hand around the bag itself. The bulky oilcloth packet was there. Her eyes closed for the briefest of moments.

"I'm ready, Sergeant," she said. She felt stronger now.

"This way, ma'am." He led the way outside.

Rance walked behind her. Her shoulders were so squared, her head lifted so high. The little feather in her hat bobbed with each step she took. She started to mount her mare alone, but Rance stepped forward and lifted her into the saddle.

His hands lingered on her waist. One heartbeat. Two. Then she raised her eyes and met his gaze.

There were so many things he wanted to say. He said nothing. He just looked at her, memorizing the curve of her lips, her dark and silent eyes. No longer did they sparkle with mischief. Now they shimmered with tears that wet her lashes like raindrops. Not a single tear spilled over, though, and he wondered how much the effort was costing her. He knew how much it was costing him.

"Carrie—"

"Thank you for helping me keep my promise," she said and pressed her heel into her mount's ribs, reining away from Rance and onto the road to Richmond.

Sergeant Kitchen was caught by surprise. He whirled his horse and sped after her just as Captain Anderson of the 4th Virginia Cavalry rode into the yard.

"Colonel Fletcher, it's Jeb Stuart, he's been shot!"

The muscles in Rance's face stiffened. "How bad?"

"Bad, sir. General Wickham wants you to take command of the 1st Virginia."

Rance ran to Cain and leapt into the saddle. "Let's go, Captain," he said and spurred the stallion toward the fight.

He didn't remember the ride, he didn't remember drawing his sabre and charging the Union line. He remembered only the face of the enemy he loved.

"What do you mean I'm riding the wrong way?" Carrie asked. Sergeant Kitchen had overtaken her and was holding her horse's reins in a determined grip.

"You're ridin' south to Richmond, ma'am. Colonel Fletcher said I was to take you north to Union lines and leave you there."

She was staggered. "He—he's letting me go?" She covered her face with her hands and bent forward over her mount's neck to fight the waves of nausea rising within her.

Dear God, please don't do this to me. I didn't tell him because I didn't want him to do this. I swear it, God. I never wanted this.

"Are you sick, Miss Blackwell?"

Her face was wet with sweat and the bitter taste of bile stained her mouth. "No, I'm not sick, Sergeant. I am paying for my sins," she said and looked at him through eyes that burned like the fires of hell.

Chapter Forty-one

She should have gone home. Instead she once again attached herself to General Grant's army and marched forward with him, one bloody inch at a time, all of them toward Richmond.

On June 3rd, 1864, the Northern and the Southern armies met across a forest clearing called Cold Harbor. In thirty minutes, seven thousand Union soldiers were killed in that clearing. That night, as Carrie moved among the dead making a list of names from the scraps of paper pinned to the soldier's uniforms, she looked up from her terrible task to see General Grant watching her.

"Was your man here?"

She looked across the field to the line of Confederate trenches. "I don't know, General."

"You should go home, Miss Blackwell.

You're wanted by the Confederate government. It's dangerous to stay here."

"I'm not going home until it's over."

He gave her a rueful smile. "I guess I knew that, but I had to try. This is no place for a woman."

"This is no place for anyone, sir."

"I know that, too, Miss Blackwell. But there isn't any other place to go."

On June 12th, General Grant did what he had promised he would never do. He backed away from a fight. On that Sunday, he pulled his army out of Cold Harbor, leaving twelve thousand dead Union soldiers in the forest clearing there. He moved his army south across the James River to Petersburg, where he began the siege of Richmond.

On December 20th, Federal troops raiding south from West Virginia captured and destroyed the Confederate saltworks at Saltville, Virginia. When they pulled out of the town, the damage was discovered to be minor. But the incident brought home to the Confederacy its desperate situation.

The country was dying for lack of salt.

If there was to be any hope at all of lasting long enough for the Union to tire of this already tiresome war, the Confederacy had to have salt.

"It is no longer a matter of just needing the Blackwell stockpile, Colonel Fletcher." President Davis rubbed his hands across the sharp planes of his weary face. "We cannot survive without it."

"I've searched every inch of West Virginia, Mr. President. I've searched Virginia and even all the way down to South Carolina."

"It's been six months since Miss Blackwell abandoned her pretense of Confederate loyalty, Colonel. Perhaps in that time she's relaxed her vigil, and now you'll be able to find her treasure."

Rance couldn't do it. It meant having to think of her instead of trying to forget her. It also meant remembering that he'd performed an act of treason when he let her go.

"I've already failed numerous times to uncover that treasure, sir. Give someone else the honor of this last search."

"It is yours, Colonel Fletcher. I have every confidence in your success."

Carrie put a hand on the pine coffin. How could something this cold and hard actually hold her grandfather? Peach Blackwell belonged in a forest filled with warm sunlight and soft breezes. Not in this box. He belonged to the sound of dogs on the trail and laughter and shouts of joy. Not the silence of a grave. Peach was the most alive person she'd ever known. How could he be dead?

It wasn't a rebel bullet that killed him. Nor was it making love to one of the many widows he courted all up and down the Kanawha Valley and most of its tributaries.

He died coughing his lungs into his pillow in the middle of the night while Riverway Cabin was being buried by a New Year's Eve snow. Pneumonia had killed Peach Blackwell.

Lucy Bream found him the next morning, and she'd brought Carrie to Peach's room to help prepare him for burial.

In the end, it had been Harris who helped while Carrie hid in the spring house, her toes freezing and her heart broken beyond repair.

It was almost the end of January before the weather broke and the Charleston ground could be opened to accept Peach. Before the first shovelful of dirt could be tossed onto the lid of the lowered casket, Carrie was on her way home, unable to watch her grandfather suffer that final indignity.

As Luke rounded the boulder in the road near Riverway, he shied and reared. Carrie got him under control, only to find herself shying back from a fearsome array of beards and moustaches, eyebrows and long hair, all bushy, all unkempt, all intimidating.

Bushwackers, she thought, but what were they doing here? The mountains in the east were their domain. Not the open roads of Charleston.

"Wait a minute," she said as recognition sparked in her memory. The tallest man in the gang had wild hair and wild eyes and a familiar face. "Aren't you Anderson Hatfield?"

He nodded. "I need your help."

"Me? How?"

"The Federals are plannin' to hang a friend of mine. I aim to save him."

"I don't know how I can help. Who is he?"

"Ransom Fletcher," Hatfield said, and caught her as she fell.

Chapter Forty-two

The tent was damp. It made Rance feel dirty and cold. He tried writing a letter to his mother. The words felt dirty and cold, too. "I am to die tomorrow," he wrote and refilled the pen with ink, but there was nothing left to say. I'm sorry I blamed you for Father's death. I'm sorry I blamed him. I'm sorry about Chance and I'm sorry about the war and I'm sorry I fell in love with a Yankee.

Those were all things he could say, but didn't, even though they were all true. All except the last part. He didn't regret anything about Carrie—not loving her, not letting her go, not even not telling her that he was about to die.

Like the confession he would not give his mother, he wouldn't say good-bye to Carrie, either. Always, he had told her, and like his love for her, the promise was true.

"Visitor," the guard outside his tent announced, and Rance stood to greet whichever Union officer was coming to gloat this time.

The tent fly was pulled back, letting in the earth-rich smell of the night and Carrie.

"Dear God," he whispered, the words both a prayer and a condemnation. How could he bear to see her now when the last hours of his life were turning into minutes?

"Baby," he said and reached out to her.

The guard had followed her in. He stepped between them. "A distance of two feet must be maintained between the prisoner and visitor at all times. Colonel Rader's order, sir."

"That's inhuman," Rance said.

"It's the condition I agreed to," Carrie said. She looked so pale and so alone. "Otherwise, they wouldn't let me see you." A ghost of a smile glimmered in her eyes. "They don't trust me."

Rance crossed his arms over his chest and gave her a skeptical smile. "Didn't you quote the Declaration of Independence to them to prove you were loyal to the Union?"

"I didn't think it would help."

"It convinced me."

"You were easy."

"I wish you hadn't come, Carrie."

She smiled, and he felt like a schoolboy being chastised for telling a lie.

"I meant it, Carrie, I do wish you hadn't

come, but I'm also very glad you're here." He uncrossed his arms and let them hang down at his sides. "I think I was more afraid of never seeing you again than of dying."

She had not cried once during the entire war, though several times he'd seen her come so close it had been painful watching her struggle to keep the tears from falling. Now, as she stood there looking across the tent at him, the tears fell freely across her lashes and down the soft perfection of her face.

He could stand anything except this. He wanted to make it all go away, the war, the hanging, all the death and all the pain. He couldn't, though. All he could do was be strong. He could give her that, even though it was almost more than he had to give, for her tears were making him so weak.

She raised those beautiful eyes to the guard. "May I please just move a little closer?"

The guard looked at Rance. "You won't try anything?"

"You have my word."

The guard nodded. "Keep the table between you."

Carrie ran to the table. Inches away from it, though, she stopped, suddenly afraid to go another step, afraid that she wouldn't be able to stop and they would make her leave and there was too much she needed to say.

There were lines of silver in his dark hair. She wanted to soothe away the worry that had put it there. She wanted to take away the hurt in his eyes. She wanted to make everything right, but she couldn't even make him free.

He had been captured behind Union lines with a map of the entire southeastern portion of West Virginia. It had been marked with the location of every known cave in the area. One particularly large cave near Sweet Springs had been used early in the war by the Confederacy for the manufacture of gunpowder. He'd been arrested coming out of it and charged with attempting to destroy by force the government of the United States of America. He was convicted by a drumhead court martial and sentenced to hang at dawn on January 31, 1865.

"They said he had a hidden store of powder which he planned to use to blow up Washington," Hatfield had told Carrie. "Only there ain't no powder in that cave. Me and my boys took what was there when we deserted Jeff Davis' war and started our own here in the hills."

Rance's hands were resting on the table, palms down, fingers spread. Carrie put her own hands on the opposite side of the table. "Anderson Hatfield wants me to help you escape."

"You told him no, I hope."

"I wanted to say yes. I tried to." She looked at her hands, so close to his, so far away. She tried to force away the pain in her throat, but it wouldn't go. "It was all so simple when it was just my life."

"It was never just your life, Carrie."

She looked up at him.

"It was every life ever sacrificed for those words you believe in."

"I keep seeing the faces of those men, Rance. And I keep hearing their voices. Their deaths have to mean something. I tried to explain that to Anderson, but he just keeps asking why I won't return the favor you did me at the Yellow Tavern." She stared down at her fingers where they touched the scarred wood of the table. "Why did you let me go?"

"Because the promise that caused you to be captured was to a Confederate soldier."

"You're a terrible liar," she said and tried to smile, but lost it when he smiled first.

"Did you know that a dimple appears in your chin every time you tell a lie?"

Her hands flew to her face. "It does not!"

"I love that dimple."

Her heart stilled within her. She turned away and stared at the tent wall. "Does your mother know you were arrested?"

"I wrote her. The letter won't be posted until tomorrow."

Carrie closed her eyes. Tomorrow.

"I don't want you to be there, Carrie."

She pretended not to hear him. "I've been thinking about Alan's graduation from West Point and I think the reason you didn't go is because you didn't want to ruin it for him by having people point and stare at you when it was his day. Am I right?"

Rance was holding onto the edge of the table with a deadly grip. "I mean it, Carrie. I don't want you there tomorrow."

The tent flap was pushed open by a black and brown coonhound. Carrie welcomed the interruption, and was surprised when she recognized the dog. "Peanut!"

"He showed up this morning," Rance said. "I don't know how he found me or even why he was looking."

Carrie fell to her knees beside the great hound and put her arms around him. "He's beautiful. It's hard to believe this is the same awkward pup who tried to knock me over."

"Whatever happened to the dress you wore that night?"

She laughed. "What a horror that was!"

"It was a little much."

"Mother wanted to have you shot for ruining it." Carrie's laugh sobered. She turned her face into the hound's warm neck. "I was glad you did it, though."

Rance had never thought much about what might lie on the other side of death. If there was something, he hoped that of all the memories of his life, he would be able to take this one with him, this moment of silence that was the last thing he would ever share with this very special woman.

"Peach is dead," she said and pressed her forehead against Peanut's neck while she drew a shaky breath. "And Pops is so worried about Mother that he actually asked me how things were at Greyston the last time I was there. Hannah made snow ice cream even though it wasn't my birthday and Lucy Bream tied big red bows all over the house for Christmas. She even tied one on the back of Pops' chair. He fussed about it, but didn't take it off. The Kanawha River iced over on New Year's Day and Charlie Littlepage almost fell through it. Our brine wells froze up the next day and the pipes all broke. Pops says he doesn't care because he's tired of making salt anyway." Carrie looked at Rance. His eyes were soft, his lips were smiling. "That's what you were looking for in that cave, wasn't it? You were looking for salt."

"But there is no salt to look for," he said. "It finally dawned on me during my trial."

"I increased production, but cut sales. Businessmen only looked at my decreased sales and believed I really needed to buy all the slaves I was bidding for."

"Which you paid for with the proceeds from

the salt you were selling illegally."

"You're pretty smart for a rebel."

"Not smart enough to see the obvious."

"That's always the hardest part to see," she said.

If only once more she could feel the touch of his hand on her face. *Just once more, God, grant me this one wish and I'll never need to ask you for anything again.*

"Don't be there tomorrow, Carrie."

She stood, but kept her hand on the dog's head. "Peach told me once that if I didn't look directly at the things I was afraid of, the day would come when I wouldn't be able to look in the mirror, either. So I've always looked directly at my fears, only now I'm afraid to look in the mirror because without you, there isn't any me to look at."

Twice before in his life, Rance had felt this helpless. When his father committed suicide, and when he learned that Chance had been killed. Now it was his turn to die, and he couldn't let it end like this, he couldn't let her hurt the way he had been hurt.

"That will change, Carrie. Someday you'll look in the mirror and you'll see yourself again."

She almost smiled. "Your chin doesn't have a dimple, but I know you're lying anyway."

He wanted to touch her so much.

"I love you, Carolina."

The air tightened around her.

"Always," he said, and saw her shatter in front of him. She trembled, her body quivering like a reflection in water. Then she turned and ran.

Rance had promised he would break her, and he knew that if there were memories after death, it would be that promise he would remember and forever regret.

Chapter Forty-three

Day came slowly, the misty mountains refusing to give up their hold on the night. The morning twilight was so quiet, so still and quiet, like a breath being held, like a heartbeat hesitating.

No smell of campfires. No crackle of warming flame. Not even a glimmer of blue sky to warm the day. Footsteps were hushed by pine needles and damp earth. A horse blew out a steaming breath.

There should have been a band playing, a drumbeat marching. There should have been a parade and a speaker in a tall hat and long tails and there should be a crowd to watch and a preacher to read from Revelations.

There was just a quiet lining up of soldiers. A slow walk from tent to tree. A wait for the coffin to be brought up and a creak of wood as Rance climbed the three steps to the makeshift gallows. It was just a raised platform with a trap and a tree limb overhead over which was strung the rope. It was a new rope. Tight and strong, a mean-looking rope with a hangman's knot tied at its end.

His heart was hammering in his chest, the force of it causing his ears to pound and his knees to feel numb. He glanced up at the tree limb and the rope, then stood on the trap and looked out at the faces watching him.

Where was she? He'd told her not to be here, but he knew she would be. He looked for her hair, its color like sweet, summer hay. In four years of trying, he'd never found a better description.

Colonel Rader was approaching the waiting assembly. And there she was, walking between him and Peanut, her head held high, her dark eyes actually looking pale in the morning light. Rance's own eyes ached at the sight of her pain.

She did not flinch as their gazes met, but tried instead to smile. Tears spilled from her lashes and his heart beat louder, deafening him with its loss.

Carrie twisted her fingers so tightly together that they burned.

He looked brave, tall and handsome and wonderful and brave. His own hands were already tied behind him. His legs were still spread wide, a captain riding the deck of his ship, a soldier riding the sea of his fate.

His eyes were bright with the tears she was crying. His lips were set in a thin, hard line, unlike hers, which were swollen and trembling and aching to tell him that she was sorry, that she would help him, that she had to save him.

But when she tried to speak, nothing came out.

Colonel Rader was on the gallows platform now. He was holding a Bible and a black cloth mask.

Everyone in camp was there. Even the pickets were coming in, the sound of their breathing harsh and loud as they hiked in from the forest and down from the tops of the mountains surrounding the camp.

Anderson Hatfield had asked Carrie to create a diversion so he could get close enough to the camp to save Rance. Here it was, the best diversion of all, only it was too late to tell him.

I couldn't help him, God, so please, please do it for me. Tell Anderson now!

"Any last words, Colonel Fletcher?"

Rance tried to memorize her face, to hold her with his gaze, to touch her one last time with the love in his eyes.

"It's all been said. I do wish the day had been clear. I'd like to have seen the sky once more."

The mask was put over his face. His last sight was of Carrie trying to draw a breath, her eyes so bright, her lips open and trembling.

The rope was settled around his neck, drawn tight, tighter. The smell of the cloth. The taste of his fear. That last brief glimpse of her pain stinging in his eyes and burning like fire in his heart.

His arms were bound close to his sides. His feet were pulled together and tied. His breath sobbed in his constricted throat.

One more second, he prayed, but there were no more seconds left. The floor fell out from beneath him.

Carrie's hands grabbed at her throat. "I love you!" she cried and flung herself at the image of him falling.

And over the cry of her heart, a sound like the rippling of thunder, the sound of a single long range rifle shot. The white clouds opened and an achingly blue sky exploded across the heavens, sending a stream of sunlight bright and golden to flash like lightning on a gleaming barrel of steel.

Then horses and men were descending from

the mountains. There were shouts and fighting and people running and the hound beside Carrie disappearing and an arm grabbing her around the waist, stopping her as she tried to run to him, to see his body lying on the ground, to die at his side from the battle that raged around her and in her.

But she didn't make it. The blue that had appeared overhead disappeared, the clouds went from white to sudden gray, real lightning flashed, real thunder roared, and a rain so powerful it felt like bullets exploded from the sky. The battle turned into a running watercolor of motion that ended as suddenly as it had begun. The arm disappeared from around Carrie and she found herself surrounded by the bodies of dead men dressed in Union blue, in rags and tatters, in blood and silence. No gray, though. Not under the gallows. Not in the coffin. Not in the mud or the rain. Only in Carrie's fear and in her heart.

She sat where he had sat. Put her hands on the table where his hands had rested. Wondered at what he had felt, if he had felt anything at all, except anger.

He told her not to help him. When she was with him, it had been easy to believe he meant it.

He thought women undermined men, drained them of will and destroyed their morals. That's what she'd done to him. Not in fact, for she had asked nothing of him. He had given her his love and her freedom, maybe her life, willingly.

And yet he had blamed his mother for his father's death. Emma had not sired the late-life child she bore. Emma had not locked the study door or pulled the trigger that killed Nelson Fletcher. Still, Rance had blamed her.

What did he blame Carrie for?

The tent flap opened and Colonel Rader entered. "Not a sign of them," he said. "These mountains and this accused rain has helped them completely disappear."

Carrie pressed her palms against the top of the table. "Is it possible he's alive, Colonel?"

Rader took off his hat and slapped the rain off. "The rope was shot clean through. If it happened before his neck broke, the answer is most likely yes. If not, well, most men don't die instantly. Some do. It depends."

"On what?"

"Luck. Fate. God. Whatever you believe in."

She didn't believe in anything.

"There's something you might like to know, Miss Blackwell. Congress passed the 13th Amendment today."

She looked up at him.

"That's to abolish slavery," he said.

She couldn't make his face come into focus.

"It's what we've been fighting for, Miss Blackwell."

Carrie lifted her hands from the table. "Yes, I know," she said, and turned away from him to listen to the rain.

Chapter Forty-four

She went to Richmond for the same reason she went to Greyston last year. She didn't want to be where he could find her. Then, when he didn't try, she wouldn't be disappointed. And even though last year he had found her, this year she knew it wouldn't happen.

I believe a person is allotted only so many miracles in life.

If Hatfield's shot had been in time, that would be the only miracle she could ever want. Expecting Rance to still love her would be one more than she was allowed.

Richmond was still under siege, so she went instead to General Grant's city of entrenchments south of the Confederate capital. It was there among the man-made hills and valleys that she waited for the fourth Valentine's Day of the war to pass. It was muddy and cold, and the sky cried down upon her as she sat, huddled and alone, among the press of Union troops.

Twilight came unexpectedly. One moment the day was dark with weather. The next, dark with the coming night.

A light, a small one, was suspended from the pole that supported the front of a hospital tent. It shed a glaring light into the ditch where Carrie sat, and it was in that harsh and ugly light that she took out the oilcloth packet. She had not opened it since that day at the Yellow Tavern. She'd been afraid to open it, afraid it no longer held the promise he had made her. It was easier to pretend it did and to take the strength she needed from the lie.

The first glimpse of the paper-lace heart with its delicate blossoms and sugar-crystal snow made her breath catch and her heart ache with the same spasm of pain she'd felt two weeks ago when first she saw Rance standing on the gallows.

Always.

The promise was still there. If he was alive, would he still mean it?

Beneath that single word, she saw something new.

"My sweet, I will love you always. Rance."

Silence. Falling around her like the rain. Like the first breath of morning. Like the dance of the snow and the music of the rime as it gave its life to the sunrise. Silence, like a mountain sunset. Like a blue sky on a summer day. Like day melting into night. Like a heart slowly breaking.

With the card, a feather, her feather, shot from her hat that spring day so long ago. It was a promise, too, a hope reaching out to her from across the years that said maybe, somehow, he might be alive.

"My sweet . . ."

Carrie lifted the feather and touched it to her lips.

". . . I will love you always . . ."

It tasted of rain and tears, of yesterday's promise, a memory of laughter, and a time when war had been very near, yet seemed so far away.

Chapter Forty-five

On April 2nd, the government of the Confederate States of America abandoned Richmond. The city exploded with their leaving. Mobs and fires, theft and terror reigned the streets. The destruction continued through the day and into the night. The next morning as dawn's first light began to streak the eastern sky, the warships in the James River were exploded. The arsenal was next. Several carloads of shell were set fire and a most terrific explosion tore through the city, lending a greater frenzy of panic to the already rioting city.

Carrie watched the horror from the south shore of the James River beside the charred remains of Mayo's Bridge. Fires still burned in the ravaged city. Flames as red as the rising sun leaped from building to building. Black smoke smothered the town.

For hours, people had been fleeing the destruction. Boats and barges, carts and carriages, slaves and servants all staggered beneath the crushing weight of baggage and possessions as the frightened and the privileged fled west in the wake of their country's leaders.

General Grant rode up beside Carrie, his horse steaming in the early chill. Another mighty explosion shook the ground. "More ammunition," he said. "That's quite a party they're throwing over there."

"I was here the night Richmond celebrated Virginia's secession. There were real parties that night, and fireworks and parades and dances." She closed her eyes. "Is this really it, General? Is it really over?"

"I don't know how they lasted this long. As for it being over, Miss Blackwell, I don't think it will ever be over. But it is finished." He pulled his horse around. "Go home, girl," he said and rode away to finish the fight.

Carrie wanted to go home, but first she went to Grace Street. The homes there were set back from the street with pretty wrought-iron fences and little gardens that invited the imagination to stroll among their wandering paths. That was before the war. Now there were dead plants and broken gates and boarded-over windows that kept the people who lived in the houses from looking out at what their world had become.

The Lewis home was made of brick with high

windows and had a little duck pond in the front yard. When Carrie was in school in Richmond, it was to this house and Lisset's family she had gone on holidays and long afternoons and bright Sunday mornings. Here was where she first saw what family life was like. Two sisters, two parents, love and laughter, and a peaceful way of caring. And though Carrie had longed for this quiet, refined style of daily life, she was not the quiet, refined type of person required to fit into the picture. Not until she sat in the grass of Richmond's fortifications and watched the Fletcher family laugh and love and play had Carrie known where she belonged.

The chimes on the front door were not working. She used the knocker and heard the sound of running footsteps and Lisset's voice calling, "I'll get it, Mama!"

Carrie backed down the two steps to the yard. The door opened and Lisset looked out. Her face tightened.

"You aren't welcome here."

It was not an unexpected reaction, but still it hurt.

"Why did do you it, Carrie? Why did you betray us?"

"I did what I had to do, Lisset. You've always known how I felt."

"You'll be happy to know that all our slaves have run away, the ungrateful wretches, and after us showing them nothing but kindness their entire lives."

"Even the girl you had whipped when she fell and broke the eggs you wanted cooked for your breakfast? She's run away from all that kindness, too?"

"Yes," Lisset said, her voice frigid with anger. "Even Poll. Good-bye, Carolina." She stepped back inside to close the door.

"Lisset, wait. Please."

She hesitated.

"General Weitzel is to be the Union commander of Richmond. If you go to him, he'll furnish you with a safeguard for your house. He'll give them to anyone who asks, but I told him about your family and Alice's, so he will be expecting you." Carrie started to leave, but she couldn't, not without asking. "Have you heard anything about Rance?"

"If I had, I wouldn't tell you."

"I'm not asking you to betray a state secret. I just want to know if he's—" She had to stop and force herself to take a breath. "I need to know if he's alive, Lisset."

"I don't know, Carrie. Honestly."

"If you hear anything, could you let me know?"

"Mama wouldn't allow it."

Carrie gave a sad smile. "You're twenty-four years old, Lisset. You shouldn't be worried about what your mother does or doesn't allow. Don't forget to get that safeguard." She walked out of the yard and closed the gate behind her.

"Wait!" Lisset ran down the steps, then stopped, as though uncertain what to do next. "If I hear anything, I'll write."

"Thank you," Carrie said. She walked a few steps, stopped, and turned back. "If you don't hear anything, maybe you could write anyway."

Lisset almost smiled. "Maybe."

"I hope so, my adored and adoring friend. I really and truly hope so."

Chapter Forty-six

Carrie reached Charleston on April 9th. She sat on her horse on the north bank of the Kanawha River and watched its water swirl slowly around the remains of the *Julia Maffitt.* Her charred and broken ribs were a sad reminder of days that used to be, of old dreams and forgotten youth and a time when being kissed was more important than rights and causes.

The sound of thunder rolled across the valley. It came from Cox's Hill, where the occupying Union troops had installed a battery of guns. Carrie went to see what the firing was about.

People all over town were rushing toward the sound of the guns' salute. Even the flag over Kanawha Court House was in a hurry, flapping and crackling and waving in a quickening breeze as it reigned over the excited town.

Carrie followed the crowd up the carriage road to where a parade was making its slow way to the top of the hill. An old hearse led the procession. Painted in large letters on both sides was "Secession." Behind the hearse was a wagon with a tree propped in the back. A sign that read "Sour Apple Tree" was nailed to the gnarled trunk, and from a limb hung a rag-doll body with a rope tied tight around its cotton neck.

Captain Gregg of the 7th West Virginia Cavalry was sitting on his horse at the edge of the road. Carrie rode up beside him. She couldn't stop staring at the awful rag figure, at the garishly painted hearse and the jubilant faces of Charleston's citizens.

"What's going on?" she asked.

"A funeral, ma'am," Gregg said. "We are burying the Confederacy."

"You're—why? What's happened?"

"Haven't you heard? The war is over. General Lee has surrendered."

The wagon with its horrid load trundled past.

"Who is that, Captain?"

"Old Jeff Davis, of course!"

Carrie turned her horse and walked him away from the terrible scene.

"Wait," Gregg called after her. "Don't you want to hear the eulogy?"

Riverway. Home. Carrie climbed the steps past the naked branches of the wind-tossed lilacs. Inside, she went straight to the little music room. Harris was sitting at his desk. Not working. Just sitting.

"It's over, Pops."

"I thought so. I heard the guns."

From somewhere inside the house came the sound of a clock ticking. Carrie had never heard it before. She'd been too busy living to notice that time was passing. Now, that's all she could hear, as though that were the only sound in the world, the sound of seconds and minutes, of hours and weeks, of years and lifetimes passing away.

"Why didn't you go after Mother, Pops?"

"I did once. I went all the way to Greyston, even rode part way up the drive. There was a woman walking out on the lawn. She was too far away for me to see if it was your mother, but I knew it was her. She looked like part of the landscape, a stroke of the painter's brush that made the picture complete."

"So you left."

He nodded.

"Think you'll ever go back?"

"Maybe. When you don't need me anymore here."

She sat on the floor beside his chair and laid her head in his lap. "I don't need you now," she said, and he stroked her hair with soothing caresses.

"I miss Peach," she said after awhile.

"You're not getting my trouser leg wet crying all over it, are you?"

"Want me to stop?"

He stroked her hair again. "No, honey, you just go ahead and cry it out."

She turned her face into the soft corduroy. "Will that make everything all right again, Pops?"

"No."

"You could've lied and said yes just to make me feel better."

"I've never lied to you before, girl, no reason to start now just to save my pants."

She smiled and wiped her tears on his trouser leg. "I guess you're right, Pops."

Chapter Forty-seven

The day was clear, the valley warm with an early summer sun. The Great Kanawha River swept past Charleston in a bright rush of water and reflected light that made Carrie squint when she looked to see if the *Northern Belle* had docked. No sign of her yet. She reined Luke away from the river and rode to the Court House.

The mail had been sorted. She picked up hers and her father's. Business mostly. An offer to buy the saltworks. An offer to buy salt. A new and improved and better-than-ever method to repair broken well pipes. A few personal items, an invitation to visit White Sulphur Springs, an advertisement from a clothing store in New York offering the latest in Paris attire to "Fashion-Starved Southern Gentlewomen."

"Is this all?" she asked. William Gramm, the postmaster of the unofficial post office, glanced at her, then down at his desk before nodding. He never seemed to be quite able to meet her eyes.

The telegraph room was next. "Anything for Blackwell?" she asked. The operator shook his head and Carrie left.

The whistle on the *Northern Belle* announced her arrival at the landing. Picking up the newspapers from Cincinnati would be the last stop on what had become Carrie's daily routine. Mail, telegrams, newspapers, then home to wait until tomorrow for word that never came.

The Army of Northern Virginia had surrendered April 9th. The tragedy of Abraham Lincoln's assassination was April 14th, Good Friday. On the 26th, Confederate Gen. Joseph Johnston surrendered to Gen. William T. Sherman at Durham Station, North Carolina. May 4th, the Confederate forces of Alabama, Mississippi, and East Louisiana surrendered. And on May 10th, the President of the Confederate States of America was captured near Irwinville, Georgia, by the Fourth Michigan Cavalry.

With Jefferson Davis' capture, President Andrew Johnson had declared "armed resistance to the authority of the Government in the said insurrectionary States may be regarded as virtually at an end."

It was June now, June 1st, a day proclaimed for humiliation and prayer in honor of Abraham Lincoln. The American flag rippled and curled in a freshening breeze above the Court House. Carrie stood on Front Street and gazed up at the white stars on a field of blue and the stripes of red and white fluttering above her.

She wanted to think of the flag as just cotton threads and colored dye. It was so much more, though. It was something worth dying for. She'd always believed that, she believed it now. But it had become more than a symbol of a country, more than a promise of equality and freedom. It had become a token of her heartbreak. If Rance were alive, he would contact her. Maybe not to put a happily-ever-after ending on their unfinished story, but he would still contact her, even if just to say that it was his promise that died at the end of that rope instead of him. So, with every day that passed without word from him, that waving symbol of America added another bar to Carrie's prison of pain.

The *Northern Belle* was unloading. There were boxes of books shipped from New York for the new Capital Book Store. A courier with a case held tightly against his chest and an armed guard stalking along beside him came ashore, then headed off at a fast walk for Mr. Stolle's jewelry store. And there were Carrie's newspapers piled on a crate at the edge of the landing.

For some reason, she couldn't make herself go near them. She didn't want to read the stories and search the lists of names who died in the final days and were still dying in isolated skirmishes. She wanted to sit in the sun and wait for the sharp edges of her pain to dull with rust, like she'd tried to do after Gettysburg. And even though it wasn't the sun that had cured her that day, she left the newspapers beside the river and turned Luke toward Burning Spring.

The day was hot, the sky so blue, it brought tears to the eyes. The grass was growing high and wild, and it smelled of summer. Bees hummed and butterflies floated on stirring breezes, and flowers the color of valentines carpeted the meadow.

The sun was bright and yellow, and it flowed like liquid light down the river of her unbound hair as she sat beside the dappling stream with toes tucked beneath its rippling waters.

How long had it been since he'd last seen beauty? A moment before, a day ago, an entire lifetime? Not until he first saw her had he known what beauty could be. And love. Had he known what it was before she smiled into his eyes? Had he known what pleasure was before she laughed and filled his heart with music? Had he ever felt happiness or dreamed dreams or believed in forever before she stepped into his arms and into his heart?

He had once asked God for one more second, and been denied. Now he wanted that second again. He wanted to hold it to him, to fill it with this moment, to remember forever the sight of her in this meadow where Washington had walked, and they had loved, and the memories of Gettysburg had begun to fade. It was here among these grasses, here in the embrace of these ever-watching hills, that he had first truly known her. And it was here that he had made her a promise, an oath no longer than a single word, and had carved it for her on a tablet of stone, not in Latin, but in love.

Carrie closed her eyes and listened. The wind was singing to her. One note, two, bringing a memory of rain and horses and the man she loved whistling this song soft and low.

Her heart hushed within her. Her hands stilled their restless stirring in the grasses by the stream, and she turned to look through startled eyes at the forest behind her.

In the shade of the chestnut tree, tall and mighty with its creamy blossoms tossing in the wind against the sky, there he stood. Was it really him or a wish come to haunt her, a hope come to tease?

"I believe this is our dance, Carrie."

She came to her knees. She wanted to reach out to him, to run to him, to prove he was real.

She was afraid to move, afraid the image would disappear. "Am I dreaming?" she asked.

"It could be a nightmare," Rance said. "Isn't that what you told Lisset? That I was more like a nightmare than a dream?"

"You're real," she said and was on her feet and running. Then she saw it, his right arm suspended in a sling. And his uniform, the tattered and worn Confederate gray cloth was stained dark with blood on his shoulder and sleeve. She stopped, inches away, a touch away.

"It's not in great shape, but it's still there," he said. "It almost wasn't, though. Task saved it. He saved me, too."

"Where?"

"The first time at Five Forks."

She had been there. She had cared for the Union wounded after Lee's desperate attempt to move his army south to join with Johnston's. The result of the action had been Richmond's surrender and the Confederacy's fall.

"And again at Irwinville," he said, "when they captured President Davis."

With fingers numb with wanting, Carrie reached out to place a hand on his wounded arm. "Does it hurt?"

"No," Rance said, but couldn't stop the wince of pain that her gentle touch sent shooting through him. Her eyes smiled at him through a shimmer of unshed tears.

"I love you, Ransom Fletcher," she said.

He lifted his left hand to touch her cheek. She turned her lips into his palm and wet his fingers with her tears.

"I never doubted it for a minute, baby."

She couldn't look at him. She kept her eyes closed, filling her senses with his touch. If this was the last time, so be it. He was alive. That was all she'd wanted, and now she had his caress, too. The bargain she'd made with God was one more touch and no more begged favors, ever. She was on her own, now, and more frightened than she'd ever been in her life.

"Not even when you heard the trap spring open beneath you?" she asked, her voice a whisper.

"Especially then," he said, and her breath sobbed in her throat.

She turned her face away from his hand and met his gaze. "You could hate me, and I'd understand."

Her lashes were so wet with tears, she looked like a drowning kitten. "I don't hate you, Carrie."

"Just because you carried a shot-off feather around for an entire war and made me a paper-lace promise, you're under no obligation."

He wrapped her in his smile. "You remind me of a parrot I heard about once that traveled around with a shouting preacher. Every night, when the preacher finished shouting, the parrot would squawk, 'Save yourself, save yourself.' "

Carrie lifted her chin slightly. "Is there a moral to this story?"

"I'm not a preacher and you're not a parrot."

"You blamed your mother for your father's death, Rance. I want to know if you blame me for your almost death."

"I was wrong to blame Mother, and I don't blame you."

She wanted so much to believe. "And the first time we have an argument, you're not going to suddenly realize you hate me because I didn't help Anderson Hatfield save you?"

"We're not going to have any arguments. Every time we disagree, I'm going to make love to you." The flush of color that spread across her lily-soft skin made Rance's heart ache with tenderness and love.

She was so overcome by the light in his eyes, she dropped her gaze to the tarnished buttons on his jacket. "Why didn't you write me that you were alive?"

He slipped his fingers into the sun-warmed silk of her hair. "I did, baby. Bredon stopped my letters."

"James? How could he—"

"Wrong Bredon, Carrie. It was his father who caught onto your Southern belle charade and provided me with an extensive collection of your letters. He has more spies in the post office than Lincoln did in the whole Confederacy. After he stopped collecting your letters, he started collecting mine. When I found out, I escaped from Task's one-bed hospital and here I am."

"Franklyn Bredon." Carrie was astounded by the revelation. "I guess he wanted to repay me for helping so many of his slaves escape."

"Any more doubts I need to explain away, Miss Blackwell, or can I hold you now?"

Those dark, beautiful eyes answered him with a smile, and he pulled her to him. For a long moment, he just held her, filling his heart and his soul with the touch and the feel and the reality of her.

"I never thought I'd hold you again, baby. That day at Sweet Springs, I thought I would die just from wanting to touch you."

She buried her face in his jacket. "I wanted to die with you. I almost did when the trap opened. And all these months of not knowing if you were alive, a little bit more of me died everyday."

"Would you make the same choice today you made that day, Carrie?"

"I don't want to ever have to make a choice like that again, Rance. Please, promise me I'll never have to."

"Would you change anything, Carrie? I have

to know."

She pressed her forehead against his chest. "No."

"I love you, Carrie."

The sun was inside her again, warming and healing her, filling her with hope, filling her with happiness. The razor-sharp edges of her doubt were gone, replaced forever by the feel of his heart beating against her lips, and the beauty of those four words.

She looked up at him and lifted her hands to his face. If she lived forever, this would be the moment she wanted most to remember, "I will love you forever, Rance. When the last memory of this war has faded from the hearts and minds of the country, when the last comet has disappeared from the sky, when the last valentine has turned yellow with age and the lace that decorates it has turned to dust, I will still love you."

He bent to kiss her. Her lips tasted of tears and promises.

"Always," he whispered.

"Always," she answered.

"Dance with me, Carolina."

"There's no music."

"Yes, there is, baby. Just listen to your heart."

She heard a flag waving in the wind and the sound of a quill pen writing the words that had made America free. She heard Peach's laughter and her mother calling her darling and her father telling her that he would never lie to her. And she heard Rance saying he would always love her, and she heard herself swearing to always love him, and suddenly there it was, a warm flow of music rising up from inside her, a song of light and life and happiness, a song of forever, a song of always.

"I hear it," she said and looked at Rance with eyes wide with wonder and delight.

He touched his lips to her forehead. "I knew you could, baby."

He led her out into the sun-washed beauty of the meadow, and there they began to waltz to the music of love.